Samantha Towl[e] ... [USA Today] and *Wall
Street Journal* bestselling auth[or]. [She began] ... novel in
2008 while on maternity leave. She completed the manuscript
five months later and hasn't stopped writing since.

She is the author of contemporary romances, The Storm
Series and The Revved Series, and standalones, *Trouble*,
When I Was Yours, *The Ending I Want*, *Unsuitable*, *Wardrobe
Malfunction*, *Breaking Hollywood*, *Under Her* and *Sacking
the Quarterback*, which was written with James Patterson.
She has also written paranormal romances, *The Bringer*
and The Alexandra Jones Series. All of her books are
penned to the tunes of The Killers, Kings of Leon, Adele,
The Doors, Oasis, Fleetwood Mac, Lana Del Rey,
and more of her favorite musicians.

A native of Hull and a graduate of Salford University,
she lives with her husband, Craig, and their son and
daughter in East Yorkshire.

Keep up with Samantha and her upcoming releases
at **www.samanthatowle.co.uk**, find her on
Facebook: **www.facebook.com/samtowlewrites**
or follow her on Twitter: **@samtowlewrites**.

By Samantha Towle

Gods Series
Ruin
Rush

Standalone
The Bringer
Trouble
When I Was Yours
The Ending I Want
Sacking the Quarterback (with James Patterson)
Unsuitable
Wardrobe Malfunction
Breaking Hollywood

Revved Series
Revved
Revived

Storm Series
The Mighty Storm
Wethering the Storm
Taming the Storm
The Storm

Alexandra Jones Series
First Bitten
Original Sin

RUSH

SAMANTHA TOWLE

HEADLINE
ETERNAL

First published in Great Britain in 2018
by HEADLINE ETERNAL
An imprint of HEADLINE PUBLISHING GROUP

1

Cataloguing in Publication Data is available from the British Library

ISBN 978 1 4722 5149 7

Typeset in Sabon LT Std by Jouve (UK), Milton Keynes

Printed and bound in Great Britain by CPI Group (UK) Ltd,
Croydon, CR0 4YY

Headline's policy is to use papers that are natural, renewable and recyclable
products and made from wood grown in well-managed forests and other
controlled sources. The logging and manufacturing processes are expected
to conform to the environmental regulations of the country of origin.

HEADLINE PUBLISHING GROUP
An Hachette UK Company
Carmelite House
50 Victoria Embankment
London EC4Y 0DZ

www.headlineeternal.com
www.headline.co.uk
www.hachette.co.uk

RUSH

Chapter One

"**Y**OU'VE GOT TO BE kidding me!"

I glance up to the sky. Big, fat raindrops splash on my face. Dark clouds have rolled in from nowhere and opened up to let out water like it's the sequel to the Great Flood.

"Jesus effin' Christ," I grumble to myself as I quickly dig through my bag, looking for my umbrella ... which isn't there. "Crap. Shit. Crap."

This is just perfect. Frigging perfect.

I don't even have a jacket on. I'm wearing my new white silk shirt, black skinny jeans, and black heels.

The weather was forecast warm, and when I got on the bus at Port Authority half an hour ago to travel to East Rutherford, the sun was shining.

Global warming for you. *Sigh.*

My first day at my new job—the job that my dad got for me—and I'm about to turn up, looking like a drowned rat.

Perfect.

I quickly start walking away from the bus stop,

heading toward my new place of work. The New York Giants headquarters and training facility. My dad is Eddie Petrelli, the head coach of the Giants, and he's hired me to be an assistant to the team. Basically, I'm a lackey. And my dad has totally made up the job, no matter how he denies it, and he did that because I'd lost mine at the gallery, due to me being a total screwup.

I was surprised that he wanted me working here. I've embarrassed him enough of late. But I guess he wants me where he can keep an eye on me.

I'm an alcoholic. A sober alcoholic, thanks to time spent in a detox and rehab facility and the ongoing support of Alcoholics Anonymous and my sponsor, Luke.

The push to rehab came because, a little over six months ago, I was arrested for driving under the influence after I caught my ex-boyfriend, Kyle, in a compromising position at a house party. Basically, his pants were around his ankles and someone I'd thought was a friend was on her knees in front of him. I'm guessing you get the picture.

I left the party, climbed into my ex's car, and took off. I was drunk off my ass and upset, and I crashed his car into one of the neighbor's garden walls.

I lost my license—hence why I ride the bus now— and was charged with criminal damage and received a hefty fine.

The gallery sacked me. And trying to get another job since I got out of rehab with a criminal record has been nearly impossible.

Not that I didn't try because I really did. But no one wants to hire an ex-drunk.

So, when I started running out of money to pay my bills, I took the job my dad had offered. I also need to pay my dad. He hasn't asked for the money he spent on putting me through rehab or paying my fine, and he rebuffs me when I tell him I'm going to pay him back. But I need to start taking responsibility for my actions.

Getting sober was the first step. Paying my dad back is the next, and now that I have this job, thanks to him, I can start doing so.

It takes me fifteen long, rain-soaked minutes to walk to the Giants headquarters.

When I finally get there, I'm drenched through to my underwear, and my hair is plastered to my head. The hour I spent this morning putting on makeup and styling my hair was a total waste of time.

I fish the ID badge that my dad gave me out of my bag as I approach the security booth.

The glass on the booth slides back, revealing a middle-aged guy with a kind face.

"You got caught in the downpour, huh?" He gives me a grin.

"Can you tell?"

He chuckles. "I'd offer you an umbrella, but I don't think that's going to help you now."

"No." I laugh. "But I might need to borrow it later, if it starts back up."

"You got yourself a deal. So, how can I help you today?"

"I'm, uh, starting work here today. My name is Arianna Petrelli." I hand over my ID badge.

"Coach Petrelli's daughter." His voice booms with

a smile. "Of course. He told me you'd be coming in today."

At his pleasant greeting, a knot I didn't realize I had in my stomach eases a little.

I guess it has been on my mind a bit—how people here would treat me. Without a doubt, they all know about my DUI and rehab stint.

My dad wouldn't have talked about it. Man of few words, my father.

But the daughter of the coach of the Giants charged with a DUI was a journalist's dream.

Since it happened—aside from the people in rehab, who were pretty much all like me—normal folk are generally disgusted by my behavior, and some aren't afraid to let me know. Don't worry; I'm disgusted with myself. I could have killed someone that night.

That's what I remind myself of when the urge to drink gets too strong.

It's just hard to have people look at you like you're a piece of shit, reminding you of what you already think of yourself. And I worried it would be the same here. So, it's nice for the first person I encounter to look at me with nothing but a smile in their eyes.

I return his smile.

"I'm Patrick," he tells me.

"It's nice to meet you," I reply.

He hands me back my ID badge. "If you need anything, like an umbrella"—he grins—"I'm your man."

"Thank you," I tell him and mean it. His kindness is appreciated. "Is my dad here yet?" I ask him.

"No," Patrick replies. "He usually gets here around nine."

I glance at the clock behind him on the wall. Eight thirty.

I've got half an hour to clean up and dry off before my dad arrives.

I want to look presentable.

Not that getting caught in the rain was my fault. But Dad has been bugging me about moving back home. He only lives a ten-minute drive from here, so I would get a lift in every day with him. And me getting caught in the rain like this will only give strength to his argument that I move back home.

I know he wants me away from the temptation of alcohol and all the bars in the city.

But I like living in New York, being so close to the art galleries and culture, and I love my apartment. It's tiny, but it's mine.

And, if I'm going to stay sober, I have to get used to being around alcohol.

My sponsor, Luke, says hiding from alcohol can actually have a detrimental effect. I think he's right. I need to get used to the fact that it's around but that it's something I don't do anymore.

Not that I'm actively going into bars anymore or browsing the liquor aisle in the supermarket, but I make sure to remind myself that it's there, and it's a part of life. Just not a part of mine anymore.

"Well, I'd better get inside and dry off," I tell him, stepping back.

The rain has eased a little. It would now that I'm here.

Stupid weather.

"Have a good first day," he tells me.

I thank him again and then speed-walk toward the building entrance.

Opening the door, I walk inside, dripping water all over the tiled floor.

There's no one at the reception desk. Damn it. I have no clue where anything is. This is the first time I've ever been here. My dad might work here, but I've never had a reason to come here before today.

I was hoping there would be someone—preferably female—who might be able to point me in the direction of, at the very least, a hand dryer.

I glance around for a sign of a restroom, but nothing. So, I start walking, going straight ahead through the lobby.

My heels click on the tiled floor, echoing loudly. I have the urge to take off my wet shoes, but I really don't want to walk around barefoot.

I walk past the staircase and down the hallway. I see a sign that shows the restrooms are on the left.

Bingo.

Although I don't know what the hell I'm going to do because there's no way a hand dryer is going to dry my clothes, but it's better than nothing.

I locate the restroom, which is empty, and—shit! Effing crap! No hand dryer. Only paper towels.

As I turn, I catch sight of myself in the mirror.

Christ almighty.

I look a mess. My makeup has practically washed off. Thank God for waterproof mascara because it's the only thing on my face that's stayed intact.

My brown hair is a wet, stringy mess.

My white shirt is clinging to my body, and you can totally see my lace bra through it.

My cheeks flame with embarrassment, knowing that Patrick could see my bra through my shirt.

I can't start my first day, meeting the guys on the team, looking like this.

I need clothes. Even if it's just a different shirt. I can live in damp jeans and panties if I have to but not a wet shirt, showing off my chest.

They must have team shirts here. Anything is better than my soaking wet top that I'm currently wearing. I look like I'm entering in the world's first solo wet shirt competition, and I really don't want to embarrass myself—or my dad—any more than I have already.

And, wearing a team shirt, at least I'll look committed to the team.

I almost laugh out loud at that thought.

I don't like football. At all.

As a coach's daughter, people assume I love the sport. But it's because of football that I had to move around a lot while growing up. That my dad wasn't around much. That my mom—

I cut off that thought.

It wasn't my dad's fault. My mom was sick. And the choices she'd made were hers and hers alone.

But it was his fault that he wasn't there for you when you needed him most, the voice in the back of my mind whispers.

No, I'm not going there today.

Today is going to be a good day despite the fact that it's started off crappily.

I'm going to fix up my hair, and then I'm going to find a shirt to wear.

Dumping my damp bag on the counter, I pull out my hairbrush and a hair tie.

I brush it through as best I can and then tie it up into a makeshift bun. I drop my hairbrush back in my bag, and clutching it to my chest, covering my peekaboo bra, I head out of the restroom and go in search of a storeroom or somewhere they might keep spare shirts. But I need to be quick before people start arriving.

I wander for a few minutes and stumble across the locker room.

There's got to be a shirt in here somewhere.

I open the door, letting myself in, and—holy shit, this room is huge. It's bigger than my apartment. Well, most places are bigger than my apartment. But, still, it's massive.

I wander in letting the door close behind me.

There are team shirts hanging on hangers at each player's station. Multiple shirts.

I could borrow one from one of the players, then find where they keep the spares, and replace it; no one would be any the wiser.

I walk into the locker room, scanning the names on the placards above each station as I pass them.

Kelly . . . Maxwell . . . Thompson . . . Kincaid.

Ah, Ares Kincaid. The star quarterback. The one they call the Missile because he throws the football with the effect of a heatseeking missile. He never misses his target.

I might not know much about football, but I do know who he is.

The golden boy. Mr. Perfect.

The guy who paid for his younger siblings' college education. I know this because my dad told me once.

"He's responsible, that one. Got his head screwed on." This was all said with a pointed look at me.

I wasn't responsible. I didn't have my head screwed on. I could barely look after myself, let alone be responsible for anyone else.

I still can't.

My dad thinks the sun shines out of Kincaid's butt.

I know my dad loves all his players like they're family—probably loves them more than his own family . . . well, me because I'm all he has left—but I'm pretty sure my dad thinks of Ares Kincaid as the son he never had but always wanted.

And who could blame him? Kincaid would never get in a car drunk and drive it into a wall.

Nope, that's all me. The screwup.

I reach out, fingering one of Kincaid's shirts.

I have this sudden urge to know what it feels like to be like him. To not be a screwup. To be someone people admire. Look up to.

Maybe, if I put on one of his shirts, some of his goodness might rub off on me.

Okay, that just sounded really dirty.

But it can't hurt to try, right? Wearing his shirt to try to soak up some of his good sense . . . and that just sounded gross.

I'm going to quit while I'm ahead. Or not.

I kick off my damp heels, drop my bag to the floor, and begin unbuttoning my wet shirt. I peel it off my skin, letting it fall to the floor with a wet thud, and it feels like heaven. The air is cool, drying my damp skin.

I really, really want to take my bra off as well, but I can't have the girls coming out to play. My chest isn't huge, so jiggling boobs wouldn't be an issue, but my nipples do have a tendency to play peekaboo at the most inopportune moments. Not that my bra is exactly concealing much in its dampened state.

God, what a day, and it's still early.

I really need to not screw up today.

Please let today go well.

Needing to find my calm, I place my hands on my hips and lean my body forward, slowly letting my hands slide down the sides of my legs until they're resting on the floor, and my chest is pressed to my thighs.

I hold the pose and breathe in. Then, I exhale.

I've been practicing yoga since I got sober. My therapist suggested it, and it really helps me.

I know it might seem strange to pull a yoga move here in the locker room, but I need a moment to relax and find my focus, and this is how I do it nowadays. The old me would have just done a shot.

"Ahem." The sound of a deep, timbral voice clearing behind me has me shooting upright and spinning around.

And, oh dear God, no.

Ares Kincaid.

He's standing right there, across the room from me.

And I have no shirt on.

Crap.

Chapter Two

"**O**H JESUS, SHIT-FUCK!" I wheeze out in complete horror, my arms clamping over my chest.

"That's a lot of expletives for one sentence." Ares's head tilts to the side, a look of amusement on his face.

"I-I . . ." I'm floundering. I have no clue what to say. I'm all like, *Jesus, take the wheel.*

I'm half-naked in front of Ares Kincaid.

My dad is going to be so pissed when he finds out.

Please don't let him find out.

"I didn't think anyone was here," I finally manage to get out.

"Clearly."

His eyes drop from my face and start to trail down my body. I see a spark of interest in his eyes, and I'm surprised by the flash of heat I feel between my legs.

Did I mention that Ares Kincaid is good-looking?

I've seen him on TV and in pictures, but this is the first time I've seen him in the flesh. He's all rippling muscles, hard edges, and golden skin. Dark scruff covering his strong jaw, like he hasn't bothered to shave in days. Striking blue eyes, which are still working their way over my body, and dark hair, which is shorter than it used to be. I remember him having longer hair.

Anyway, he's hot. If you like that kind of thing—jocks—which I don't.

What do I like?

Honestly, I have no clue anymore.

Before I was sober, I used to go for guys who liked to party. Dirty, rough guys. Guys I could get drunk with. The quintessential bad boys.

Sporty, serious, and stable was never in my repertoire.

Maybe it should be.

Not with him, of course.

And not anytime soon. Relationships are not something I'm interested in. Staying sober is.

"So . . ." His eyes finally land back on mine, and I give him an irritated look due to him blatantly checking me out. The bastard doesn't even have the courtesy to look embarrassed. He just smiles and shrugs his big shoulders. "This might be a crazy question"—his lips are now twitching with amusement—"but who are you? And why were you bent over and shirtless in here?"

"I, um . . . look, do you mind if I put my shirt back on?" I take a step back, angling down to look at my shirt, which is still on the floor in a damp heap.

"No. Go ahead." He gestures a hand in my direction but makes no move to give me any privacy. He just stands there, watching me with his blazing eyes burning right through me. The color reminds me of a flame when it's reached its hottest temperature.

"Could you turn around?" I give him a pointed look, tightening my arms over my chest.

Shaking his head, he rumbles out a chuckle, which makes the muscles in my stomach clench. "Sure," he says. "I've already seen *everything* . . ."

His eyes drop to my chest before slowly lifting back to mine. The heat in them is undeniable. And so is the sudden throbbing occurring between my thighs. It's been a while since I had sex. That's why I'm responding like this. It's all it can be.

"But I can be a gentleman."

"Wow. Lucky me," I mutter sarcastically as he turns away.

I hear him laugh again.

And I experience another stomach clench.

I bend to retrieve my shirt and quickly pull it on, wincing at the feel of the wet fabric against my now-dry skin. I fasten the buttons, starting at the top and working my way down.

"You can turn around," I tell him as I fasten the last button.

"So . . ." he says, turning to face me. A smile lifts his lips. It's a smug look.

His thick arms fold over his massive chest. I can see the veins running beneath his golden skin.

I have a thing about men's arms and veins. I find them incredibly hot. On the right man, of course.

Weird, I know.

"So . . ." I echo.

The smile widens. "I hate to tell you this. But I can still see as much as I could before you put the shirt on.

Well, more now since your arms aren't in the way, blocking the view."

My eyes drop. "Shit!" I bark out, arms covering my chest again.

I forgot it was totally see-through.

"Wet shirt," he says. "Rain outside. I'm guessing you got caught in the downpour."

"You're right," I grind out.

He's starting to annoy me a little.

His arms unfurl, and those bright eyes of his darken. I'm not sure what with.

Then, he starts toward me, those long legs eating up the space between us. My heart starts to beat in staccato.

He stops a few feet away.

Sweet Jesus, he's huge.

And I'm small.

Ridiculously small. Five feet one to be exact. And I don't currently have my heels on for the added height. I stupidly took them off.

Ares is well over six feet tall. Probably closer to six and a half.

I am a dwarf, standing in front of him.

His eyes stare down at me, probing. I feel like he can see every part of me. Even the bad parts.

"Still doesn't explain who you are or why you stripped off and decided to do your morning stretches in my locker room." His voice is lower, deeper. The sound rushes over my skin, like a cold breeze on a hot day, making my skin cover in goose bumps.

I have to hold back a shiver.

"Your locker room?" I question, lifting a brow.

"Are you a football groupie?"

"No!" I bark out a laugh.

"Because, if you broke in here, I'll have your ass hauled out with one phone call," he continues, clearly ignoring me.

I slam my hands on my hips, momentarily forgetting I need them to cover the girls, and then I put them back over my chest.

He smirks at me.

Asshole.

"Look, I'm not a groupie, okay? It's my first day here. I got caught in the rain. I came in here, looking to borrow a shirt, as I can't wear this one. You caught me about to change into one."

"And you were bent over for the fun of it?"

"No, I was doing yoga."

"Yoga?" He looks at me like I'm mental.

He wouldn't be wrong.

"I was stressed about my shitty start to the day, and I practice yoga to de-stress. I thought I was alone. I was literally just doing the one pose to help clear my mind, and then I was going to put on a shirt and get out of here."

"And which shirt were you putting on?" He glances over at his changing spot and then back at me, brows raised.

"Uh . . ." I'm stumbling. Deep breath. "Okay, I was going to borrow one of yours. But I was going to find another to put in its place."

"Okay," he says.

"Okay?" My brows draw together as I look up at him.

"Yep. It sounds plausible. Weird as fuck. But plausible."

I can't help but laugh at that. He laughs, too.

"I'm going to go." Freeing one arm, I stand my heels up and slip my feet into them, appreciating the extra height they give me, but I still look like a child next to him.

"Don't you need a shirt to wear?" he says.

"I'll figure it out."

"Here." He reaches over and grabs a white dress shirt from one of the hangers. "Wear this. It'll be big on you, so you'll have to roll up the sleeves, but it's better than a team shirt."

"Thank you." I smile genuinely. "I appreciate it. I'll wash it tonight and bring it back tomorrow."

"No rush," he tells me.

"Thank you," I say again.

I start to walk past him when he says, "I'm Ares, by the way."

I stop and slide my eyes up to his. I feel a jolt at the visual contact. "I know who you are, quarterback."

He smiles at that. "You said it was your first day."

"Yes," I say slowly, my mouth suddenly drying.

"I didn't know we had a new staff member starting."

So, my dad hasn't told any of the players that I'll be working here. Great.

"What will you be doing?" he asks.

"Oh, this and that," I reply.

He laughs. "You don't give much away, do you?"

I shrug.

His eyes glitter with amusement and challenge. "Do I get your name at least?"

I take a deep breath. "Ari. Arianna . . . Petrelli."

I watch as my name filters in, and realization dawns on him.

The light fades out of his eyes. His expression shuts down.

And my stomach suddenly feels very empty.

He steps away, putting a good amount of distance between us. His arms fold over his chest, like a barrier. Jaw gritting. "You're Coach's daughter."

I swallow past the dryness in my throat. "Yes."

"I didn't know you'd be working here."

"I . . . it . . ." I lift my hands, unsure of what to say.

There's a beat of silence. A moment of nothing. Neither of us says anything.

Then, he abruptly turns to his changing station, giving me his back.

Wow. Okay.

I'm used to people looking at me like shit. But not this kind of reaction. Like I have an infectious disease.

I take a deep breath and find my voice. "Is . . . is there a problem?"

"Nope." He pulls a team shirt off a hanger.

I stand here, knowing full well there is a problem, but not really knowing how to handle his adverse reaction to me.

He glances over his shoulder at me. There's none of the warmth or humor from before. His eyes are blank and narrowed, looking at me like I'm an inconvenience. I'm gum on the sole of his new shoes.

"I need to change," he states, voice cold.

"Sorry." I step back, holding his shirt to my chest.

His eyes drop to it with a flash of something akin to

anger, and for a moment, I wonder if I should offer to give him his shirt back.

But I don't. I keep my mouth shut, turn on my heel, and head for the door.

Before I reach it, I pause and turn back to him. "Ares?"

His eyes flash over to mine. His expression is tight.

I take a small step forward. "Could I ask a favor?"

He blinks slowly and exhales a harsh breath. "What is it?" His voice is irritated.

"I just wanted to ask . . . could you not mention this to my dad . . . that you saw me in here—"

"Without your top on."

My face heats. "Yes. It's just . . . I . . ." *How do I say this?* "It's just that I . . ." *Don't want to disappoint him again.*

"I won't say anything," he growls and then turns back to his station. "There's nothing to tell."

"Thank you," I say softly.

He huffs out a brittle laugh, shaking his head, and I feel like I'm missing something.

I want to ask why he's so pissed off by me. But I'm too chickenshit to do it.

So, I once again keep my mouth shut and head for the door.

"Arianna."

I stop and glance back over my shoulder. He's facing me now, the same stoic expression on his countenance.

"What?" I say.

"I want the shirt back tomorrow. Clean."

Something in the way he says *clean* pokes at me.

He thinks I'm a dirty drunk.

I inhale through my nose.

I am not that person anymore.

I'm clean and sober.

And I don't need his stupid shirt. I'd rather walk around with my boobs on show than wear his clothes.

I lift my chin and walk back over to him.

When I'm a foot away, I toss the shirt back to him. He catches it with a single hand, eyes not moving from mine.

"Turns out, I don't need to borrow *your* shirt after all." Then, I spin around and walk out of there.

Chapter Three

I STEP INSIDE MY APARTMENT and close the door behind me, locking it.

I cast a glance toward the corner of my room where my paints and easel are set up. I stare at the blank canvas sitting there on the easel, praying that I'll feel something. Anything. Even a spark of interest or inspiration would be a start. I'd be grateful for that.

But nothing.

I haven't painted in six months.

Not since I've been sober.

Painting is all I've ever known. All I've ever done.

I'm an artist who can't paint.

It feels like I've lost a limb.

Since I quit drinking, I can't bring myself to put brush to canvas.

There has been only one other time in my life when I stopped painting. After my mother killed herself.

I was the one who found her. Hanging from the clothes rail in her and my dad's walk-in closet. It was a high rail. The one my dad used to hang his shirts on.

My dad's tall. Six feet three. My mom was small. Like I am. I look like her, too. I sometimes wonder if that's part of the problem. That I remind my dad of her.

She had used her vanity stool to stand on.

I had come home after studying for a test at a friend's house. My dad was away with the team.

She had known it would be me who found her.

And she hadn't cared.

I took my first drink of alcohol on the day of her funeral.

I was fifteen. My uncle, my mom's brother, handed me a glass of brown liquid. He told me it was brandy and to go ahead and drink it, that it was good for shock, that it would help me get through the day.

He was right.

That single glass of brandy got me through her funeral.

And, when I woke up the next day and everything felt difficult, even just getting out of bed, I had another glass of brandy to help me get through the day.

And where was my dad, you might ask? Well, he was at work. Back with his team. His *real* family. He'd left me a note tacked to the fridge, saying he wouldn't be long.

And I was left home alone, in the house where my mother had killed herself, only five days ago.

Alcohol was my comfort through a difficult time, and it helped me get back to painting. I felt alive and inspired when I drank.

It made everything easier.

And, now that I no longer have that . . . I'm blank.

Like the canvas that's sitting there, waiting for me.

Sighing, I kick off my shoes. I put my bag on the kitchen counter as I pass. Then, I tug off the shirt I borrowed from my dad as I pad down my tiny hallway. I stop by the bathroom and toss the shirt in my laundry hamper. I take off my bra and my jeans, followed by my panties, and toss them in the hamper, too.

I take a quick shower. Leaving my hair wet, I dress in clean panties, an old college sweater, and shorts.

I head for the kitchen and grab a glass from the cupboard. Go to the tap and fill it with water.

Leaning back against the counter, I take a sip.

My apartment is so quiet. Too quiet.

Peace isn't good for me. Too much time to think.

I take another sip of my water, my eyes closing on a blink as I do.

I swallow slowly, letting the water run down my throat.

My mind drifts . . .

Vodka.

Sliding down my throat.

The burn of the alcohol.

You remember how good it felt, Ari.

The feel of it coursing through your body, taking the pain away. Freeing you—

Stop!

I flash open my eyes, turn, and pour out the water into the sink, setting the glass in it.

I grip the edge of the counter and swallow in a lungful of air.

Breathe, Ari. Slow and deep.

I take a breath in through my nose and let it out through my dry mouth.

Dry from the need to drink.

No.

My grip on the counter increases. My arms start to tremble from the force, but I don't let go. Because I'm afraid of what will happen if I do.

I don't have alcohol in the apartment, but I'm within a ten-minute radius of pubs and bars. Five minutes if I run.

And I'm afraid that, if I let go of this counter, I'll start running.

I squeeze my eyes shut and slowly count to ten.

I don't need to drink.

I am in control of my life.

Six months, Ari. Six months sober.

Don't blow it now.

You've gotten through the worst.

Detox was the most horrific experience of my life. I don't ever want to go through it again.

And, if I have even one drink, I'll be right back where I started.

I can't go there.

I *won't* go there.

I was what is called a high-functioning alcoholic. I used alcohol as a coping mechanism. I would find any reason to drink. I would drink alone at home. Too much, too often. I could drink a couple of bottles of wine at home or go out and party like it was 1999 and wake with no hangover and head into work. Some people might think that was a good thing, being able to drink with no hangover. But it really wasn't. It meant that I'd built a tolerance over the years. I'd been drinking too much, for too long.

I couldn't go a day without a drink, and even then, I still didn't know I had a problem. If someone had asked me seven months ago if I could stop drinking, I would've answered yes without hesitation.

It wasn't until it was too late when I realized I had a problem.

No, it's not too late.

I made a terrible mistake because of the disease I have.

And that's what alcoholism is . . . it's a disease.

But I'm getting better. Every day, I'm getting stronger and stronger.

It will not defeat me.

I want a life. I want to be able to paint again. I want to have a career as a professional artist. Maybe even get married one day and have children of my own.

But, to have all of those things, I need to stay sober.

My count is up to fifty when I feel able to actually let go of the counter.

I get my cell from my bag and sit down on my kitchen floor. I open up my music app and press play on my relaxation music. I adopt the lotus position and close my eyes.

I don't know how long I've been sitting like this when my cell starts to ring with an incoming call.

I open one eye, glancing at the caller display, and see it's my dad.

I really don't feel like talking to him at the moment, especially not after my little episode. And it's hard, feeling like a disappointment all the time. Not that he says so. I can just hear it in his voice.

But I know, if I don't answer, he'll just keep calling.

So, I pick up my cell and swipe to accept the call. "Hey, Dad."

"Hey. How are you doing?"

Oh, I'm currently sitting on my kitchen floor in the lotus position after a bad moment, but aside from that, peachy.

"I'm good," I say. I stretch my legs out and lean back against the cupboard door. "I was just going to start thinking about what to have for dinner."

"We could have had dinner together," he says. "I thought you might have come to see me after you finished work. I was gonna give you a ride home, so we could grab dinner together in the city."

"Sorry, I didn't realize." *If you'd told me, I would've known though.* "I wasn't sure where in the building you were"—*lie*—"and I had to rush to catch my bus." *Another lie.* "Maybe tomorrow?" I suggest.

"I can't tomorrow. I've got a late meeting with Bill."

Bill is the owner of the team.

"The day after," I suggest.

"Sure." Pause. "So, how did you get on today?"

"Okay. It was . . . good."

"I'm sorry I didn't get to spend much time with you today. I was busy with—"

"It's fine, Dad." *I'm used to it.* The words are on the tip of my tongue, but like usual, I don't say them.

My therapist in rehab told me that I should air my grievances with my dad, tell him how I've felt like second best all these years. The resentment that I feel toward him for never being around to help with Mom when she was still alive.

I knew he couldn't handle Mom's mood swings. He would spend as much time out of the house as possible. So, it was mostly just me and her.

When she had a high mood, she was great, fun. But, when she was low . . . it was bad. Sometimes, she couldn't get out of bed for days.

Mom was diagnosed with bipolar disorder when I was seven.

Her problems started after I was born, and I wonder if I was the catalyst for everything that went wrong for her. I know she'd had a bad childhood, which was where most of her problems stemmed from. But it seems that it got worse for her after I was born. I sometimes think that she blamed me for her depression . . . her illness, and that was why she let me be the one to find her in the closet on that day.

I was angry with her for a long time. Angry with my dad for not being there. I guess I still am.

But he was there when I screwed up. It was him who cleaned up my mess. Hired the lawyer. Put me in rehab. Gave me this job.

I owe him for that.

And I don't want to fight with my dad over the past. He's the only family I have left.

He might not be perfect, but who is? Well, aside from Ares "Mr. Perfect" Kincaid.

"Did Mary show you around?" Dad asks, cutting into my thoughts.

After Dad introduced me to all the players and assistant coaches—which didn't go as bad as I had expected. Well, except for Ares, who acted like we hadn't met, which I guess was good because I would've had to explain to my dad how we'd met, and I definitely didn't want to do that. So, I guess in a way, he was only doing what I was asking and keeping our encounter from my dad.

It was just the way he was looking at me when Dad was introducing me to him ... clear disgust in his eyes. A hardness to his voice that my dad didn't seem to notice.

But I did, and it made me feel like shit.

Dad disappeared once I met everyone, and I was palmed off to Mary, his PA. She's well into her sixties but doesn't look a day over fifty. She's one of those really classy, glamorous women, who I aspire to look like when I'm her age. She was really nice to me, too. Never once brought up my problems. She spent most of the time telling me all about her new granddaughter, Rosie.

"Yeah, she did," I answer him. "She gave me a tour of the building and pitches and gave me a rundown of my duties."

"Did she give you your work cell and iPad?"

"Yes. They're in my bag."

"Good. Well, the players all have your work cell number now—I had Mary send it to them—but only take calls during work hours. Don't let them take advantage, okay?"

"I won't."

There's a beat of silence. The awkwardness that's always existed between us, which has only worsened since the crash. I wonder if it'll ever go, if we'll ever just have an easy, flowing relationship.

"Right, well, I'll let you get to it," he says.

"Okay, Dad. I'll see you tomorrow."

We hang up, and I push up to my feet.

I search through my cupboards, trying to decide on what to eat, and I end up with a bowl of Cap'n Crunch, like usual.

I take my cell, bag, and cereal bowl into the living room with me. I put my bag down on the floor. I sit down on the sofa, legs tucked underneath me, cereal bowl resting on them, and put my cell down beside me. I glance at it.

The cell that only rings with my daily call from my dad and my sponsor, Luke.

The friends I used to have, I had to leave behind. They like to party, and I don't do that anymore. My old colleagues from the gallery, who were friends, too, haven't made contact since the crash, and I have a feeling they don't want to hang out with me.

So, I'm friendless.

I'm lonely. It's pathetic but true. I've gone from a life of constantly having somewhere to be—a gallery event with hors d'oeuvre and champagne or dinner with friends and endless glasses of wine or parties with my cheating scumbag ex-boyfriend—to now staying in every night with Netflix for company. Well, except for the one night a week when I go to my AA meeting where I spend an hour listening to people who are just like me.

I was hoping maybe I might be able to make friends at my new job, but so far, the two people I have gotten along with are the middle-aged security guard and my dad's sixty-year-old PA.

Leaning down, I reach into my bag and pull out the

iPad that Mary gave me. I eat some cereal while it loads.

It's already been set up, and there's a link to the Giants website. I click on it, and when it loads, I go to the photos tab.

I click through a few of the pictures, seeing my dad on the goal line and some of the players I met today in action on the field.

I click on the video tab and scroll down until I come across an interview titled "Giants Insider: Quarterback Ares Kincaid."

I spoon more cereal into my mouth and press play.

It's only two minutes long, and it's basically him being charming as he talks football.

I saw some of that charm today before he found out who I was, and then that changed.

If I'm being honest, knowing he doesn't like me is bothering me, considering how highly my dad thinks of him.

My dad didn't notice today that Ares was off with me, but he will soon enough, if Ares keeps on with his cold attitude toward me.

Ares Kincaid has formed an opinion of me because of what he heard or read in the press.

But he knows jack shit.

He doesn't know a single thing about me. He doesn't know that I dislike myself way more than he ever could.

He might not like who I used to be or what I did, but I haven't personally done anything to him, so I don't get why he dislikes me so much.

I resolve to clear the air with him tomorrow. Start

fresh and all that. I don't want to be at odds with a guy I have to work with—or for or whatever.

And who knows? Maybe, if it goes well, I might even make a friend out of him, a friend my own age—and a responsible one at that. God, my dad would be ecstatic.

I laugh out loud at the absurdness of my thoughts.

Honestly, if I can just get Ares to stop being so frosty toward me, I'll call that a win.

I grab the remote and turn on my buddy Netflix, settling back into the couch to watch the latest episode of *Riverdale*, spooning some more cereal into my mouth, looking forward to a better day tomorrow.

Chapter Four

I'VE BEEN WORKING HERE for a week now, and I still haven't managed to get a chance to speak to Ares. The guy avoids me. Like, seriously, he saw me a few days ago in the hallway. He'd just come out of the locker room, and I was walking that way.

I was heading to the gym to take Hector, the veteran center, a special protein shake that he has every day, which is made up by the Giants' resident chef, Pierre. Bonus about working here: the food is amazing. Pierre is awesome. Early thirties, very handsome, and from France. His accent is divine. He moved here ten years ago to be with his husband, Eric. They'd met when Eric was in France on business.

Pierre has been wrapping me up food to take home every day, so I've been well fed this past week.

Anyway, Ares saw me, and he did an about-face. I shit you not. He saw me. His expression darkened like thunder, and then he just turned around and went straight back into the locker room.

I'll admit, it stung.

No one wants to be disliked. Especially when I haven't done anything to him. Well, except for flash him my bra. But I wouldn't say that's a hate-worthy crime.

I really do need to sort this out with him because it's getting silly now.

I don't want him to have a problem with me, and I don't want one with him. But the way he's acting toward me is making me dislike him.

So, I endeavor not to let this drag on for much longer, and I'm going to corner him the second I get a chance.

And it must be my lucky day because Ares has just walked into the screening room where I'm currently setting up the laptop with the game my dad wants the players to watch on the cinema-sized projection screen.

"Uh"—he halts in his tracks when he sees me and looks around the empty room—"where is everyone?"

"Still on the field. Practice ran over. Weren't you there?"

"No." He doesn't elaborate more, and I don't ask.

"When will they be here?"

"Another ten minutes, I think."

"Right. Well, I'll"—another step toward the door—"go and do, um . . . yeah." He turns for the door.

"Wait," I say, my voice coming out a little too squeaky, too desperate-sounding.

He stops and glances back at me over his shoulder. He doesn't turn around or let go of the door handle though.

I move around the laptop table and walk a little

closer to him. "Look, I was, um ... hoping we could ... clear the air."

He lets go of the door handle and turns to face me, but he doesn't say anything.

"Okay"—I let out a breath—"so I know you don't think very ... highly of me. I'm guessing most of your opinion is based on what you've heard or read about me."

He cuts me off with a laugh, only it doesn't sound funny, and it makes my eyes narrow.

"What?" I bite.

He folds his arms across his mammoth chest. "I just think it's funny that you assume that's how I formed my opinion of you."

"Isn't it?"

"No."

There's a beat of silence. Both of us staring, neither speaking.

Naturally, I'm the first to break it. "Are you going to elaborate on that?"

"I'm not sure you want to hear what I have to say."

"Don't spare my feelings. I'm a big girl. I can take it."

He sighs out a breath, making me feel like an inconvenience. Like having to talk to me is taking up too many precious minutes of his time when he could be, I don't know, looking in the mirror, telling himself how amazing he is.

"Fine," he says, looking me dead in the eye. "I don't like people like you."

"People like me?"

"Alcoholics."

Okay.

"And is there a particular reason you don't like alcoholics—aside from the obvious."

His lips press together, body rigid with tension, and it's abundantly clear that he's not going to answer my question.

"Okay. So, no answer on that. Well, can I ask . . . is it all alcoholics you don't like, or could a person in recovery maybe get a reprieve? I've been sober for six months now." Well, six months, two weeks, and three days, but who's counting?

He laughs, and it's derisive. It makes me feel smaller than I already am. "And what do you want, a medal?" he says coldly.

Wow. He really hates alcoholics.

I'm smart enough to realize that he's had someone in his life who had a problem with liquor, and I'm really trying not to take his attitude personally, but it's hard not to. Especially when his venom is currently being direct right at me.

"Usually, it's a chip. They give them to you in AA. I just recently got my six-month chip. It's dark blue. I'm now working toward my nine-month chip. That one is purple. But, if you want to get me a medal, I'm cool with that." I give a loose shrug of my shoulders and a big smile even though, inside, I'm hurting, but I don't want him to know that.

I figure, if he knows he's hurt me, he'll win, and I won't let him win.

"Sure. I'll get right on that," he deadpans with a shake of his head.

"It doesn't have to be this way, and it would be

much easier if we could get along. I work for you—
indirectly. And a bad atmosphere is just unnecessary.
I haven't done anything to you personally. And I
understand that you don't like *people* like me." I point
at myself. I don't know why I do that. I might as well
have gone full-on dork and air-quoted the words.
"But I'm trying here, and it's just really unfair of you
to hate me based on a general idea of 'my people.'" I
do air-quote that time. *Jesus Christ.*

He laughs that hollow laugh again, and it makes
my skin prickle.

"I don't hate you. I don't *anything* you. I just don't
trust alcoholics. And that *includes* sober ones."

"Why?" I can hear the plea to my tone, and I hate
it and don't understand it. *Why can't I just let this go?
Why do I want him to like me?*

"Look, Jailbird—" His hands lower from his chest
on a sigh.

My eyes widen. "What did you just call me?"

"You heard exactly what I called you, so why are
you asking me to repeat it?"

"Because I can't believe you would call me . . . *Jailbird*. I haven't been to jail!" I can feel myself starting
to tremble from his barb.

His expression narrows. "Yeah, well, you should've
after what you did. Climbing into that car, drunk off
your face." He shakes his head with disgust. "You
could've killed somebody."

Shame covers me like winter frost. I don't say anything because . . . what can I say? He's right.

"I know drunks, and I know you can't trust them.
The only thing they're loyal to is the bottle."

I want to argue with that. Tell him that he's general-izing. But he's not wrong either.

In most cases, it's true that alcoholics only care about where their next drink is coming from. When I was going through detox, I realized that had been true of me, too. There were moments back then when I would have literally done anything for a drink.

But that's not who I am now.

Are you sure? the voice in the back of my mind whispers.

"That's not me," I say, and I don't know if I'm talk-ing to him or myself in this moment. "I'm sober, and I intend to stay that way."

His shoulders lift. "I hope that works out for you. Statistically, it doesn't look good. But I hope you do stay sober, for your dad's sake. He's a good man, and he doesn't need you putting him through the kind of shit you put him through earlier this year."

Has my dad said something to him?

"And there's no reason for you and me to get along. We both know that Coach made up this job for you because he wants to make sure you don't relapse. I get that, and so does the rest of the team. But you must know that we don't actually need anything from you. Everything is covered by the staff already here. And some of the guys have their assistants. You're only getting jobs from some of the guys because we respect Coach, and he asked us to make you feel useful. And, as much as I like Coach, I'm choosing not to do that, for my own reason. We don't need to com-municate. So, there's no reason for us to get along. There's no reason for anything. I suggest we just stay out of each other's way for the foreseeable future. Okay."

Shit.

My heart is racing. Mouth dry. My face is burning. My eyes stinging.

I can't speak because, if I do, I'll burst into tears.

The door opens, and a barrage of voices comes into the room as it starts to fill with players.

I turn away, moving back to the laptop.

Don't cry. Don't cry. Don't cry.

I hit select on the video my dad wanted, and then, using my hair as a curtain to shield my face, I quietly slip out the door.

I walk quickly to the restroom. Into a stall.

And burst into tears.

Chapter Five

I LEAVE MY YOGA CLASS, waving good-bye to the instructor, Martin, and step outside into the warm air. The sidewalk is bustling with people. The day has such a positive vibe about it. I'm calm and relaxed after my class, and I don't want to lose this feeling.

There's a farmers' market a block over. I think I'll take a walk over there before heading home and buy some cheese and fresh bread. Then, I can spend the rest of the day gorging myself silly on it.

Sounds perfect.

Well, okay, not perfect. It sounds lonely. But it's not like I have many other options.

I hitch my bag up my shoulder and start walking.

As I approach the market, the aromas of fresh food invade my senses, and my stomach rumbles.

When I used to drink, my appetite wasn't very big. The alcohol suppressed my desire for food. Now that I'm sober, I've been discovering a big love for food. It took a while to get to this point. When I first detoxed,

the thought of eating made me want to throw up. But,
now that I'm over the worst of it, I'm able to enjoy
food.

The market is bustling. People browsing and making purchases.

There are couples, moms and dads with kids, and
solo people like me all milling around.

In a way, being here, surrounded by these strangers
all going about their day, makes me feel less lonely.

I inhale through my nose, my eyes briefly closing as I
absorb the smells and sounds around me, and—*ouch!*

My shoulder just connected with a wall.

My eyes flash open, and it's not a wall. It's a body.
A very hard male body.

I step back, a *Sorry* on the tip of my tongue, but
the word dies in my mouth as my eyes connect with
flaming blue eyes glowering down at me.

Ares.

Jesus Christ.

Seriously, you couldn't write this shit.

The one person guaranteed to kill my mood, and I
somehow manage to bump into him in this city of
eight and a half million people.

Just my luck. Maybe this is Karma's way of finally
getting me back.

And I would be wearing my yoga pants and oversize off-the-shoulder *Namast'ay In Bed & Watch
Netflix* sweatshirt over my sports bra. No makeup
and my hair tied back into a ponytail.

Why is it you're always looking at your worst when
you bump into the one person you really don't want
to see?

He's wearing an NY Giants ball cap, khaki cargo shorts, and a white linen shirt. The top few buttons are undone, the sleeves rolled up, dark hairs and veins covering his forearms.

God, he's attractive. I hate that he's so gorgeous to look at.

An asshole like him doesn't deserve to be this handsome.

It makes me want to dislike him even more.

Mr. Perfect.

I haven't spoken to him since our little *chat* in the viewing room.

And, apparently, we're not speaking now.

He's currently scowling at me like I'm the spawn of the devil. And I'm staring back with a mixture of hurt and anger in my chest.

"What are you doing here?" he asks in that hard tone he always uses when he's forced to speak to me.

What?

"Um, the same thing you're doing here ... shopping."

His eyes go down to my empty hands. "You haven't bought anything." His tone is accusing, and my back is instantly up.

"Because I literally just got here!" I'm exasperated. God, this guy is a dick.

He stares down at me, those intense eyes narrowing. "Are you following me, Jailbird?"

"What?" I sputter, my eyes going wide. "Why in the hell would I be following you?" Honestly, I've been doing my best to avoid him. "God, you're a jerk," I hiss. "For your information, I just finished my yoga class, which is the next block over, if you'd like to check, and I came here straight from there to pick up some cheese." Why am I telling him this? I don't have to explain myself to this goober.

He smirks. "Oh, yeah. I forgot that you liked to do yoga." The tone in his voice hints at amusement and actually stuns me into silence.

I part my lips to speak, but nothing comes out. I'm like a goldfish, just opening and closing my mouth, no sound coming.

"Hey," I hear a sweet female voice say.

It yanks my eyes from his to her, and standing beside him is a tall, beautiful woman. Long, dark hair. Sunglasses covering her eyes. Looks to be about my age.

I must look like a toddler, standing here with these two gorgeous skyscrapers.

She's wearing cutoff jean shorts, showing off her long, tan legs—I'm not jealous at all—and a T-shirt that says, *I'm Not Smart for A Girl. I'm Just Smart.*

I like her immediately. Any woman who wears a shirt saying that has my admiration.

She's looking between us.

She must be wondering who the hell I am and why he's looking at me like he would like to strangle me with his bare hands.

"A, are you going to introduce me?" she says with curiosity in her voice.

She called him A. She's clearly familiar with him.

I wonder if she's his girlfriend.

My stomach fills with battery acid.

I choose not to think about why.

But, if she is his girlfriend, then she deserves a medal for putting up with him. Although I imagine he's nice to her.

She pushes her sunglasses up to the top of her head, revealing her eyes. Bright blue. Exactly like his.

Maybe she's not his girlfriend after all. Maybe they're related.

Ares lets out an aggravated-sounding sigh and folds his arms over his mammoth chest. The fabric of his shirt stretches over his huge biceps. "She's Coach Petrelli's daughter."

Coach Petrelli's daughter.

Wow, don't go overboard there with the introduction, Mr. Perfect.

Seems I'm not even deemed worthy enough to have a name. Actually, come to think of it, I can't remember him ever calling me by my name. He's called me Jailbird, but that's it.

I get that he has a strong aversion to alcoholics, but his hatred for me is something else altogether.

"Well, hey there, Coach Petrelli's daughter," she says in a teasing voice, which is aimed at Ares and his lame introduction. "I'm Missy. This grumpy ass's sister." She thumbs in his direction.

Ares frowns in her direction.

And I smile. My smile has nothing to do with the fact that she's his sister and everything to do with her calling him a grumpy ass and the fact that her expression hasn't dropped at the introduction of who I am. I can't imagine he's talked about me to her. Either that, or she's not a hater of ex-alcoholics.

And my stomach most definitely has not emptied of the battery acid it was filled with.

"I'm Arianna," I tell her.

"Well, it's nice to meet you, Arianna," she says, sounding like she actually means it. "Guess I don't need to ask how you know my brother. Coach Petrelli being your dad and all."

"We actually only met recently," I tell her, avoiding his hard stare. *And he hates my guts.* "I just started working for my dad."

"Cool. And how's that going?"

Um . . .

You know, aside from my dad, she's the only other person who's asked me that question.

"It's . . ." I risk a glance at Ares, and his eyes are staring off into the distance, his jaw clenched so tightly, it looks like it might shatter. I look back at Missy, and her eyes are sparkling with something that looks a lot like mischief. "It's okay. I guess." I shrug.

"Mmhmm. I can imagine, being surrounded by all those big, strapping football players—barring my brother, of course—must be a real hardship."

She gives a teasing roll of her eyes, and I laugh.

"I'm just not a big fan of football," I say.

"You're not?" That's Ares, and the sound of his voice surprises me. I thought he was done with his participation in this conversation.

"Oh Christ, don't say that." Missy laughs. "Not if you don't want to endure a lecture on how football is the greatest game in the world."

I've had enough of Ares Kincaid's lectures to last me a lifetime, so I'll pass on that one.

"Got it," I say. "Well, I should head off. It was nice meeting you, Missy—"

"Hey, we were just about to go for some gelato, if you want to join us?"

My eyes dart to Ares.

He shakes his head ever-so subtly, ensuring his sister doesn't see.

My face goes hot with embarrassment.

I knew he wouldn't want me to go, but I never thought he'd be so cold and actually tell me to say no.

That feeling of being disliked and my complete and utter loneliness hit me at a whole new level.

"I, um . . ." I'm stumbling over my words. "I can't. I have to . . ." I can't think of anything to say; my mind has gone blank. "Cheese," I suddenly blurt out. "I need to buy cheese."

Missy chuckles. "So, we'll get your cheese on the way to the gelato place. We're not taking no for an answer, are we, A?" She nudges him with her elbow.

He frowns at me. "Apparently not."

Chapter Six

Aɴᴅ ᴛʜɪs ɪs ʜᴏᴡ I find myself sitting on a stool in a gelato shop across from a scowling Ares with his smiling sister, Missy, next to him.

Aside from the pissed-off football player there, throwing daggers at me, it's actually nice, talking to his sister. I can't remember the last time I did this . . . just hung out and ate ice cream.

Probably before my mom died.

"So, you guys have another brother?" I say to Missy. "The boxer. Zeus, right?"

"Yep. Zeus is our big brother. And there's also my twin brother, Lo," Missy tells me.

"Wow. You have a twin. So cool."

"Not as cool as you'd think. He's like a menstrual cycle—"

"For fuck's sake!" Ares groans.

She rolls her eyes at him, and I laugh.

"A menstrual cycle?" I cough out.

"Yep. He's like this thing I have, and I wouldn't

function right without him, but he gives me serious cramps."

My eyes are watering with laughter by this point. I can't think of the last time I laughed this hard. Honestly, I can't remember the last time I laughed for real.

I wipe at my eyes, my laughter dying down.

"What about you, Arianna? Any brothers or sisters?" Missy asks me.

"No. No brothers or sisters. And call me Ari. Everybody does," I say. *Well, people who actually call me by my given name.*

"An only child. I've always thought that would be incredibly lonely," she says, sounding genuinely concerned for me.

You have no idea.

"It was okay." I shrug. "It meant I didn't have to share any of my stuff."

"Well, I was reading this article the other day, and it said that only children are overachievers, and they tend to be leaders."

"Yeah, and they're also selfish and spoiled."

"Ares Kincaid!" Missy cries out. "Ari is not spoiled."

My cheeks are hot with embarrassment.

"I never said she was. But you don't even know her either to make that assumption," he tosses back at her before his eyes shift to mine. And those judging eyes of his are saying, *But I know you. I know who you are. A worthless drunk.*

I want to tell him that he doesn't know a thing about me, but what would be the point? He's already made his mind up about me.

"I've seen enough to know that she's a sweet person," Missy says, smiling kindly at me.

I try to return her smile, but it feels off.

Ares stares at her, his eyes softening in that way only a sibling's can. Then, he wraps an arm around her neck, pulling her to him, and presses an affectionate kiss to her forehead.

She pushes him away, feigning irritation, but I can tell she secretly loves it.

I know I would if I had a brother who cared for me like he clearly does her.

"Ignore my brother. He's being a butthead today." She turns back to me. Elbow on the table, she rests her chin in her hand. "Tell me about you," she says to me.

"Uh . . . there's not really much to tell," I say around a spoonful of salted caramel gelato, trying to cool my heated face down.

She is so bright and positive, like a ray of sun, and her positivity is infectious, unlike her asshole brother.

I'm sitting here, trying to soak up as much of her zeal as I can. I really don't want to bring down the mood with tales of my miserable existence.

"Sure there is!" She rings out a laugh. "Okay, I'll ask questions. Are you from New York?"

"Nope." I shake my head.

"Didn't think so. You don't sound like a native."

"I'm from Atlanta originally," I tell her. "But we moved around a bit with my dad's job, so I've lived in quite a few places. My accent is a bit of a mixed bag."

"Best place you've lived?" she asks.

"Here." I smile.

I jolt when I hear Ares's voice talk in my direction. "Makes sense. There are a lot of bars in New York. Plenty of places to party." The dig is blatant and cruel.

My eyes flash up to his. His are on me. Steady and hard and judgmental.

My face burns with humiliation. I dig my spoon into my gelato, staring down at it.

"Speaking of bars," Missy says, obviously unaware of the tension between us, "we're going to check out this new club tonight. Ares got VIP tickets. You should come with us."

Shit.

"Oh. Um . . ."

"If you haven't got plans already, that is."

I could say I have plans. I should say that. But I don't want to lie to Missy. She's being so nice to me. And it's not like Ares won't tell her anyway after we've left here.

Honestly, I'm half-expecting him to say it now and beat me to it.

But I won't give him the satisfaction.

I am who I am, and I shouldn't be ashamed of that. I'm sober now, and that's what matters.

I look up at Missy and try to smile, but I'm not sure that I pull it off. "Bars aren't my scene anymore. I'm in recovery. Six months sober. But I really do appreciate you inviting me."

"Oh," she says, her bright eyes dimming a little as they move to Ares, who's surprisingly staring at me.

When she looks back to me, the expression on her brow . . . it's like she's just figured something out.

That I'm a mess. A loser. And definitely not the kind of person she wants to befriend.

Oh well. It was nice while it lasted.

"That's amazing, Ari. Not the drinking problem, of course." She slaps a hand to her head. "Sorry. That came out sounding wrong. I meant, you being sober. That's a big deal. You should be really proud of yourself."

Warmth glows in my chest. The only other person who's said that to me is Luke.

"I am." I smile.

I don't look at Ares, but I can practically feel him burning holes into my head with his fire eyes.

"Have you celebrated the milestone?" she asks me.

"Um . . . no. Well, Luke, my sponsor, brought in a cupcake for me when I received my six-month chip, so there was that."

"Okay, so we're totally doing something. Oh, I know! We should go to the movies. Have you seen *The Greatest Showman*?"

I shake my head.

"Me either, but I've heard it's amazing."

"Honestly, you don't have to change your plans on my account."

"She's right. Listen to her," Ares says low.

Missy gives him a dirty look. "It's just a club. It's not going anywhere. You can use the tickets anytime, right?"

He folds his arms. "It's not the point."

"It's totally the point. But, if it bothers you so much, you still go. Ari and I will go to the movies together."

His eyes flash to me, a look of distrust in them.

Then, he heaves out a sigh. "Fine. We'll go to the movies."

He doesn't trust me with his sister.

That cuts me to the core.

What does he think I'm going to do? Turn her into an alcoholic?

"Really, it's fine," I say quietly. "You should totally go to the club."

"I'm not really in the mood to go clubbing tonight anyway. A date with Zac Efron sounds so much more appealing."

"For fuck's sake," Ares grumbles.

"And I'm guessing you don't already have plans," she says to me, ignoring Ares. "Otherwise, you would have said so by now."

"I don't have plans," I admit.

She grins. "Then, it's settled." She claps her hands together. "We're going to the movies."

Chapter Seven

I'M STANDING OUTSIDE THE movie theater where I arranged to meet Missy and, unfortunately, Mr. Perfect at seven thirty. My hair is down and wavy. I'm wearing a little makeup, my black skinny jeans with ripped knees, a gray sweater, my leather jacket, and my pink Dr. Martens. I have my bag slung over my shoulder, containing all the usual stuff, plus an umbrella because my luck with rain recently has not been good.

I'm stupidly excited for this evening. I spent way too much time getting ready for a night at the cinema. But, when you get out as little as I do, you have to make the most of it.

I got here a bit early, so I've been waiting a while. But they are a little late. I check the time on my phone again. Seven forty.

The movie starts at seven forty-five; that's why we agreed to meet at seven thirty. Give us time to get tickets and food.

A sinking feeling of being stood up starts to take root.

Maybe Ares told Missy what I did. The drunk driving, crashing my ex's car into that wall. I wouldn't be surprised if he did tell her. It's no secret that he hates me, and I got the distinct impression he doesn't want me spending time with his sister.

Maybe he told her all the bad things about me, and she changed her mind about coming. I wouldn't blame her.

No. She's a good person. She wouldn't do that—stand me up like this. Ares would. But not Missy.

And she's only ten minutes late, for goodness' sake. Chill out, Ari.

A gust of wind blows past, kicking up my hair. I wrap my arms around my chest and shift on my feet, trying to ward off the chill.

"Jailbird."

I turn at the sound of Ares's voice saying my name. *Christ, not my name!* The jerk even has me responding to it now.

"Please don't call me that." I frown at him, not even able to feel relief that he's here and I haven't been stood up, like I feared.

He doesn't say anything, just stands there in front of me like a big tree.

I glance past him. "Where's Missy?"

"She's not coming. She had me come tell you that she's sorry, but her best friend's having a baby, and she went into early labor a few hours ago. She tried to call you on your work phone, but it went straight to voicemail."

"Oh . . ." Disappointment swells inside me. "My dad told me to turn it off when I'm not working, so I don't get calls from any of the players at stupid times of the day."

"Well, whatever. She left you a voicemail, explaining."

"Oh. Okay. Well, thank you for coming to tell me. I know you probably didn't want to. But I appreciate it all the same."

He's staring down at me, arms folded over his chest.

"Well"—I step back away from him—"bye then."

I turn to leave, but his voice stops me.

"Where are you going?"

I glance back at him. "Home."

"Didn't you want to watch this stupid movie?"

"Well, yes . . ."

"So, why are you going home?"

Good question.

I can still watch it even though Missy couldn't make it. I'm an independent woman. I can go to the movies alone. If I don't, I'll just go home and probably watch a movie on Netflix. I might as well watch a movie here, where I'll be surrounded by other people for a few hours even if they are strangers.

"Yeah, I think I will still watch it," I say more to myself than him, turning toward the cinema. "Thanks again for coming to let me know about Missy. And would you please tell her that I said congratulations to her friend on her new baby?"

I don't wait for his response as I turn to go inside the theater.

I reach the door when I realize that he's behind me.

I stop and glance back at him. "Um, what are you doing?"

"Same thing you are. Going to watch the film."

"You want to watch this movie? You just said a few minutes ago that it was stupid."

"I have no desire to watch this movie at all. But I promised my sister that I wouldn't let you watch it alone. So, here I am." He spreads his hands out, and I frown.

"Seriously, you don't need to do me any favors."

He frowns back at me. "I'm not. I'm doing it for my sister."

"Well, I let you off the hook. You can go home." I gesture toward the street.

He follows the direction of my hand, like he's actually considering it. Then, he looks back at me and shakes his head. "No can do. If Missy finds out I left you here, there'll be hell to pay. And I could really do without having my ear bent by her."

"Don't worry; I won't tell her you didn't stay. And you won't tell her. So, there you go. You're free to leave." I let my hands go wide.

He lets out a low laugh. "My sister will question me to the tenth degree about the movie when she gets home. She'll know instantly if I haven't seen it."

"Wikipedia. You can get the whole plot on there. There you go."

"Missy can smell a lie at fifty paces. She's like a sniffer dog for bullshit. Seems like we're stuck with each other for the next few hours."

"No, we're really not. Just because you promised your sister you'd stay doesn't mean I have to go along with it."

He laughs again, eyes widening with humor. "You

really don't want me here, do you?" His hand slaps his chest. "You're starting to hurt my feelings, Jailbird."

"Good," I bite. "And why the hell would I want you here? You've been nothing but an asshole to me since the moment I met you."

"Well, not the moment I met you . . ." He grins, his eyes brightening, reminding me of my semi-naked bent-over moment, and I snap.

"Oh, I'm sorry! I should've said, the second you realized who I was. So, please, excuse me if I don't want to spend my evening with a judgmental, bigoted asshole who can't see past the end of his own so-called perfection to understand other people and their problems!"

When I break off, I'm breathing a little harder, and his face is blank.

"I never said I was perfect."

I let out a humorless laugh. "Whatever. Just . . . what-the-fuck-ever. Good-bye, Ares."

I spin on my heel and stomp into the theater.

It's not until I reach the queue for tickets when I realize that he's standing right behind me.

For fuck's sake!

"Stop following me," I hiss at him.

"I'm not." He gives me a look of innocence, shoulders lifting. "I'm just going to watch the movie."

"The movie you don't want to watch."

His lips widen into a grin.

"God, you're such a jackass! Just go away and leave me alone, *please*."

My voice hitches on the word *please*, and afraid I might burst into tears or punch him in his handsome, arrogant face, I turn around, moving forward, as the queue shifts.

A moment later, I feel heat at my back and almost jump out of my skin when I feel his hot breath against my ear. "Now, now, Jailbird, there's no need to be so bitchy."

I almost bite my tongue off at that. I turn my head to him to tell him to fuck off, but I misjudge actually how close he is. My nose bumps his, our lips literally centimeters apart.

My breath catches. My body freezes. My nose floods with his scent. Woodsy-scented aftershave and the smell of mint on his breath.

Every feminine part of me comes to life. It's like my body is suddenly wide awake after a long stretch of being dormant and is saying, *Well, hello there, man with a penis. It's been a while. Wanna come play?*

I hear him suck in a breath, and his eyes flicker down to my lips.

I lick them without conscious thought, and his eyes ignite with fire, causing a tightening in my lower belly. *Jesus.*

I exhale a ragged breath. His eyes lift to mine.

"You want to kiss me, Jailbird?" he whispers and inches closer. So close that I feel his lips brush mine when he talks again. "Yeah . . ." he breathes out. "That's never going to happen."

Everything good I was feeling inside dies. My face stings with embarrassment.

I straighten up, arms crossing over my chest. "I know it wouldn't because I would rather kiss herpes than you, you arrogant prick."

"God, I love it when you talk dirty to me."

He smirks, and I give him the middle finger.

I face forward and walk straight toward the now-open ticket booth, ignoring the rumble of laughter behind me.

"One to see *The Greatest Showman*, please," I say to the girl at the counter.

I pay for my ticket and walk straight in the direction of the food, not giving him a backward glance.

After buying a large tub of popcorn and a soda with no more sightings of Ares, hopefully meaning he got the message and left, I head into the theater.

There are a few people already seated. I wander down and take a seat in the middle of the theater, a couple in from the end of the aisle.

I put my soda in the cup holder and my popcorn on the ground by my feet while I dig my glasses out of my bag.

I need them for reading and watching TV. I mostly forget to wear them, but I need them for the movies, as the screen is bright and big, and I'll get a headache if I don't use them.

I slide them on, pick my popcorn up, and sit upright. Just as someone takes the seat right next to me.

Ares.

"For fuck's sake," I hiss at him. "Go away!"

"Can't." He shrugs. "I made a promise to my sister, and I don't break my promises."

"She won't know that we didn't sit together, you goober."

He laughs a surprised sound. "Did you just call me a goober?"

"You heard what I said. Why are you asking me to repeat it?" I toss back the words he used on me the first time he called me Jailbird.

He laughs again. "Touché." He settles back into his seat, setting his long legs out, clearly having no intention of moving. "And no can do, Jailbird. I have to sit here. I told 'you, Missy knows when I'm lying, and she'll know if I didn't sit with you."

"Argh! You're insufferable! Is it your current mission in life to make my life miserable? Because, news flash, Mr. Perfect: my life is already shitty, so there's not much more you can do!"

His head tilts to the side, like he's seeing me for the first time. "I didn't know you wore glasses," he says, totally throwing me off course.

"What?" I snap.

"Glasses. I didn't know you wore them."

I touch my hand to them. "Why would you? It's not like you know a single thing about me."

"Well, you know that's not true, Jailbird. I know you like to crash cars in your spare time."

"Fuck you," I hiss.

He lets out a low rumble, the sound reverberating in his chest and straight into mine. "Jeez, the mouth on you. I'm just messing with you. But I do know something else about you."

"What? That I like to drink? Ha-ha. Yeah, you're frigging hilarious."

"That's not what I was going to say."

"Okay, fine. Go on then; enlighten me, Mr. Perfect." I throw out a gesturing hand. "Get it out of your system, and then leave me the hell alone."

He leans his head over, closer to mine. His eyes are bright in the darkness, and my body stills. Every molecule that makes me up is frozen solid.

"I was going to say"—his minty breath brushes over my skin—"that you look pretty when you wear glasses."

My mouth drops open. Then, closes. Then, opens again.

"Wha . . ." I eventually manage to get out.

"Hush." He admonishes, eyes flicking toward the screen. "Movie's starting."

Then, you know what the cheeky son of a bitch does?

He digs his hand into my popcorn and takes a handful of it, stuffing it in his mouth, eyes smiling at me.

He's stunned me into silence. I'm just sitting here, staring at him, goldfish gaping.

"Close your mouth, Jailbird, and watch the damn movie."

"You look pretty when you wear glasses."

I finally move my eyes from him to the screen to watch the movie with my heart beating a brand-new rhythm.

Chapter Eight

"**W**ELL, THERE'S TWO HOURS of my life I'm never getting back," Ares complains as we leave the theater.

"An hour and forty-five actually. And are you being serious? I loved it."

"It was crap, and you know it, Jailbird."

My brows crash together. "Pfft. You wouldn't know a good movie if it came up and smacked you in the face."

He stops walking and stares down at me. "And you would?"

"Yep." I give him a knowing grin and start walking, leaving him behind.

I exit through the door, into the throng of the other moviegoers, and out into the chilly night.

I stop outside the theater, zipping up my jacket, and start debating on whether to walk or grab a cab.

"I'm driving you home." Ares's voice comes from beside me.

I slide a glance in his direction. "You drove here?"

"Yep. Come on." He starts to walk away, expecting me to follow him.

"No, thanks. I'll take a cab."

"I'm driving you home," he repeats with a firmness that irritates me.

"Don't tell me . . ." I put a hand on my hip. "Missy said you had to."

"She actually said I had to make sure you got home okay, and by that, she meant, see you safely to your front door, and I know you don't drive, so I'm driving you."

"Don't you ever tell her no?"

He laughs loudly. "If only. I learned years ago to just do as she says; it makes my life a whole lot easier."

I sigh and roll my eyes. He might be an asshole, but he loves his sister. Can't fault him for that.

"Fine. Where's your car?"

"Just over here."

I follow him toward a big, shiny black truck. Surprisingly, he opens the door for me.

"Erm . . . thanks," I say as I move past him to get in.

And . . . sweet Lord, it's high. And I'm vertically challenged.

Okay, I can do this.

I'm just thanking foresight that I wore jeans tonight.

I lift my leg, managing to get my foot on the edge of the car. One hand on the door, the other on the seat, I try to hoist myself in . . . and fail.

I hear him laugh behind me, so I scowl at him over my shoulder.

He shrugs and smiles. "You need a boost in?"

"Fuck off," I bite.

"You and your filthy mouth." He tuts, head shaking, amusement in his eyes.

"Fuck off, *please*." I give him a saccharine smile.

He laughs loudly, his eyes sparkling, and I hate the glow in my chest that I feel, knowing I made him laugh.

"You're funny when you want to be, Jailbird," he tells me, still chuckling. "But you are ridiculously small."

"I am not ridiculously small." I glower at him.

"Mmhmm." He nods, lips pressed together. "You keep telling yourself that."

"It's a fact."

"You can't even climb in my truck, Jailbird."

"Stop calling me that!" I snap. "I can't get in your truck because it's ridiculously big!"

"It's a normal-sized truck. You're just undersized."

"Ugh, shut up, you big . . . tree."

"Original." I can almost hear his mental eye roll from here. "Now, stop being bitchy, and let's do this." He steps over me, and I hold out a hand, stopping him.

"And what exactly are you doing?" I eye him suspiciously.

He raises a brow. "Helping you in my truck. I'd like to get home at some point tonight."

"If your hands touch anywhere near my ass, I *will* kick yours."

"Don't worry, Jailbird. I have zero interest in touching your ass. You're not my type."

Before I can register his words, large hands grip either side of my waist and lift me like a toddler into the car.

"There. That was easy, wasn't it?" he says smugly.

I give him a fake smile and the middle finger.

Laughing, he shuts the door and rounds the truck, climbing in the driver's side.

Engine on, the radio comes to life with Fall Out Boy's "Alone Together," and I want to laugh out loud.

Apparently, I do because he says, "What?" He pulls the truck out onto the street.

"Oh, nothing. Just this song."

"You don't like it?"

"No, I do. It's just . . . the lyrics remind me of . . . getting sober."

He goes silent. Then, he says in a quieter voice, "I didn't know that's what this song was about."

I glance at him. His eyes are fixed on the road ahead.

"I don't know for sure that it is. It's just the way I interpret it—addiction and the road to recovery. It probably means different things for different people."

He doesn't say anything for a long moment. The only sound is Patrick Stump's voice flowing through the car.

"So"—his voice sounds gruff—"where am I taking you?"

I rattle off my address, and then that's it for the rest of the ten-minute journey it takes to get to my apartment. We don't speak another word.

He pulls up near the sidewalk across from my apartment building, and I let out an audible groan when I take in the person sitting on the steps that lead into my building.

"What?" he asks. His eyes must follow my gaze because the next thing he says is, "Who's that?"

I turn my eyes to his. The glow of the dash lighting his face.

"My ex-boyfriend," I tell him.

His eyes seem to burn brighter in this moment. "A recent ex?"

I shake my head. "We broke up before . . . it was his car that I crashed that night. We were at a party. I caught him . . . with his pants around his ankles . . . and a friend of mine was . . . yeah, anyway, I left the party, got in his car, and . . . you know the rest."

"Well, he sounds like a real . . . catch."

I let out a laugh. "I honestly don't know what he's doing here. I haven't seen him since that night."

"Let me see you to your apartment." He takes off his seat belt.

"No, it's fine. Kyle's harmless. But thank you. And thank you for the ride home."

He's staring at me, saying nothing. His jaw is tight. He looks like he's angry with me, and I don't know what I've done now to piss him off.

And, honestly, I don't want to know.

It was surprisingly not a bad night—once the movie got going, and he stopped talking. I don't want it to be spoiled.

Although I have a feeling that Kyle is going to ruin it for me when I get out of this truck and go over there.

"Well, I'll see you," I say to Ares. I retrieve my bag from the floor, hang it on my shoulder, and open the truck door.

"You gonna be able to get out okay?" He doesn't sound like he's being sarcastic for once but actually asking a genuine question.

I glance over at him. "I'll be fine. But, if I break my ankle on the way down, I'm suing. Just so you know."

I grin, and he chuckles softly.

I shift my butt to the edge of the seat. Holding on to the door with one hand, I jump down, landing steadily on the sidewalk.

"See? Easy," I tell him with flair before shutting the door of his truck.

I cross the street, walking toward my building. As I get closer, I make my footfalls a little heavier, so Kyle will hear me.

And he does. His head comes up. The moment he spots me, he stands up. Then, I spot the bottle of beer on the step beside him.

He's been drinking.

Of course, he's been drinking.

"What are you doing here?" I say to him as I approach, coming to a stop at the bottom of the steps.

My eyes take him in for the first time in almost seven months.

He looks the same—but also different.

It's like I'm seeing him through fresh eyes, which I guess I am. His once-spiky blond hair is now overgrown and looks like it hasn't been washed for days. Dark circles ring his eyes. His cheeks are hollow. His clothes look disheveled.

Is that how I used to look? A mess.

Kyle comes down the steps to me. I see the sway in his movements, telling me that he's had a lot more than one beer. He stops on the bottom step, standing before me.

The smell of beer on his breath instantly hits me and throws me back to another time.

A bad time.

I take a step back, and he notices, a dark frown crossing his face.

I wrap my arms over my chest. "What are you doing here?" I repeat, more forcefully this time.

"I came to see you. I've been waiting for over an hour. Where have you been?"

"Out."

"Okay," he says when he realizes I'm not going to elaborate. "I tried to call you after that night. But I kept getting your voicemail. Then, it said the number had been disconnected."

"I changed my number."

"To keep me away?"

"That was one of the reasons."

His shoulders slump. "I, um . . . heard you went to rehab."

"I did. But you didn't come here to talk about my time in rehab. So, what is it you want?"

His eyes lift to me. "I miss you."

Oh, hell no.

"And it took you almost seven months to realize that?"

"I haven't just realized. I've never gotten over you. I've only just found the courage to come see you."

"Sure, Kyle. And does Cherry know you're here? I'm assuming you guys are dating. I'd hope so after I found her with her mouth around your cock."

He winces. "It was a stupid mistake, babe. She'd been hounding me for months, trying to get with me. I resisted, but that night, I was ... I don't know." He pushes his hand into his hair. "I loved you. I *love* you."

"Funny way of showing it. And you know what, Kyle? I don't believe you. I think Cherry saw sense and dumped you, and for some reason, you thought it'd be a good idea to come and see me because you figured I'd be dumb enough to take you back. Well, news flash: I'm sober now, meaning I'm not as stupid as I used to be."

"Come on, Arianna Banana."

"Don't call me that."

"You used to love it when I called you that."

"Nope. I always hated it. I just didn't want to hurt your feelings at the time, so I pretended to like it. Guess what? I don't give two shits about your feelings anymore."

"You're being a bitch." He steps close, getting in my face, but I refuse to move or show any signs of weakness. He's not huge by guy standards—five-ten—but he's still a hell of a lot taller than me. "What? You think you're better than me now because you're all sober and shit and working for your daddy?"

How does he know I work for my dad?

"No," I say, staring up into his face. "I've always been better than you. You're a loser, and I was an idiot to ever think you weren't."

I go to move past him, but he grabs hold of my arm, stopping me.

"Let me go," I firmly tell him.

He ignores me. His grip on my arm increases. "We're not finished here, Arianna."

"Yes, we are! Now, let me go!" I yell, hating the tremble I hear in my voice.

A second later, I see a shadow to my right, and then Kyle is moving, being pulled away from me and tossed backward where he stumbles on the lower step, falling on his ass.

Ares.

And I've never been so relieved to see him.

"Are you okay?" he asks, his face lit with anger.

"Yeah." I swallow. "Yes, I'm fine."

His eyes move to Kyle, who's just scrambled up to his feet.

"I know who you are." Kyle points a finger at him. "You're that quarterback . . . Kincaid . . . who plays for her dad's team." Kyle looks past Ares to me. "You with this prick, Ari? Hooking up with Daddy's players now? Being the good girl?"

"Shut up, Kyle."

"You seriously want this guy over me?"

"Are you fucking deaf, dickhead? She told you to shut up," Ares barks at him.

"Ari . . . please . . . I know I messed up, but I love you. So fucking much. I didn't press charges when you smashed up my car. The cops wanted me to, but I didn't. I wouldn't. I told your dad when he came to see me—"

"I'm sorry, what?" I step around Ares to stand in front of Kyle.

"Your dad. He came to give me money to fix my car up."

"And you took it?"

He looks sheepish. "I needed to fix my car up."

"So, that's why you didn't press charges. Because my dad paid you not to."

Kyle says nothing.

"How much did he give you?"

Still nothing.

"How much?" I yell.

"Ten grand."

I almost choke. "And that's all gone now, right? That's why you're back here, sitting outside my apartment. You need more money."

"No." He lunges toward me, grabbing me again. "I need you! I love you."

"Get your fucking hands off her." Ares shoves him back away from me and advances on him, looming over him. "You don't put your hands on a woman ever, dick face. And especially not her. If I hear you've come near Ari again, they'll be finding parts of you all over the city."

Kyle tries to straighten up, lifting his chin, acting like he's not afraid, but I know him better than that. "You threatening me, quarterback?"

Ares looks at me and lifts his shoulders. "Did you hear me threaten him, Ari?"

"Nope." I shake my head, staring back at Kyle.

"You're a fucking bitch," Kyle spits at me. "And you, quarterback, you'll get what's coming to you."

"What did you call her?" Ares takes a menacing step forward, his foot stomping on the ground, and Kyle takes off running.

It would be almost comedic, if it wasn't so pathetic.

"Wow." Ares barks out a laugh. "He can really run for a guy who's half-cut."

"Impressive, isn't it?" I say as we watch Kyle leg it around the corner of my block. "Well, I think you scared him off."

"Fucking pussy," Ares grinds out. "He's got no problem picking on a woman half his size, but he runs like Usain fucking Bolt when a guy fronts him."

"Honestly, I think he was more half of your size than me, his."

Ares's eyes come down to me, the look in them softer than I've ever seen before, and he chuckles. "You actually used to date that prick?"

"Yeah." I sigh. "But I was drunk for all of the relationship, if that counts for anything." I lift my hands, palms up, giving a loose smile, and surprisingly, he laughs again.

"Come on, I'll see you up to your apartment."

"You don't need to. He's gone."

"I know I don't need to. I want to, okay? So, I'm walking you up, and then you can invite me in for a coffee."

I give him a look of mock shock. My hands go to my chest. "Coffee? That's not actually code for . . . *coffee*, is it?"

"Shit, you got me," he deadpans. "And I'll be wanting milk as well."

"Jesus, you're pushing it, Mr. Perfect. Okay, I go as far as milk. But, just so you know, you're not getting any sugar."

"Don't need it. I'm sweet enough."

"Ugh." I wince. "It was going so well, and then you ruined it with that lame joke."

He laughs, and the sound works through me in the best kind of way.

"Come on then, Mr. Perfect. Let's get inside and get you your coffee with milk."

Chapter Nine

"HERE YOU GO." I hand Ares the cup of coffee I just finished making.

He's standing in the middle of my living room. And the sight of Ares Kincaid standing in my apartment is not one I ever thought I'd see.

He looks so imposing in my apartment. Like a giant in a playhouse.

"You can sit, you know," I tell him as I take a seat in my cozy armchair, leaving him with the sofa.

He takes a seat on it, almost taking up two of the three seats that the sofa has to offer. Sitting forward, elbows on thighs, hands cradling the cup, he stares across at me.

"I know I already asked you outside, but are you really okay? That prick didn't hurt you, did he?"

"No. I'm fine," I reassure him.

"Did he . . . used to be like that with you . . . in the past? While you were together?" He seems to struggle with getting the words out, and if I didn't know him like I do, I'd think the thought of someone actually hurting me bothered him on an emotional level.

"No." I smile softly. "Kyle was a cheating asshole and could say some pretty mean things at times. But he never once got physical with me. That's the first time it's ever happened."

Ares exhales, his body seeming to relax a little. "Well, I'm just glad I was here to scare the shit out of him."

"Why were you?" He looks taken aback by my question, so I expand, "I mean, I just figured you'd left after I got out of your truck."

He gives me a disgruntled look. "I might be an asshole, Ari, but I'm not a careless one. I wasn't leaving until I saw you go inside your building. Especially not when that prick was sitting, waiting outside for you."

It jolts me when he says my name. He said it a couple of times when we were outside, but everything was crazy then, so it was hard to register, but now, in the silence of my apartment, hearing him call me Ari . . . it's nice.

Better than nice.

I bring my coffee to my lips, blowing on it to cool it. "You are an asshole," I say over the rim of the cup, giving him a wry grin. "But I am grateful that you were here. I really do appreciate it."

Because I have no clue what would have happened if he hadn't been. I would like to think that Kyle wouldn't have hurt me. But, once upon a time, I never thought he would've cheated on me.

It really is true that you never know a person.

I shiver, and Ares notices.

"You okay?"

"Yeah, I was just thinking."

"About?"

"What might've happened if you weren't here."

His face darkens. "Don't worry about that. But I do think you should think about getting a restraining order."

"Doesn't that seem a bit extreme?"

He gives me an irritated look, and I concede. "Okay, I'll consider it."

"Get a rape alarm, too. That'd scare the motherfucker off."

"I'll pick one up tomorrow. But could I ask . . . please don't mention Kyle turning up here to my dad. He's been trying to get me to move back home with him since . . . everything. Kyle showing up would only strengthen his case."

Even though I'm angry with my dad for not telling me that he gave Kyle money, I can't let on to him that I know, because then he'd know that I've seen Kyle, and I definitely don't want that.

"I don't know, Ari. Your dad should know."

"Please," I say softly, eyes pleading.

He lets out a sigh. "Okay. But on one condition."

"What?" I take a sip of my coffee.

"You let me drive you to and from work."

"What?" My head snaps up so fast that I hear my neck click.

"I don't want you catching the bus and walking home alone with that prick loitering around."

"First, how do you know I catch the bus? And,

second, I'm pretty sure Kyle won't be coming back around. I think you scared him off for good."

"One, I know you catch the bus because you don't have your license at the moment." He ticks off on his finger. And I wait for the barb about how I lost it to come . . . but it never does. "And, two, that guy isn't smart enough to give up on the first try. He'll be back; trust me."

"I don't need you babysitting me, Ares. And why would you even want to?"

"Because you won't let me tell your dad about what happened with that dipshit tonight. And because, believe it or not, I do have a conscience, and I would never forgive myself if something happened to you, and I knew what was going on and did nothing about it."

"There's nothing going on."

"That out there wasn't nothing." He jabs a finger in the direction of the window. "That guy was drunk and aggressive with you. He grabbed you, for fuck's sake. So, it's either me driving you or we tell your dad." He stubbornly folds his arms.

I stare at him, furious. I don't like being backed into a corner.

And since when did he turn into a decent guy who cared about my welfare?

"What's it gonna be?" He pushes. "I have your dad's number right here . . . so we can call him now . . ." He reaches into his pocket for his phone.

"Fine!" I yell. "Fucking fine! You win. I'll ride with you to and from work."

He pushes his cell back into his pocket and smiles smugly at me.

I don't know whether I should be pissed off or thankful that he now cares about my welfare. And he's not a bad guy, size-wise, to have as a pseudo body-guard. He's built like a tank.

He drains his coffee and puts the cup down on the coffee table. Then, he toes off his sneakers, which are huge, by the way.

Big feet, big—

Don't even go there, Ari.

Cheeks flush, I mutter out, "Um ... are you staying?"

"For a bit, in case that fucknut decides to come back."

"And do I have a say in this?" Clearly, I'm still feeling pissy about the corner he backed me into a minute ago.

He sits up. "Of course you do. It's your place, Ari."

"Well, I didn't have a say a minute ago." I fold my arms over my chest.

"You had a choice. You always have a choice. Would I prefer it if you told your dad about what happened with that asshole? Yes. But you won't, so you're stuck with me for the time being until I know Kyle the cunt has gotten the message and is not gonna come back and bother you again. Now, if you want me to go home now and leave you alone, I will. Just promise me that you'll lock up after I'm gone. And, if he turns back up, you'll call the police and then me. In that order."

I watch him reach for his shoes to put them back

on, and I have this odd, tight feeling in my chest at the thought of him leaving. The word *alone* rattles around in my mind.

I'm tired of being lonely.

"Wait . . ."

He stops and looks over at me. I can't meet his eyes. I stare down at my hands in my lap.

"I, um . . . you . . . can . . . stay for a while. If you want." I make it sound like it's me doing him the favor when actually it's the other way around.

I'm so pathetic; it's laughable.

I risk a glance at him through my lashes.

"Okay." He nods and sets his shoes back down.

I decide not to dig too deep into the fact that I'm not ready for him to leave. I've just . . . I've never had someone care about me . . . well, care about my safety, like this before, and it's . . . nice.

He's nice.

And there are two words I never thought I'd say in relation to Ares Kincaid.

How things have changed in such a short space of time.

"Do you, um . . . want to watch some TV?" I ask him, needing to break through the weird atmosphere currently residing in here.

"Sure," he says.

"What are you in the mood for?"

"Football," he says.

I groan, and just like that, we're back to normal.

"Oh, yeah, I forgot that you don't like it."

I don't believe for a second that he forgot. The smirk on his face is telling me that.

"Seriously though, how can you not like football? Especially when your dad is a football coach. You must've spent your whole life around it."

Not really. My dad was hardly ever home to share his love of football with me.

Of course, I don't say that. I don't want to get into the specifics of that with him. And it's not that I don't like football per se. It's just that I resent the fact that my dad chose it over his family.

"It's just not my thing."

"So, what is your thing? Painting?" He nods his head in the direction of my easel, sitting in the corner of the room.

"Oh." I swallow. "No. That's just a . . . hobby."

I don't know why I lie. I guess . . . I just don't want to tell him about another thing I've been failing at.

Ares stares at me for a long moment, like he's trying to see what's really inside my mind. "Hmm," he murmurs. "Well, I guess I'll have to see what I can do to change your mind about liking football."

"Ha!" I laugh. "Good luck with that."

"That sounds like a challenge, Jailbird. You should know I love a challenge."

Jailbird. Ah, so he's back to calling me that. I guess not everything has changed then.

"So, what do you want to watch?" I ask, changing the question, trying to hide my disappointment.

His eyes assess me. Then, he shrugs those big shoulders of his. "I don't mind. What are you watching at the moment?"

"*Riverdale.*"

"What's it about?"

"A bunch of high school students who—"

"Pass."

"I didn't even get a chance to tell you what it's about!" I laugh.

"You lost me at high school students."

"Okay. So, no shows about schoolkids," I say, scrolling through the listings. "Oh, have you seen *Dexter*?" I ask, coming to a stop on it.

"Nope. Is that the show about the serial killer who's a cop?"

"Blood spatter analyst, but yeah. I've not seen it, but I've heard it's amazing. I've wanted to watch it for a while, but I've been too chicken to watch it alone," I admit on a laugh.

"Okay, put it on. We'll watch the first episode and see if it's any good."

"You want anything to eat before I put it on?"

"Whatcha got?"

"Chips, um . . . some cookies, I think. Oh, and ice cream."

He looks at me. "Chips are good."

I push out of my chair and head into the kitchen. I grab the two bags of chips that I have in my cupboard.

"Which do you want?" I ask him, holding them up for him to see. "Cheetos original or Doritos Nacho Cheese?"

"Doritos."

"Good. 'Cause I want the Cheetos."

"I could change my mind."

"Too late." I toss the bag of Doritos to him, and he chuckles.

I sit down in my chair and press play on *Dexter*.

"How many seasons are there of this?" Ares asks as I open my bag of chips.

"Um . . . eight, I think."

"Fuck. That's a lot of TV." He laughs.

"Don't worry; I'll only make you endure this first episode."

He glances over at me, giving me a steady look. "I'm not worried." His voice is deep and sure.

I try to ignore the shiver I feel and fail miserably.

We don't speak for the whole episode, both too engrossed. When the pilot ends, we both look at each other, wide-eyed, and Ares tells me to put on the next episode.

Before I do, I go for a bathroom break and grab us both a couple of sodas on the way back to the living room.

I grab the blanket I have from the back of the chair and cover myself with it before putting on the next episode.

We're on the fourth episode, and I can feel my eyes getting heavy with sleep when I glance over at Ares and realize that he's asleep.

He's slouched down, head tipped back on the top of my sofa, long legs sprawled out on the floor. It does not look comfortable at all.

I look at him for a moment. He looks so much younger in sleep. Face relaxed. Dark lashes shadowing his cheekbones. His hair falling onto his forehead. I wonder if it's as soft as it looks.

I turn the TV off midway through the episode and push my blanket aside, climbing off my chair.

"Ares?" I say softly.

"Mmhmm?" he mumbles.

"You've fallen asleep."

He makes a sleepy sound. It's actually pretty cute.

"If you're tired . . . you can stay here, if you want?" I bite my lip.

"'Kay . . ." he mutters, eyes still closed.

I grab the blanket off my chair, and when I turn back to him, he's shifted. Head on the arm of the sofa, long legs dangling off the other end, and he's already snoring lightly.

I smile and then cover him with my blanket.

I make sure the front door is locked and put the chain on. I flick the light off and then head into the bathroom to brush my teeth.

When I'm done, I get changed into my pajamas and then climb into my bed, content in the knowledge that, for the first time in a long time, I'm not alone.

Chapter Ten

I WAKE TO THE SOUND of someone inside my apartment, and my heart stills.

Shit.

Then, I remember that Ares crashed on the sofa last night, and I relax.

I reach over to my phone and check the time. Half past six.

A smile tugs at my lips. I slept right through the night.

I haven't done that since before I was sober.

I guess having Ares in my apartment helped.

I clamber out of bed to go see him. I open my bedroom door and step into my little hall, and Ares is there.

Inside my hallway closet, which is filled with my paintings.

And he's looking at them.

"I was looking for the bathroom," he says, glancing back over his shoulder at me.

And he doesn't look guilty at being caught.

Asshat.

His clothes are wrinkled from sleep. His hair is all mussed up. His eyes are bright. And I would be thinking about how handsome he looks right now if I hadn't just caught him snooping through my paintings.

"I thought it was just a hobby?" he says.

"I thought it was none of your business," I throw back at him.

He laughs a deep, rumbling sound that affects me in a way I don't want to examine right now.

"Didn't anyone ever tell you it's rude to snoop through people's things?" I place my hand on my hip, and my oversize bed tee slips off my shoulder.

He turns, holding one of my paintings in his hand, and I see his eyes go to the bare skin there. Scorching hot, they trail over my chest, and then they move up to my face.

A burst of heat explodes inside me, like he's just lit me.

"Technically, it wasn't snooping. It was an accidental discovery," he says.

His jaw is tight, but I'm getting the impression he's not angry. Well, he might not be, but I am.

"Oh, well, that's all right then." I fold my arms over my chest. And then I remember I'm not wearing a bra.

Christ on a cracker.

I close my eyes on a groan.

He chuckles a dark sound. "Don't worry, Jailbird. It's nothing I haven't seen before."

My eyes flash open, accusing.

"Locker room. Your bra didn't exactly cover *all* the goods."

He slowly runs his eyes down to my chest and then

back up, and I can see the memory of that moment in his eyes.

He looked at me like he wanted me back then. Before he knew who I was.

The crazy thing is . . . he's looking at me in the exact same way right now.

And I'm dying. From a blazing inferno of embarrassment and something that has my thighs clenching and my nipples pebbling.

I tighten my arms over my chest.

"You're cute when you're embarrassed."

"And you are where you're not wanted."

I go to grab the painting out of his hand, but he's faster, and he holds it out of my reach. Then, I remember . . . *nipples* and clamp my arms back over my chest.

He's holding the painting I did of a ballerina a year ago. A teenage girl, facing away, a tutu on and her ballet slippers hanging over her shoulder, and on her feet are a pair of pink Dr. Martens.

I got the inspiration when I saw a teenage girl entering a ballet studio, close to the gallery I used to work at. She was all dressed up in her ballet garb, hair up in a bun, her ballet shoes hanging over her shoulder with bright pink Dr. Martens on her feet.

I thought she looked amazing. Perfectly made up with a hint of the rebel inside of her only visible on her feet.

I went home and worked through the night on that painting. It took me two days. And then I went out and bought myself a pair of pink Dr. Martens. Later that night, I wore them when I went out to a bar with

Kyle where I got totally trashed and he puked on one of my new boots.

We had a fight about it. Then, Kyle took off, leaving me in the middle of a street alone.

I had to walk home, as there were no cabs to be seen. And I scrubbed my boot clean when I got home.

He turned up the next day with flowers, a bottle of wine, and a lame-ass apology. And I forgave him.

"Why did you tell me it was just a hobby?" Ares says. "It's clearly so much more than just that."

"Again, none of your business."

"Did you study art?"

I realize that he's not going to stop asking questions until I at least give him an answer.

"Yes."

"You're incredibly talented."

"I'm okay," I say in response.

"Okay?" he repeats, brows furrowing. "So, that's your thing."

"What is? Painting?"

"No. Putting yourself down."

Ah.

I bite my lip, sucking it into my mouth, and turn my eyes from his.

I hear him putting the painting down, and the next thing I know, he's standing before me, and his fingers are holding my chin, turning my eyes to his.

I stare up at him, holding all of my pain inside of me. Pain that is begging to escape.

"You shouldn't hide your talent away like that," he says gently.

A dry laugh escapes me. "And why would I have

them out on display when all they do is remind me of what I can no longer do?"

Shit.

His brows come together in confusion. "What do you mean?"

Christ. Me and my big mouth.

"Why do you even care?" I toss at him. "You still hated me this time yesterday."

Confusion turns to anger. "I never hated you, Ari. But this isn't about me. So, don't try to distract us from the issue. Tell me what you meant by that."

"I can't paint anymore, okay!" I push his hand away from my face. Stepping back, I bump into the wall. "I stopped drinking, and now, I can't paint anymore. Happy?"

"No, I'm not happy." He leans against the opposite wall, eyes watching me. "Why can't you paint?"

"Weren't you just listening?"

"I was listening. I just think it's bullshit."

"Fuck you."

The bastard smirks. "There she is. Foulmouthed little Jailbird."

"Stop calling me that!" I yell, my hands going into my hair and making two fists. "God, you're so infuriating!"

He laughs this time, and I want to take a fist from my hair and use it to punch him right in his perfect jaw. "I'm glad my life is a joke to you."

His humor disappears, replaced with irritation. "Trust me; the last thing I think you are is a joke."

What the hell is that supposed to mean?

"Tell me the real reason you can't paint."

"Because the alcohol made me good. I don't drink anymore. Ergo I can no longer paint."

"How long have you been painting?"

"Since I was a kid."

"When did you start drinking?"

"When I was a kid."

He frowns. The look in his eyes makes me want to shrink in on myself. Disgust laced with consternation.

"I was fifteen," I add quietly, my eyes lowering.

It takes a good minute before he speaks again. I wonder for a time if he's actually going to say nothing and just walk out of my apartment. I wouldn't blame him.

"But I'm guessing you started painting before you were fifteen. A gift like that, it's always in you, right?"

"Yes . . ." I say, slowly looking back up at him. "I've always painted. Since I was small."

"Then, you still can. You just think you can't. But your talent is still in there."

"I don't know . . ."

"Do me a favor. Stop punishing yourself with the blank canvas out there."

"I am not—"

He holds a hand up, stopping me, giving me a look.

Am I punishing myself? I thought it was to try to inspire myself. But wouldn't I have the paintings where I could see them to remind me of what I could do . . . what I might be able to do again? Not the blank canvas.

"Hang the paintings up. Remind yourself of what you're capable of. Of what you're good at. What you love. Well, all of them, except for this one." He reaches for the ballerina painting, picking it up. "I want this one."

"Why?"

"My niece is obsessed with ballet. She'd love this."

"I didn't know you were an uncle."

"Two nieces. They're Zeus's kids. Gigi is five and ballet-obsessed. And Thea is only six weeks old."

"Cute," I say.

"Ridiculously so."

"I bet you spoil them rotten."

He gives me a look. "All the damn time. Case in point." He nods down at my painting. "So, can I buy this from you? It doesn't matter what it costs."

"No." I shake my head.

"Ari—"

"Take it. Call it a gift for, you know, your help last night."

"You don't owe me for that."

I shrug. "Whatever. I still want you to have it. Well, your niece."

"You have to let me give you something for it. I can't just take it. It doesn't feel right."

"Honestly, I don't want anything, but if it bothers you that much, make a donation to a charity instead."

"Okay. I can do that." He nods. "Which charity?"

"American Foundation for Suicide Prevention," I say without thinking.

He's watching me, wordlessly. Like he's trying to fit all the pieces of me together, but he's coming up short.

"Okay." His voice is rough. "I'll make the donation today."

"Thank you," I say softly.

We're quiet a moment. All of the unspoken words hanging silently between us.

He's the first to speak, "Well, I guess I should take off."

"Right. Yeah. Of course."

I follow him into my living room and watch quietly while he puts his shoes on.

Then, I follow him to the front door. He unlocks and opens it, stepping through, my painting in his hand.

"So . . . thanks again for the save last night."

He shakes his head in silent reproach. "You don't need to thank me, Jailbird. I did what any guy would."

"Well, not any guy. I don't think Kyle would threaten you to save my ass."

"Good point," he says.

I chuckle.

"Don't forget I'm driving you in the morning."

I tap two fingers to my head and salute. "Why do you get there so early anyway?"

He's always there first before all the other players, and he is always the last to leave.

"I like to do cardio before training starts."

"And after? You stay way later than the other players."

"Weights. Sometimes, I have a massage. And I like to spend time watching tape."

"Geek," I say.

He laughs.

"Well, at least I know why my dad thinks you're the shit. You're certainly his most dedicated player."

"You don't think I'm the shit?"

"Nope." I smirk. "I think you are shit."

"Low, Jailbird." He slaps a hand to his chest. "You almost hurt my feelings." He steps back. "Tomorrow morning. Eight o'clock. Be ready to go."

"Yes, boss."

"And don't go watching *Dexter* without me," he throws over his shoulder as he heads for the stairs.

Does this mean he wants to come back? Not just to drive me to work, but to watch TV with me? Maybe be my friend?

I feel a little glow inside of me at the thought.

"Got it. But you don't need to worry. I wouldn't dare watch it alone. Seriously. I'd *shit* if I did."

That earns me a laugh. "Later, Jailbird."

"See ya, Mr. Perfect."

I shut the door on the sound of his deep chuckle and lean against it, feeling a little lighter and a lot happier.

Chapter Eleven

IT'S FRIDAY. I'M IN a great mood. It's been a good week.

Ares has been giving me a ride into work every day and dropping me home, just like he said he would.

He even walks me up to my apartment when he takes me home, like he thinks Kyle is going to jump out from behind the wall and get me.

There's also been no sign of Kyle since that night, which is a good thing.

Ares and I are getting along well. No more sniping or shitty comments from him.

We're actually talking like normal people. And I'm finding that we have more in common than I would've thought.

Well, not tons in common. But we like a lot of the same movies and music.

Okay, so that's it. But I like him. I like what he has to say. I like listening to him talk.

I find that I look forward to our chats in the car.

And I haven't had a bad moment once this week.

Don't get me wrong; the need for alcohol is always there, in the back of my mind. It's just not been as strong.

Ares hasn't once mentioned us watching *Dexter* together again though. And I don't want to be the one to ask him. I don't want to push a friendship onto someone who doesn't want it. So, the ball is in his court.

Although I am dying to watch more episodes of *Dexter*, I'm wondering if I should just watch it alone. During the daytime, of course.

I've seen Missy a few times this week, which has been fun. I like her a lot.

We had lunch together on Sunday. She had called a few hours after Ares left to invite me to lunch. We met at a cute little café in Times Square. She apologized for missing the cinema, which I told her she didn't have to. I mean, her friend was having a baby; that was way more important. She told me that her friend, Amanda, had a boy called Freddie. Missy showed me a picture of the baby on her phone. So freaking adorable.

Then, she asked me about Kyle. She said that Ares had told her. I mean, I'd asked him not to tell my dad, which he hasn't, but I hadn't thought about other people. I guess Missy knowing isn't a problem, and she told me that he'd only told her because she was staying with him at the moment, and she'd just gotten home from the hospital early in the morning when he came in from being at mine.

After that, I focused the conversation toward her. She talked about her nieces, Gigi and Thea. She practically glowed about them, clearly a besotted aunt. She showed me photos of them, too. I swear, I had baby fever by the end of that lunch.

Missy never mentioned the painting that I gave Ares for Gigi though, so there's something he did keep to himself. And I'm grateful for that. I don't want to talk about my art with anyone right now—or the lack of it.

Missy also told me that she was a psych major at Dartmouth. She's home for the summer, staying with Ares, like she always does. She told me that her twin brother, Lo, is currently in Europe, travelling with his buddies. He's at Penn State, earning a law degree.

She told me tons of stuff.

One thing I noticed she never mentioned was her parents. And I never asked.

I don't want her asking about my mom, so I'm not going to ask her questions about her parents.

But I do know that Ares pays for hers and Lo's college tuition, as my dad once told me that. So, either their parents aren't financially able to help toward their education or they're not around.

Something tells me it might be the latter.

Missy and I also finally went to the cinema together on Tuesday evening. Just me and her, no Ares this time. We went to see *The Greatest Showman* again. Well, again for me, first time for Missy. But I was more than happy to watch it for a second time.

I've had quite a busy week, by my standards, and it's been really good.

I'm on my way to the players' meeting room right now to set up for the weekly team meeting.

The meeting room is on the other side of the gym.

I'm just walking by there when I hear my name—well, a variation of it—being said, and I stop, near the partially open door.

"So, Kincaid . . . you and Coach Petrelli's daughter."

I don't recognize the voice, but it's one of the players on the team. They're the only ones who use the gym.

"Me and Ari, what?" That voice I do know. It's the one I've grown to like listening to in his car every morning and evening.

"Oh, Ari," the voice singsongs. "So, you're on a first-name basis with her. I guess you should be when you're screwing her."

What?

"I'm not screwing her, dick face. And I don't refer to her as Coach Petrelli's daughter because she has a fucking name—*Ari*."

It was only a week ago that he referred to me as Jailbird. He still does from time to time, but I now take it as something that changed from a barb to cheeky.

"Hey, man, I wouldn't blame you if you were. She's hot as hell."

"I'm sure your wife would love to hear you saying that."

"Hey, I might be married, but I'm not fucking blind. And Arianna Petrelli is rocking some serious curves." A pause then. "You don't think she's hot?"

"She's okay, I guess. If you like that kind of thing."

"If you like that kind of thing."

Wow. Thanks, quarterback.

"Um . . . pretty face, great ass. Sure, her rack's not huge, but there's a definite handful there."

"You have issues. Like, seriously, you should talk to a doctor."

A chuckle. "Look, all I heard is that she's been seen in your car a lot this past week, and if I'm hearing, so is Coach."

"So? All I'm doing is giving her a ride home."

"Is that what the kids are calling it nowadays?"

It's Ares's turn to laugh. "Don't be a dick, Thompson." *Ah, so it's the fullback he's in there with.* "Ari doesn't have her license anymore, and she was taking the bus. I live in the city, not far from her, so I offered to drive her."

There's a pause. Then, "So, you're really not hittin' it?"

"Do I look stupid to you?"

And the compliments just keep coming.

"Is that a trick question?"

"Fuck you." Ares chuckles. "And, no, I'm not hittin' it."

"Then, you are as stupid as you look, quarterback. 'Cause, if I were single, I'd be tapping that in a heartbeat."

"Nah. She's Coach's daughter. That's a recipe for disaster in itself. And all the shit that went down with her earlier this year . . . she has baggage a mile wide. And baggage doesn't interest me."

Chapter Twelve

PEARL JAM'S "BLACK" IS playing in Ares's truck. And it's apt because it's the color of my mood right now.

"Baggage doesn't interest me."

The words have been on repeat in my head all day, and I've been getting angrier and angrier.

I don't know why it bothers me so much. It's not like I'm interested in him in that way.

Sure you're not, Ari. You keep telling yourself that.

Fine. I do like him. A little bit. But I know he has no interest in me in that way, so I'm paying attention to my feelings. I'm tamping them down.

And, yes, it stings when I hear he's not interested in me. More so because I have *baggage*.

But, mostly, I'm pissed because I don't like being the topic of conversation for him and his buddy while they're doing reps.

It's disrespectful.

Yeah, but it's not like he respects you. Remember how he used to talk to you? The things he said?

I know, but I thought things had changed after that night with Kyle. I thought he saw the real me now. Not just the screwed-up girl who's clinging on by her fingernails to stay sober.

But, clearly, nothing has changed. He still sees me that way.

I didn't want to ride home with him tonight. But I also didn't want him to know I'd overheard.

So, here I am, sitting in his truck.

Angry and hurt and a million other things. Fingers curled into my palms in quiet contemplation.

"You okay over there, Jailbird?" he asks, finger tapping on the steering wheel in time to the beat of the song.

"Mmhmm."

"Sounds like it."

"I'm fine." I grit my jaw and stare out the passenger window.

I can feel his eyes on me again, but I ignore him.

"I meant to tell you this morning . . . Gigi loved the painting. I gave it to her last night."

"I'm glad." I'm speaking as few words as possible because, if I don't, my anger will come spilling out.

"I made the donation to AFSP."

"Good."

He swings the car to the right and firmly hits the brakes, stopping by the sidewalk, and we're still a five-minute drive from my apartment.

"Okay, what gives?" he says in a frustrated tone.

"Nothing."

"Nothing. Sure." He nods, disbelieving. "So, nothing is the reason you've barely said a word for the last half an hour and you won't look at me now."

I turn my eyes to him. "I didn't know it was a pre-requisite to talk."

He looks annoyed, but there's a flicker of something else there in his eyes that I can't decipher. "It's not, but I can't usually get you to stop talking."

Nice.

Maybe, if he'd kept his mouth shut, then I wouldn't be feeling like I do right now.

Shitty.

And like I really want to drink.

No, I don't. I'm not going to let his carelessness with words lead me down the path of spiraling thoughts.

"Are you going to tell me what's eating you anytime soon?"

"Why?"

"Why?" he echoes, brow rising.

"Yeah, why? Why do you even care if something is bothering me?"

He looks surprised. Like he's not actually sure of the answer himself. "I just . . . do."

I laugh humorlessly. "Good answer."

"Fucking hell, Jailbird." He tosses his hands up, irritated. "Because we're friends; that's why."

"I thought I had too much baggage to be your friend."

He frowns. "What are you talking about?"

"I heard you . . . in the gym, talking to Thompson about me."

"So?" His face doesn't change. Not a trace of guilt there.

Then, what did I expect? This is him I'm talking about. I don't think the guy has it in him to feel guilty.

"So?" I laugh again, and it still hasn't got a trace of humor in it. "I don't like being fodder for you and your buddy."

"You weren't fodder. Thompson was being a dick, and I was just trying to shut him up."

"You did a stand-up job of that."

"For fuck's sake," he snaps. "It's just locker-room talk. That's what guys do. I'm not going to stand there and tell him things that will give him ammo to wind me up about later."

"Oh, well, that's okay then."

"Stop being so fucking sensitive!"

"Fuck you, Kincaid. You ever think that maybe this isn't me being sensitive? And that it's you being an insensitive prick!" I yell back.

He pushes his hand into his hair, gripping the strands. "It was a nothing conversation, and you're getting all bent out of shape for no reason. I didn't bad-mouth you. I just stated facts."

"Yeah, what was it again? 'So, you're really not hittin' it?'" I say, imitating a male voice. "'Do I look stupid to you?' So, that's a fact, is it? That someone would have to be stupid to be with me?"

"That's not what I said!"

"You just said, you stated facts! And that was one of the *facts* that you said to Thompson this morning!"

"You're taking it out of context."

"I don't think I am."

"Jesus! See, this is why I avoid women like you—"

"Women like me?" I let out a dry laugh, cutting him off. "You mean, women with baggage. Women with substance abuse issues, right?"

"Yes." No hesitation, and the chill in his voice is enough to refreeze the melting ice caps in the Antarctic.

I swallow hard, past the lump in my throat. "Well, you don't need to avoid me anymore." I grab my bag and open the door.

"Where are you going?" He sounds irritated, maybe even bored. And that makes me feel a million times worse.

God, I was so stupid to think that he would ever be my friend. He hasn't changed one bit from the person I met that first day.

He's just the same judgmental asshole as he was then.

"Somewhere you're not," I bite and clamber down out of the truck.

"You're being stupid, Ari. It's still six blocks to your apartment."

I turn to face him, my hand on the door, ready to shut it. "Sounds like me, right, Mr. Perfect? Stupid with baggage a mile wide." Then, I slam the door shut before he can say any more to hurt me, and I take off, striding away in the opposite direction from him.

Chapter Thirteen

NSYNC's "Bye Bye Bye" is blaring out of the speakers from my iPod docking station in my living room.

I should be doing yoga. Relaxing. Focusing. Clearing my mind. But I can't.

I've got too much anger inside me to even attempt to do yoga.

So, I'm currently doing exercise in my living room to rid myself of the adrenaline tearing up my body, so I can relax enough to do yoga.

I could've gone out for a run to burn off the hot energy, but I don't feel sure that I might not run straight into a bar right now.

How I managed to get home without going inside of one was a goddamn miracle.

Did I stop outside a pub and stare at it for a good five minutes?

Yes.

Did I go in?

No.

And, for that, I deserve a fucking medal.

I wanted to go inside so bad. It would have been so easy.

But I didn't give in to the urge, and that's what counts.

Instead, I walked away and speed-walked home. The second I got inside my apartment, I stripped off my clothes and changed into a sports bra and shorts. Pushed my coffee table up to the wall and turned on my music.

I must have been listening to NSYNC the last time I'd had my iPod on, so I left it playing. Can't beat a bit of old-school boy band to do old-fashioned exercise to. Sit-ups. Push-ups. Jumping jacks. Anything to burn off my anger. And it's slowly working.

My heart is pumping. I'm sweating. Getting that anger right out of my veins and mind.

I start jogging a circuit around my apartment, singing along with the music.

I probably look like a crazy person right now. But I'm doing the best I can.

I'm not used to dealing with emotions. In the past, whenever I felt something I couldn't handle, I would drink, and then it would disappear.

It's like learning how to handle my emotions without a crutch all over again.

But I did it.

I'm doing it.

"Bye Bye Bye" comes to an end, and "It's Gonna Be Me" starts to play. I chuckle to myself, thinking of the It's Gonna Be May memes.

God, I'm sad.

I start singing along when I hear what I think is a knock on my front door.

I stop and tilt my head in that direction, wondering if I actually heard it or not.

Yep, I did because it comes again but harder this time.

Must be one of my neighbors. I hope they're not coming to complain about the music.

I go over and turn the sound down. Then, I pad over, barefoot, to the door.

Reaching up on my tiptoes, I check the peephole.

I suck in a surprised breath when I see who's standing outside my door.

Ares.

How the hell did he get in my building? You have to be buzzed in. And what is he doing here? Probably come to have a go at me and get in the last word.

Well, he can just piss right off.

I step away from the door, having no intention of opening it.

Like he knows I just thought that, he says through the door, "Ari, I know you're there. I just heard you turn down the shit music."

Ugh. Asshole.

I stubbornly fold my arms over my chest. "I'm not pretending not to be here. I'm just choosing to ignore you."

"But you're not ignoring me right now." He sounds smug.

Jackass.

I flip him the bird even though he can't see me.

"Will you open the door?"

"No."

"Please."

I don't think I've ever heard him use the word *please* before. Especially not to me.

That makes me open the door. But I'm frowning when I swing it open. And I hate how my heart switches up tempo at the sight of him standing there. Traitor heart.

I see his jaw clench as he takes in my appearance. And you know what? I don't even care that I'm only dressed in a sports bra and shorts, all sweated up. I'm not trying to impress him right now.

Actually, I've never wanted to impress him, period.

All I've ever wanted was for him to like me. To be my friend.

When he finally lifts his eyes from my body to my face, his brow rises. "NSYNC? Really?"

"You got me to open the door, so you could pick apart my choice of music?"

"No. I wanted to make sure you were okay, and—"

"You mean, you came to see if I was drunk. Well, I'm not. Sorry to disappoint you."

His eyes darken, jaw tightening to shatter. "The thought didn't even cross my mind."

That does surprise me.

"I actually came to apologize."

No, *that* surprises me. I have to grip the door to stop from falling backward from shock.

"You were right. I shouldn't have discussed you with Thompson. The moment he brought it up, I should've shut him down. I let myself get pulled into the locker-room banter, and it was wrong. I'm sorry for that."

"Thank you for apologizing. But there was truth in it. You think I have baggage."

"Doesn't everyone?"

True.

"I guess. But you used it as a reason to not be with me."

His head tilts to the side. "Do you want . . . that?"

"God, no!" *Liar.* "It just hurt me to hear that I'm undateable because of my alcohol abuse problems."

"You're not undateable, Ari. Far from it."

My heart spikes.

"But I can't date someone like that . . . like you."

And plummets.

"Because of my own reasons. But I shouldn't have said it as a slight against you when I was mouthing off to Thompson."

I hate the ache I feel in my chest right now.

I know he doesn't want me. I've always known that from the moment I met him.

Sure, he probably thinks I'm fuckable.

I see the way he checks me out sometimes. He's doing it right now. I'm not blind.

But thinking someone is screwable is completely different to seeing them as dating material.

I am the complete opposite of what he wants.

I know this.

So, why is it bothering me so much?

I get to have him as a friend, and that is huge. I don't have many . . . okay, I don't have any friends. But, now, I have him and, because of him, Missy, too. And that means everything.

"So, am I forgiven?" he asks in a gentle voice.

Knowing that he cares enough to come here and apologize makes up for everything that happened this morning and in his truck on the way home.

"Sure." I smile, and so does he.

"Does that mean I can come in now?"

"Oh. Okay." I step back, letting him into my place. "How did you get in my building?" I ask, closing the door as he makes his way over to my sofa.

"Your neighbor let me up on his way out," he tells me as he removes his jacket, laying it over the arm of the sofa and sitting himself down, kicking off his shoes.

I love how comfortable he already is in my apartment.

"Great security," I quip.

"He's a Giants fan."

"He would be." I roll my eyes, and he chuckles.

"Are you hungry?" he asks me.

After that workout, I'm starving. "Yep."

"You like pizza?"

"Does the Pope shit in the woods?"

He bursts out laughing. "I knew there was a reason I liked you, Jailbird," he crows. "Shit, now, I wanna watch *The Big Lebowski.*"

"Nope, we're watching *Dexter*," I tell him. "Because you've made me wait nearly a whole week to watch the next episode, and I'm dying here."

"You mean, you didn't cheat on me and watch it already?" His laughter has stopped, and the tone in his voice is so serious, it makes me stop and look at him.

There's something in the way he's looking at me that makes me feel like it was some kind of test.

A test he expected me to fail.

But I didn't.

"Of course not." I give him a faux-annoyed look. "When I say I'll do something, I do it."

Something akin to relief flickers in his eyes, and it leaves a warm feeling swirling inside me.

I walk over and turn NSYNC off, and then I pick up the TV remote and toss it to him. "You set up the next episode of *Dexter* while I order the pizza. Anything you don't like?" I ask him.

"Anchovies. They're the devil. I'm good with everything else."

"See, I knew there was a reason I liked you, quarterback." I smirk, using his earlier words back on him.

He gifts me with a wide smile that reaches all the way up to his eyes.

I feel that smile all the way down to my toes, like a rush of adrenaline.

And I know I'm in trouble.

Chapter Fourteen

I'VE BEEN SUMMONED TO my dad's office. I don't know what he wants me for. I don't usually get called to his office. If he wants something, he just rings me. I've only been in his office once since I started working here, and that was on the day I started, so I can't say I have a good feeling about this.

As I walk up the stairs to the second floor, where my dad's office is, I look at the photos hanging on the wall of players in action from over the years. There's one of Ares hanging up there, and it makes me smile.

I'm going to the cinema with Ares tonight. After saying that he wanted to watch *The Big Lebowski* after my "Does the Pope shit in the woods?" quip, he told me a few days later that he saw that it'd be showing at a cinema in Greenwich Village that did late-night screenings of old movies and asked if I wanted to go.

My answer was ... "Does the Pope shit in the woods?"

Clearly, I'm hilarious.

I never got to see *The Big Lebowski* when it was

first released because I was only three at the time, so it will be cool to see it on the big screen. And, of course, I'll be with Ares, which will make it even better.

We've been getting on brilliantly after our disagreement. He practically spent the whole weekend over at my place, watching *Dexter*. We got through a serious amount of food and episodes. We're on season three already.

Although I did have to kick him out on Sunday, as I had arranged to go shopping with Missy.

Well, it was more like window shopping for me, as I'm trying to save money to pay my dad back. It was fun. I hadn't had a girlie shopping day in forever.

I'll be sad when Missy goes back to Dartmouth, but we've promised to message all the time, and she even invited me to come visit. No frat parties though.

But, when she goes back, I'll still have Ares here to hang out with. Actually, I think I've spent more time with him these past few weeks than I have Missy.

Although the more time I spend around him, the more my feelings for him grow. I'm keeping them under wraps, but I need to get a handle on them because unrequited feelings for someone who is turning out to be a good friend is not a path I want to go down. I need to keep my head straight.

Because I'm allowing myself to mistake friendly things he does as something more, which it isn't. Like, when he passes me something and his fingers brush over mine, my wanting mind tells me that he did it on purpose. Or, when I think I'm feeling him watching me, but when I look at him, he's not.

My stupid heart is whispering foolishness to my brain, and I need to put a stop to it.

Ares sees me as a friend only. And that's enough.

It's more than enough.

It's way more than I ever thought I would have.

After the crash, I thought my life was over.

But look at me. I have a job. It might not be the one I want, and I still might not be painting. But it's a start.

I haven't had a drink in seven months.

I have two new, great friends in my life. I might have the hots for one of them—Ares—but that's just a crush, and it will pass soon.

Life is good.

I'm still smiling when I reach my dad's office door. I knock once and then walk in.

He's on the phone when I enter, so I just go over and take the seat across from him, putting my bag on the floor by my feet.

He lifts a finger, telling me he'll be a minute, and I nod.

I take a moment to watch him while he's on the phone.

My dad is a handsome man.

He'll turn fifty next year, but he looks like he is in his early forties. His hair is full and dark with only a hint of gray at the sides. He's this tall, gigantic beast of a man. Still in great shape for his age.

He still gets women checking him out. The hostess at the restaurant he took me to the other night was openly flirting with him. Not that he even noticed. I actually felt a little bad for her.

God, I remember the arguments it caused between him and my mom when she was still alive. I always felt bad for him because it wasn't like he ever did anything to incite those women looking at him and flirting with him, and he never noticed back then either.

But then he never noticed my mom. Maybe that was the problem.

He's more interested in football. Always has been, and he always will be.

He played professional football before I was born, but a knee injury took him out early in his career.

When I was a little kid, he would pick me up with one hand and sit me up on his shoulder, and I remember how safe I used to feel up there because I knew he would never let me fall.

I thought nothing and no one could ever hurt me while I had a dad who was as big and strong as he was.

How wrong I was.

"Yep, sounds good, Bill," he says, finishing off his call. "Next week. Yep . . . yep. See you then." He hangs up the phone and looks at me. "How are you doing?"

"Good. You wanted me?"

"Yeah." He leans back in his chair, elbows on the armrests, and steeples his fingers together. "Ares has been driving you to and from work." It's not a question; he knows it's fact. "Is there anything I need to know?"

I frown. "Such as?"

"Are you dating him?"

"No."

"Sleeping with him?"

"Jesus Christ, Dad." I shake my head, annoyed. "Not that it's any of your business who I date or sleep with—"

"You're my daughter, so it is my business. And especially if it's one of my players that you're seeing."

Right. So, this is actually about his precious player, not his daughter.

Why am I not surprised?

"Well, you can rest easy, Dad. I'm not doing anything with Ares Kincaid, except riding in his truck—and not *riding* in the biblical sense. He knew I lived in the city and that I was taking the bus in, so he offered to give me a lift."

"So, you're just friends?" He seems surprised that would even be an option.

Gee, thanks, Dad.

I don't want him knowing that Ares and I hang out. If he has a problem with me riding in his truck, then he'll definitely have a problem if he knows Ares spends time at my apartment.

"I wouldn't say friends . . . but I have hung out with his sister a few times." I say this to put his nose on a different scent.

"Missy. Yeah, I've met her." He nods. "She seems like a nice girl."

Unlike me.

"She is."

He pauses a moment, tapping his fingers together. I stare at him, waiting for him to say whatever he thinks he needs to.

"Look, Ari . . . I just don't think it's a good idea for you to be riding around in Ares's truck."

"I didn't know I needed your permission."

His lips tighten. That's his tell when he's frustrated. "He's my quarterback. You're my daughter. People talk."

"News flash: people always talk. It's the beauty of the gift of speech."

"Don't be smart, Ari. You know exactly what I'm talking about. You're in a vulnerable place right now, and you don't need people talking about you."

"More than they already have, you mean? I'm pretty sure everyone in New York knows the worst of what I've done. But that's not it, is it? No, this is about Ares. You don't want people talking about him, especially not in the same sentence as me, right? It's bad press if people think the quarterback is lowering his standards to the coach's messed up daughter. Well, don't worry, Dad; Ares is most definitely not doing anything with me that will bring disrepute to his name." Tears are stinging the backs of my eyes, so I stand. "And I'll go back to taking the bus home from now on. Don't want to tarnish the shiny reputation of your star player."

"That's not what I'm saying, and you know it."

"Bullshit. That's exactly what you're saying. Trust me, Dad; I know where your loyalty lies, and it sure as hell isn't with me."

Hands on his desk, he pushes to his feet. His face is tight with anger. "My loyalty isn't with you? Right, so it wasn't me who pulled you out of the mess you'd gotten yourself into. Got you in rehab. Got you cleaned up. Gave you this job. News flash: all me, Ari, whether you like it or not."

"Yeah, you saved my ass! Well done, you. But where the hell were you when I needed you after Mom died? Before she even died, when things were bad at home?" I slam my hand to my chest. My face is hot. I shouldn't be saying these things, but I can't seem to stop. "On the football field! That's where you were. Where you always are! So, let's not pretend that you didn't do it out of anything but obligation and to get a handle on the bad press it could bring to you. Not because you actually give a shit."

His eyes darken. "I give a shit, Ari."

"Like you did with Mom."

He looks like I just slapped him.

It was a low blow, and I know it, but I'm angry and hurt, and I don't care right now.

I turn and walk out of his office, slamming the door behind me.

My eyes are stinging as I descend the stairs.

Don't cry. Don't cry.

I don't stop when I reach the bottom step. I walk straight through the lobby and past the reception desk where Marissa, the receptionist, is talking on the phone. I hide my face behind my curtain of hair, and I walk out of the building.

Fortunately, Patrick isn't at the security gate, so I don't have to stop and talk to him about why I'm leaving early.

And I keep walking as it starts to rain, and the irony isn't lost on me right now. And I guess it won't matter if I cry. No one will be able to tell the difference. So, I let the tears fall.

I intend to stop at the bus stop, but when I reach it, I keep walking.

And I keep on walking right into town.

And straight into the first bar I see.

Chapter Fifteen

"**H**OW'S IT GOING?" LUKE takes the stool next to me, resting his arms on the bar top.

"I've been better," I answer quietly.

My arms are on the bar, chin resting on them, my eyes fixed on the glass of wine sitting on the bar in front of me.

I called Luke five minutes after I ordered the wine. He told me to sit tight, and he'd be there soon. He wasn't kidding. That was twenty minutes ago, and he lives in the city. He must've broken all the speed laws to get here.

"I haven't drunk any," I tell him, my eyes still fixed on the wine glass, seeing the distorted reflection of my face in it.

My real face.

"I know," he says gently.

"I want to though."

"I know that, too."

I let out a sad-sounding sigh.

"Do you want me to get rid of it?" he asks.

"Not . . . yet." My eyes slide to his. "I'm not going to drink it, but . . ." I trail off. *I'm not ready to let go yet.*

"I know," he says in understanding. "If you were going to drink that wine, you would have done it by now, and you definitely wouldn't have called me. Trust me; I know."

Luke is eight years sober—drugs and drink. He's in his early thirties. A self-made millionaire. He owns a tech company. Nearly lost it all on drugs, alcohol, and women. It took an overdose that nearly killed him to wake him up.

"I'm sorry to drag you here."

"Don't be. You know the rules. Never be sorry for asking for help. I'm your sponsor. This is what I'm here to do—help you when you need it. And, Ari, you're seven months clean, and this is my first call to a bar from you. I'd say, you're doing great."

I snort out a dry laugh "Only you would say I'm doing great when I'm sitting in a bar with a glass of wine in front of me."

"I see the positive in everything. I'm a ray of sunshine. What can I say?"

I laugh again; there's still no humor in it.

"So"—he props his chin on his hand—"you want to talk about it?"

I shake my head.

"Okay. So, what do you want to do?"

"Drink." I throw him a wry grin.

"You're a comedian."

"I do try."

"Just don't give up your day job."

The bartender appears, asking Luke, "What can I get you?"

"Diet Coke, for me, and one for her, too. And, if you could get rid of the wine, it'd be appreciated."

"Killjoy," I mutter as the wine is moved from my line of sight by the bartender.

"I know. I'm sensible and boring."

We don't speak for a while. Our Diet Cokes are placed in front of us. Luke pays for them.

He's waiting me out. Waiting for me to talk.

He doesn't have to wait long. I fold like a cheap suit.

I let out a big sigh. "I had a fight with my dad. A big one."

"Okay. What about?"

I sigh again and tilt my chin in his direction, eyes looking at him. "Ares . . . the guy I told you about."

"Your dad's quarterback."

"Mmhmm. You know he's been driving me to and from work after what happened with Kyle."

"And I agree with Ares that you should consider getting a restraining order against Kyle and also that you should tell your dad."

I sigh, shaking my head. "Well, my dad doesn't like me spending time with Ares."

"Why? The guy's a friend, right? And a positive influence, by the sound of it."

"My dad doesn't want me spending time with him . . . for Ares's sake, not mine."

"Oh."

"He thinks it'll be detrimental to Ares's reputation—you know, the coach's screwed-up daughter hanging

with the star quarterback. He doesn't want the negative press. Not with the season about to start."

"He said that?"

"In not so many words . . . but yeah. Then, I got angry
and said some shitty things to him about my mom."

"Were they true?"

I meet his steady green gaze. "Yes."

"Then, don't feel bad for saying them. You know
that I think you should tell your dad how you feel
about him not being there when you were younger,
when you needed him. I'm not saying, if he'd been
there, you wouldn't have started drinking—no one
can say that—but he let you down when you needed
him most, Ari."

"According to him, he was there when it mattered
most—after the crash, when I hit rock bottom."

"Putting a loved one in rehab and bailing their ass
out isn't being there. It's doing something proactive
and right to help them. But being there is about giving
them your time and listening when they need it. Your
dad doesn't do that. In the past, with your mom, he
ignored the problem because he didn't know how to
handle it, and he left you to deal with it. He couldn't
leave you to deal with this, and there was no one else
to do it, so he's had to step up, but he's not doing
enough. He should be doing more."

My eyes are stinging with tears. I can't speak
because, if I do, they'll spill over. I take a sip of Diet
Coke and try to steady my emotions.

"Shall we get out of here?" Luke says.

I nod, and he slides off his stool. I pick up my bag
and clamber down from mine.

My legs tremble as I follow him outside to his car, a sporty bright blue BMW.

He unlocks it, using the key fob, and I get in on the passenger side. He climbs into the driver's seat and starts the engine.

"Where am I taking you?" he asks me.

"We could hit up a club." I give him a sad-looking grin, letting out an empty laugh. "Home," I say quietly.

I don't really want to go home to my empty apartment. But I don't have anywhere else to go.

I put my seat belt on, and Luke pulls the car out onto the street.

We're only a few minutes out of town, heading for the city, when I remember that I'm supposed to be going to the cinema with Ares tonight.

God, I can't go out with him, not while I'm feeling like this.

And I don't want him to know how close I was to drinking today.

He'd be disappointed in me, and I couldn't bear that. It'd probably tip me over the edge.

I get out my phone from my bag and tap out a text to him.

Hey, I'm gonna have to bail on tonight. Sorry. Left work early, as I'm not feeling well. Rain check?

While I wait for him to text back, I run a hand through my hair, and it gets stuck in the tangles. On my phone, I switch the camera to selfie mode to look at my hair.

I almost scream when I see myself.

Mascara and eye makeup are smudged under both

my eyes. I look like a panda. And my hair is a damp, knotted mess.

I look like I used to the morning after a heavy drinking session.

"Jesus Christ!" I whine. "I look a mess!"

"Yep." Luke nods, chuckling.

"Thanks a lot! You could've told me that I looked like this when you came into the bar," I complain, trying to rub the mess away from under my eyes.

"Sorry." He shrugs. "But I didn't want to push you over the edge by telling you that you looked like the Bride of Frankenstein. I figured you'd have downed that wine in one go if I'd told you. I know I would've if I'd been in public, looking like you do right now."

"Ass," I grumble.

He chuckles. "And that's the reason you asked me to be your sponsor."

"Because you're an ass."

"Because I'm truthful."

I look at him and smile for the first time since the argument with my dad. "True that."

Chapter Sixteen

LUKE PULLS THE CAR to a stop outside my building. I stare up at it, knowing what is waiting up there for me.

An empty apartment.

"Thanks for the lift and the save," I tell him as I take my seat belt off.

"Anytime. Do you want me to come up and keep you company for a while?" he asks.

"Yes." My response is so quick and eager, it's laughable. And he does chuckle. "God, I'm pathetic, aren't I?" I groan. "I'm a grown woman, afraid to be alone in case I succumb to the urge and run to the nearest bar and drink myself into a coma."

"You're not pathetic, Ari. You're human. And a brave one for admitting that you're afraid."

"Thanks." I give him a sad smile.

"I've been there, remember? Hell, I'm still there. I know what it feels like. And, also, I can't let you go to another bar, looking like that." He gestures to my face, grinning.

"Jerk." I chuckle.

"Come on," he says, taking off his seat belt and turning off the engine. "You can make me a coffee."

Luke follows me up the steps to my building and to my apartment. I unlock my front door, letting us in.

I kick off my shoes and go to the kitchen to turn the kettle on.

"You mind if I just take a quick shower and clean up?" I gesture to the mess that is me.

"Course not. Go ahead. Actually, are you hungry? I skipped lunch, and I'm starving."

"I could eat. What were you thinking?"

"Chinese."

"Sounds good to me. There's Chinese takeout just on the corner of my block."

"Perfect. You go take your shower, and I'll go grab us some food. Anything specific?"

"Chow mein."

"Egg rolls?"

"One for me."

"Got it." He heads for the door.

"You want some money?" I ask him.

He gives me a look that tells me it's a definite no.

"Okay. Well, take my keys with you in case I'm still in the shower when you get back." I throw them over to him, and he catches them.

"Back soon."

I turn down the hall to the bathroom as I hear the front door bang shut. I close the bathroom door and turn on the shower to let it heat up.

I catch sight of myself in the bathroom mirror.

God, what a mess I am.

And I don't just mean the state of my face.

I turn away from the mirror and strip off my clothes.

I climb in the shower and put my head under the spray.

The feel of the hot water is just what I need to help clear my mind of my problems.

The only bad thing is, they'll all still be there after this shower is done.

I turn my face to the stream, and I wash the makeup off my face. Then, I shampoo my hair before combing conditioner through it, followed by soaping my body clean with my favorite raspberry-scented body wash, and then I rinse off.

I'm conscious not to be too long in the shower, as I don't want to be in my towel when Luke gets back, and I didn't bring any clothes into the bathroom with me.

I turn off the shower and wring the excess water from my hair. I grab a towel from the rail and cover my body with it.

I've just opened the bathroom door when I hear a knock at the door.

Is that Luke already? But he took my keys with him, so why is he knocking?

Men. I give a mental eye roll.

"Use my keys," I holler. "I just got out of the shower."

No answer. But another knock.

Christ.

I tighten up my towel as I walk over to the door and swing it open. "You didn't lose my ke—" The words die on my tongue at the sight of Ares standing in front of me.

"Hey," he says. His eyes do a leisurely rake up and down my towel-clad body, causing goose bumps to break out everywhere, before settling back on my face. "I didn't lose what?"

"Uh, what?" I stutter in shock that he's here.

"You said, 'You didn't lose my . . . something.' What was it I must have lost?"

"Uh . . ." Apparently, this is now nine-tenths of my vocabulary. "Nothing. I, uh, thought you were someone else."

"Oh." His eyes dim. "Are you expecting someone?"

"What? No! No, of course not." My eyes dart to the stairwell.

Why am I lying to him?

Because you're a flaky drunk and your sponsor just had to come and rescue you from a bar and he is still here because you can't be trusted to be alone.

Ares's eyes follow mine over his shoulder to the stairs and then come back to me. He gives me a suspicious look.

Crap.

"How did you get in my building?" I ask, my voice sounding unnaturally high.

"The main door was open. The security on your building sucks balls, Jailbird."

I suck my lip into my mouth and nod my head in agreement.

Then, there's an awkward, weird pause between us.

I shift on my feet, holding on to my towel. "So . . . what are you doing here?" *God, that sounded way harsher than I meant it to.*

Discomfort flashes through his eyes, and I want to slap myself.

"Oh, yeah. I didn't get your text until I got back to the city. My cell battery had died, so I had to charge it in my truck on the way home. Anyway, I thought I'd swing by and check to make sure you were doing okay. And . . . I brought you this." He holds out a takeout soup container that I didn't even realize he was holding until now. "It's soup," he tells me, sounding awkward, which is weird for him because he's never anything but confident. "Chicken noodle." He scratches his cheek. "And soup helps when you're sick, right? So, I brought you . . . soup."

"That's, uh . . . really . . . nice . . . thank you." I still haven't taken the soup from him though. I'm just standing here, staring at it, like it's going to sprout wings and fly away. "I—" I start, but Luke's cheerful voice cuts me off.

"Hey."

Ares's eyes snap around to Luke, and the look on his face . . . it's awful.

Confusion quickly morphs to understanding and then turns to anger and disappointment.

It all hits me like a punch to my solar plexus.

I feel winded. And sick.

Luke is, of course, completely oblivious to the fact that I canceled my evening with Ares, telling him I was unwell because I was a complete and utter coward since I didn't want to tell Ares the truth about my meltdown and that Luke had had to come and save me from a bar that I was sitting in, staring at a glass of wine, like the alcoholic I am.

Now, Ares is here, being sweet and bringing me soup and being a really good friend, and Luke is here with Chinese food. And Ares is going to think that I blew him off for Luke and lied to him about it.

Which I did.

But, if I tell him the truth ... why Luke is here ... Ares will be disgusted with me. He'll remember that I'm everything that he despises, and he won't want to be my friend anymore.

And I don't want to lose him.

And, also, I'm still only wearing a frigging towel in front of both of them.

Sweet Jesus, please take the wheel.

"Hey, man." Luke stops in front of Ares, who is standing next to me, and smiles at him. "I'm Luke." He holds his hand out to Ares to shake his.

Ares stares down at Luke's hand like it's covered in shit.

For a moment, I think he isn't going to shake his hand, but then he does. "Ares," he says, voice deep and rough. Shivers fly over my skin at the sound.

"The football player, right?" Luke smiles. "Well, it is good to meet you, man. Ari, I'll take this through to the kitchen and dish it up." Then, Luke walks past me and into my apartment, leaving me standing here with Ares.

Who I daren't look at.

I risk a glance up at him, and his face is like stone. Eyes the bluest I've ever seen them. Jaw set like granite.

"I—"

"I guess you won't be needing this," he says in a voice that's colder than a polar bear's ass. He steps away from me, taking the soup with him.

"Ares—"

He cuts me off with a hollow laugh and a shake of his head, like this is what he was expecting all along . . . for me to let him down. "God, I'm such a fucking idiot," he says low.

"No." The panic in my voice is palpable. "You don't understand—"

"Save it," he snaps. "I'm not interested in anything you have to say." His eyes go over my head and assumedly to Luke. Then, they come back to me, cold and hard. "Enjoy your evening," he adds bitterly. Then, he's gone, striding down the hall, jogging down the stairs and out of sight.

And I stand here, my heart beating a painful rhythm in my chest, eyes staring at the empty space where he just was.

Shit.

I've messed up bad.

He thinks I lied to him.

You did lie to him, you moron.

Fuck.

I close the door and lean back up against it.

Luke is standing in the kitchen, serving up the food. His eyes lift to mine. "Everything okay?" he asks.

"Yes . . . no."

"Want to talk about it?"

It's my turn to laugh dryly. "No."

"Okay, but . . ."

"But what?"

"Well, are you sure you two are just friends?"

"Uh . . ." Well, we were. But I'm not so sure now. "Yeah. Of course. Why?"

"Well, I'm just wondering if he knows that. Because, for a moment there, I wasn't sure if he was going to shake my hand or break it."

"Oh."

Oh.

Chapter Seventeen

AFTER ARES LEFT, I went in my room and changed into my black yoga pants and a black T-shirt. I tied my damp hair into a messy bun and then went into the living room and sat down with Luke to have the Chinese food he'd brought.

Luke's words kept circling my brain the whole time we ate.

He made small talk. I picked at my food, which I didn't eat much of because my appetite was gone after Ares's visit.

Then, I got a text.

I'd never moved so fast to get my cell, hoping it was Ares.

But it was my dad, checking on me after our fight.

No actual mention of the fight itself or the things I'd said. He was basically checking that I wasn't drunk. He didn't exactly say it—the text said, *Are you okay?*—but I've had enough of those texts from my dad since the crash that I know how to read between the lines.

That annoyed me even more. But I didn't want to leave him hanging or worrying, if he's even capable of that. So, I texted back.

I'm fine. I'm having dinner with my sponsor.

I knew that would set his mind at ease.
And it did. He responded with, *Good.*
Luke insisted on helping me with the dishes, and when they were done, I said that I was feeling better, no fear of me running to the bottle, so he was okay to take off. I was too stuck in my own head after what happened with Ares to be good company.

Luke looked at me for a long moment, but whatever he saw in my face satisfied him that I was okay, and he left with my promise to check in with him tomorrow.

And, now, I'm just sitting here, in my quiet apartment, staring at the black screen of my television that I haven't bothered to turn on, thinking about that moment with Ares. Why he was so angry. How sick I feel for lying to him about why I canceled our plans. And why Luke would even think that Ares saw me as more than a friend. He's given no indication of that at all. If anything, he has made it more than known that I am not his type at all.

I need to talk to him to, at the very least, apologize for being dishonest with him.

But, if we have that conversation, I will have to tell him who Luke is and why he was here.

It might push him away, but he's not exactly here anyway, is he? So, what do I have to lose?

"Fuck it," I say to my empty apartment.

I get up, push my feet into my sneakers, put on my

leather jacket, and grab my cell phone, bag, and my keys. Then, I let myself out of my apartment, locking the door behind me, and exit my building.

Out on the street, I start walking until I spot a taxi. I flag it down and climb in the back. I give the driver the address of the building Ares lives in; I only know where he lives because he mentioned it one time. I have no clue which apartment he actually lives in.

So, this is a pretty dumb idea.

But I have to do something. I have to see him. It's not a conversation that I want to have over the phone.

So, I'm figuring, I'll just call him when I'm at his building, letting him know I'm there, and hopefully, he won't turn me away, and I can have my chance to apologize and explain.

When the cab pulls up outside his apartment building ten minutes later, I'm jittery with nerves.

I pay the driver and climb out.

I hear the cab pull away from behind me as I stare up at his apartment building. It's really nice. A lot nicer than the building I live in.

Not that where I live is crappy. But his building screams money.

Which he has, thanks to his football career.

I walk up to the main door and push it open, stepping inside.

"Hi. Can I help you?"

My eyes lift to the security guy at the desk.

His building has security, and mine has a main door that some of the residents forget to shut.

Shit, did I close it when I left?

"Hi." I step up to the desk. "I'm here to see Ares Kincaid."

"Is he expecting you?"

"No. Would you mind calling up and letting him know I'm here?"

"Of course." He smiles. "What's your name?"

"Arianna Petrelli."

I wait while he picks up the desk phone and makes the call to Ares. My leg bouncing on the spot.

What if he doesn't want to see me?

Then, you'll go home, eat ice cream, and feel sorry for yourself. But you will be okay.

"Mr. Kincaid, it's Phillip from security. I have a Miss Arianna Petrelli here to see you. Okay."

He hangs up the phone, and I'm watching him with my heart in my throat.

"You can go on up."

I almost crack my face with the smile that hits my lips.

"Thank you," I say and then, "Which floor? I haven't been here before."

He smiles. "Take the elevator to the eighth floor. It's apartment eight-oh-two."

"Thank you."

I walk over to the elevator, pressing the button, and the door opens immediately.

I step inside and hit the button for the eighth floor.

I can barely keep still while the elevator goes up. Fidgeting, I try to figure out what to say . . . how to say it.

Just start with the truth, and go from there.

The elevator pings its arrival. The door opens, and I step out.

I don't need to wait to figure out which is Ares's apartment, as he's standing in the open doorway of it, waiting for me.

Shirtless.

Sweet Lord.

Those big arms are folded across that massive, rock-hard chest of his.

He's barefoot, wearing only dark gray sweats that sit low on his hips. I can see the happy trail of dark hair running from his navel to down into those pants toward his—

Christ almighty. I think there's drool leaking out from the corner of my mouth.

I press the heel of my hand there, just to check. And, yep, there is.

Great. Come to apologize, and start off by drooling over him.

Well done, Ari.

I take in a deep breath, gathering my wits, and I start to walk toward him.

He watches me, saying nothing. Eyes hooded, making them look darker than they actually are.

I gulp down. Heat and fear are a raging mixture inside of me.

When I reach him, I tip my chin up to look at his face.

Our height difference is so much more pronounced when I'm wearing flat shoes. Who am I kidding? It's pronounced even when I'm in heels. The guy is a giant compared to me.

I part my dry lips, moistening them, ready to speak, and I intend to say *Hi*, or, *Thank you for seeing me*, but what actually comes out is, "I went to a bar."

His eyes widen slightly, but he doesn't say anything, and then I start babbling, trying to explain my brain fart of an apology opener.

"I had a fight with my dad earlier—about you actually—and I said some things and it was awful and I was upset and I left work and started walking for my bus and it rained—can you believe it?—and then I just didn't stop walking and then I was in town and inside a bar, ordering a drink—wine," I say this like it will make everything better, which, in fact, it will do the exact opposite.

"But I didn't drink it. I promise. I don't think I ever was going to. But, after I ordered it, I called my sponsor, Luke—the guy you met—and he came and we talked and he drove me home. I was still a mess and I couldn't let you see me like that, so I texted you, saying I was unwell, which I kind of was but not the kind of unwell that I led you to believe, and I was wrong for that and I'm so sorry. But I need you to know that I didn't blow you off so I could spend time with someone else, some other guy. Luke just stayed with me, as I didn't feel ready to be alone, so he went to grab us some dinner while I cleaned up and took a shower and then you came and I was embarrassed and ashamed of what I'd done, going to the bar, and I didn't want you to think bad of me and not want to be my friend anymore and . . . I messed up. And I'm sorry."

I suck in a breath. The expression on his face hasn't changed. Still stoic, telling me nothing. His mouth fixed in a tight line.

"So . . . yeah . . ." I twist my hands together in front

of me. "I just wanted to come here and be honest with you and tell you that I'm sorry that I wasn't honest in the first place." I take a step back. "Well, thanks for letting me . . . say what I needed to. I guess . . . I'll leave you to it." I turn on my heel to leave, my face hot with sadness at his lack of response.

"Ari."

I stop and turn at the sound of his voice, soaking it up, thirsty for it.

His arms are by his sides now. His expression is a little softer.

"Do you want to come in?" he asks, and my heart leaps.

I smile. "Yes."

I walk back to him, and he moves aside, letting me into his apartment.

Sweet Jesus, his open-plan living room and kitchen is the size of my entire apartment and my neighbor's apartment, put together.

"Where's Missy?" I ask him.

"At Zeus and Cam's." Cam is Zeus's fiancée, and mother of their children. "She's babysitting for them. Staying the night." He shuts the door and moves past me. "Do you want anything to drink?" he asks.

"Water would be great. Thanks."

He walks over into the kitchen area, and I toe off my sneakers. His cherry-wood floors are too nice to walk outside dirt on.

I step further into his apartment, over to the window by the kitchen, taking in the view.

"You have a really nice place," I tell him when I hear him approach. I turn, taking the glass of water he's holding out for me. My finger brushes his, causing a zing to fly up my arm.

Ares doesn't say anything. He just leans his ass against the counter, eyes watching me.

I take a sip of water and then rest my lower back against the window ledge as I cradle the glass to my chest. Desperately trying not to look at his bare chest. It's harder than you'd think.

I'm blaming his nakedness for my brain fry and word vomit from a few minutes ago.

How is a girl supposed to think straight with all this smooth, golden skin in front of her?

Now that he's closer, I can see that he has a fine smatter of dark hairs on his chest.

It makes him even hotter.

But I'm not here to think about his hotness. I'm here to make sure I haven't screwed up our friendship with my lack of honesty.

And I'm clearly doing a shitty job of not trying to stare at his chest.

I lift my eyes to his face, and I see a raised brow and a spark of smug humor in his expression.

He totally knows I was checking him out.

My cheeks heat.

I take another drink of water.

"So . . ." I say.

"So . . ." he echoes.

"I'm sorry."

"You already said."

"I did. I just wanted to say it again."

"Okay." He nods.

No *I accept your apology, Jailbird*, or, *You're forgiven. I totally understand.*

Frustration burns my cheeks.

"You look annoyed." There's almost humor in his words.

"I'm not annoyed." Another sip of my water.

"You sure?"

"Positive."

"Good. Because it would be a bit shitty of you to be annoyed with me after what you did——"

"I said I was sorry!"

"Jailbird."

"What?"

"I'm fucking with you."

I meet his eyes, which are now much softer and smiling at me.

"Ass."

"True." He chuckles. "Thank you for coming here and telling me all of that. I appreciate you being honest with me. But don't lie to me again. I hate being lied to. Even if you think it's something I won't want to hear, I would rather hear it. So, full disclosure from here on out. Okay?"

He's still my friend. My happy heartbeat is a palpable force in my chest.

"Okay." I smile. "Full disclosure."

There's a beat of silence between us.

"So, that guy . . ."

"Luke."

"He's your sponsor?"

"Yes."

"And you guys aren't . . ."

"No! God, no! That's not allowed. Totally unethical. But, even if it weren't . . . he's not my type."

"Oh. Well . . . who is your type?"

You, apparently.

Shit. I just agreed to full disclosure, no more lies. But I can't tell him that he's my type because I'm not his; it'll be awkward as hell, and then I'll definitely lose him as a friend.

I shrug with a noncommittal answer. "Uh . . . um . . . guys."

His brow lifts. "What type of guys?"

Jesus. My whole body is getting hot. My face must be the color of a tomato right now.

"Ones who . . . don't drink."

"I don't drink."

"You don't?"

I didn't know that. We haven't been anywhere where he would drink. But I just assumed he did. I don't know why I thought that. He's not exactly a fan of alcohol.

Alcoholics. You're getting them confused, Ari.

"Nope," he says.

"Okay . . ." I trail off.

"So, what other qualities do your type of guys have to have?"

"Why do you want to know?" I'm skirting the question because I can't think of anything else to say that won't expose my feelings for him.

"I'm curious."

"You know what curiosity did—"

"I'll take my chances." He shrugs, a grin on his lips.

"Uh . . ." I rake my fingers into my messy bun, tugging on it. "They just have to . . . I don't know. Like me. Like who I am. Baggage and all."

He nods, his eyes holding mine. "You're right. He should."

My chest is starting to feel tight. I rub my hand over the ache.

"Do you want to know what my type is?" he asks.

Nope. Because the last thing I want to hear is you describe the exact opposite of me.

"Uh, sure." I stop rubbing the ache, and wrap my arms over my chest, ready to protect myself from the intentional blows he's about to throw at me.

"Usually, I go for blondes. Tall. Leggy. You know the type."

The exact opposite of me then.

I bite the inside of my cheek and make a sound of agreement.

"Women with zero baggage. Who aren't too interested in commitment, as I've really never had time for a relationship—actually, no, that's not right. What I should've said is that I'd never met anyone that I wanted to make time to have a relationship with."

I nod, still biting the inside of my cheek. I'm pretty sure it's bleeding.

"But that's changed now."

"You've met someone?" I blurt out.

He nods, steady blue eyes holding mine. "Yes."

Knife, meet my heart.

But, of course, this was going to happen at some point, if we were going to be friends. I mean, look at him, for God's sake. He's gorgeous, smart, and talented, and he has a good heart once you get past the assholery. It's not like he's going to stay single forever. I guess I just didn't expect it to happen quite so soon. And when the hell did he meet her? It's not like he's with me all the time, but this last week, we've spent quite a lot of time together at my place, watching *Dexter*. And, in that time, he's never let on that there's been anyone . . . a woman in his life.

Jesus.

God, just the thought of it hurts. What will it be like when I have to see him with her? She must be tall and beautiful and have her shit completely together. Unlike me.

I don't think I can do this.

Yes, you can. You're his friend. So, be his friend. Suck it up, Ari. It's big-girl panties time.

"Wow. That's great. I'm really happy for you."

Okay, so that wasn't so great. I sounded insincere as hell. And, if I can hear the insincerity in my voice, then he probably did, too.

But, if he did hear it, he doesn't call me on it, which I'm grateful for.

"Well, don't be too happy for me. She doesn't know how I feel yet . . . and she might not feel the same way."

She will. Trust me.

"I'm sure she will. You should tell her." I nearly bite through my lip when I say that.

Why did I say that?

"You're right." He nods, still staring at me. Actually, he hasn't moved his eyes off me once since this whole conversation started. "It's funny though," he continues, "because of what I said before—you know, about what my usual type is. Well, this girl is the exact *opposite* of that. She's brunette. Short as hell. Filthy mouth on her. Has baggage bigger than JFK. We do, however, share the same taste in movies and music— well, apart from NSYNC . . ."

I suck in a sharp breath.

He can't mean . . .

Was Luke right that Ares might see me as more than a friend?

Surely not.

"Actually, she looks and sounds an awful lot like you."

Holy shit.

"I-I don't . . . understand."

He pushes off the counter, walking over to me. He takes the glass from my trembling hand, setting it on the window ledge. Then, he takes my face in his hands, tilts it up to his, and stares down into my eyes. "Then, let me make it very simple for you." And he leans down and covers my mouth with his.

Chapter Eighteen

ARES KINCAID IS KISSING me.
He's kissing me.

Actually, mouth on mine, kissing me.

Duh. Where else would he be kissing you? Well, there are other places . . .

Nope. Not going to go there. Because I'll definitely get my panties in a twist if I do.

I just . . . can't believe this is happening. One minute, I'm thinking he's into some other woman . . . and then this.

But it is happening.

Holy hell, it's happening.

It's his tongue sweeping my bottom lip before slipping into my mouth. His hands on my face.

It's everything I imagined and more.

I know there's the stupid, gimmicky romance trope of feeling electricity and butterflies, but, God, his mouth on mine is all of those things and more.

My whole body is aware of his in a way I've never experienced before.

Maybe I haven't felt this way before because I was drinking. I always thought it brought my senses to life, but maybe it was dulling them.

Or maybe it is just him.

Because this, being here with Ares . . . this feeling, right here, this is what it's like to feel alive.

One hand leaves my face and pulls my hair free of the tie. The other hand slides down until it's cupping my chin.

His kiss slows. Lips brushing once . . . twice.

Hot breath on my skin.

I open my eyes. His are on mine, hot and dilated.

"Do you understand now?" His voice is gravelly and oh-so very sexy, making my womanly parts tremble.

A grin pulls up one side of my mouth. "I'm starting to. But I think I need you to tell me again. But more thoroughly this time." I tug his mouth back down to mine and feel his smile against my lips, and it's the greatest thing ever.

Two very large hands slide down my back, cup my ass, and pick me up, setting me on the windowsill. My back is pressed against the glass. He's in front of me. And there's nowhere else I would want to be right now.

"That's better," he murmurs against my lips, shifting closer, putting himself between my legs. "You're so small."

Something very hard and very large presses up against my stomach.

Sweet Lord, that's one hell of a boner he's rocking there.

"You're big."

Jesus effing Christ.

I mentally roll my eyes so hard, I almost give myself a headache.

"Thank you." He chuckles into my mouth.

"I meant, height."

"Of course you did."

"But you do seem big . . . down there."

"I am."

Well, there you go.

His hand slides up my side, brushing the underside of my breast, making me moan.

My hands go to his chest.

Holy shit.

Rock-hard muscle beneath smooth skin.

He's hard everywhere.

And I am a lucky, lucky girl.

I run my fingertips through the smattering of hair on his chest, tracing one of his nipples, and he shivers.

Then, he kisses me harder. One hand plunges into my hair, tilting my head back, taking control of the kiss, and I am more than willing to let him take over. The other hand skims the hem of my T-shirt, fingers running under the hem, brushing against my skin, making it my turn to shiver.

I slide my hands around his back and down to his ass and squeeze.

He has a great ass. A really, really great ass. It's as firm as it looks.

His fingers are still teasing the skin of my stomach, driving me crazy.

I want him to touch me. Everywhere.

"Touch me, please," I whisper.

He groans, biting down on my bottom lip before licking the sting away, as his hand finds its way up my shirt and cups my breast over my bra.

The first brush of his thumb over my nipple has my hips pushing forward, seeking pressure, which he willingly gives me, pressing his dick against me. Then, he starts to move his hips, thrusting up and down.

Well, this went from naught to a hundred pretty quickly.

Not that I'm complaining.

"Fuck," he chokes out as we start dry-humping the shit out of each other. "You feel so fucking good."

His hand has now left my hair and is gripping my hip, fingers digging in me in the most delicious way, holding me in place. I'm just holding on to him for dear life. The feelings running through me right now are indescribable.

"You're incredible, Ari. So goddamn beautiful. But we have to stop."

"Wha . . ." I manage to get out as he wrenches away from me.

He's back against the counter, hands gripping the edge, like he's afraid to let go, chest heavy with breaths.

And I'm panting like a dog in heat. Legs trembling. Body in an outcry at his absence.

Shit, does he regret what just happened?

"No, I don't regret it," he says like he just read my mind.

"I never said anything," I counter innocently.

"I could read it all over your face."

Okay. So, maybe I'm easy to read at times.

"So . . . why'd you stop?" I ask quietly.

"Because I was about three seconds away from fucking you on my windowsill, and the first time we do this . . . have sex . . . I want you to be a hundred percent with me."

"I am a hundred percent with you." *I think I always have been.*

"Glad to hear it. But you've had one hell of a day, babe. And, when we do this, the only thing I want you thinking about is me, you, and the way I'm making you feel. And call me old-fashioned, but I'd kinda like to take you out on a date before we get to the sex."

I can't contain my smile. He wants to take me out on a date.

"Okay. And when will this date take place?"

"Tomorrow night, if you're free. *The Big Lebowski* is showing again. I was thinking I could take you out for dinner and then to the movies."

A date with Ares Kincaid. Who'd have thought it?

"I'm free." Even if I weren't, I'd cancel my plans for him. "But, just so I'm clear on this . . . it's just the one date before we get to the fucking?"

He laughs, and it's deep and throaty; it lights me up inside.

"What do you think?"

I think I'm getting laid tomorrow night.

Chapter Nineteen

ARES HAS SEEN ME soaking wet, wearing only a bra and jeans. He's seen me in just a towel, for God's sake.

So, why is it taking me forever to decide what to wear for our date? Which he's picking me up for in fifteen minutes.

Argh!

Because this is different. You're actually going out on a date. There's going to be more kissing. And then later, sex.

Holy cannoli!

I honestly still can't believe this is happening.

That he likes me. That he wants me in this way.

It's crazy. The best kind of crazy.

I don't know what changed his mind or when he realized that his feelings for me were more than just friends, but I don't care. Because he wants me.

Okay, maybe I care a little.

I know how he feels about alcoholics. And I still am one.

But I just need to not focus on that right now. I need to focus on what to wear.

I turn back to my closet.

Okay, so we're going for an early dinner and then to the cinema. So, nothing too dressy.

Pants maybe?

I rifle through my closet and pull out my white ripped jeans. I could wear these.

What with?

I rummage through my tops and pull out my loose, silky bright blue tank top. The color reminds me of Ares's eyes. Perfect.

I go to my underwear drawer and get out my nicest white lacy underwear. I'm going for virginal.

Ha! Like that's even a remote possibility.

But the white will go better under my clothes.

So, white it is.

I take off my robe and put my underwear on, remembering just why I love this bra because of the boost it gives to my boobs. It makes them look fuller and gives me nice cleavage, which will look good with this tank.

I pull my jeans on. Put the tank on.

I decide on my highest black heels. I need the height with this guy.

I put on my gold chain, which sits nicely in my cleavage, bringing the eye to it.

I spritz my favorite perfume, J'adore, on my neck, wrists, and onto my already-done hair, which is down and curled around my shoulders. My makeup is on and light. Focus being on my lips, which are painted with my new favorite lipstick shade, Matte Raspberry.

I've just put my lipstick, wallet, and cell into my bag when there's a knock at my door.

He's here.

My heart takes off at a rapid pace.

I take my bag with me into the living room, grab my leather jacket and slip it on, and then open the door.

Hells bells, he looks good.

I mean, he always looks good, but this . . . is something different.

He's dressed up—not that he normally looks scruffy, but he's clearly made an effort. His hair is styled. His jaw is clean-shaven. He's wearing a dark gray blazer with a black button-down shirt beneath it, dark blue jeans, and black biker boots on his feet.

Maybe he looks different to me because I'm looking at him through new eyes now.

I'm looking at him as more than a friend.

I get to kiss this guy.

I'm quite likely going to see him naked later and do all the good stuff with him.

That definitely changes everything, and how I now view him.

"Hi," he says, voice deep and raspy. "You look beautiful, Ari."

"So do you. Hot. Gorgeous, I mean." *For fuck's sake.*

He chuckles and then leans down and presses his lips to mine, tongue ever-so lightly coming out to touch mine.

"Mmm," he murmurs. "You taste good, too."

He's going to kill me, I swear.

"You sure you don't want to skip the date and just get to the sex?"

He laughs a throaty sound, and I have to squeeze my thighs together.

He moves his lips to my ear. "Anyone ever tell you, the longer you wait to have something . . . *someone*, the better it will be?"

"I'm pretty sure it's, *Great things come to those who don't wait.*" I smile cheekily.

He chuckles again. Then, he kisses me. One quick, firm kiss that leaves me aching.

"You ready?" he asks, and I nod. He slips his hand into mine. "Let's go do our date, so we can come back here . . . and I can make you come. Multiple times."

Sweet Lord.

He leads me out of my apartment building and to his truck. He opens the door for me, and I get inside. I've gotten much better at climbing in this beast, and the high heels definitely help.

I buckle myself in and ask, "So, where are we eating?"

He shifts to look at me. "There's this Thai place in East Village. It's nothing fancy, but—"

"I was sold at Thai. And I don't need fancy."

"You deserve fancy. I just . . . I know you don't go to bars, for the obvious reason, and I didn't know if the same went for restaurants because they all serve fucking alcohol, but this Thai restaurant doesn't have a liquor license. It's one of those bring-your-own-booze restaurants, so there will be alcohol there, but they have outdoor seating, and you can't drink out there, so . . ."

He's babbling. Ares never babbles. And I feel bad that my problem with alcohol is causing him a problem. But I also love that he cares.

"Ares"—I place my hand over his—"I'm going to love it. I'll be there with you, and that's all I care about."

His eyes meet mine, and I smile at him.

He turns his hand over, palm up, and links his fingers with mine.

Hand-holding. So simple. But so incredibly thrilling.

The touch of that one single part of his body against mine is sending my hormones haywire.

My hand looks tiny compared to his, but I don't care. It makes me feel feminine. And I like the feeling.

He lifts my hand to his lips and presses a kiss to it. "I'm sorry, Ari." His lips brush my skin as he speaks, "I didn't see you the moment we met, and I'm so fucking sorry for that."

"I don't understand."

He looks at me, and the look in his eyes . . . anguished, makes my heart clench. "Yesterday, when you came to my apartment and told me the truth and apologized, you were so fucking brave. And I was a coward because I should have been apologizing to you, too. For all the shit I'd said to you. The way I'd acted toward you."

"It's in the past, Ares. It doesn't matter."

"Yes, it does. I judged you. I was a total asshole. And you're this amazing, talented, incredibly strong, beautiful woman, who fights and slays her demons every damn day, and I'm a coward, who let my own shit get in the way of me seeing all of that . . . seeing who you are. And I'm so fucking sorry, Ari. But I promise, I will make it up to you. I will treat you the way you deserve to be treated." Another kiss to my hand. "I like you for who you are. Baggage and all, babe."

And I'm done for.

This guy. Sweet Jesus, this guy. He slays me.

I can feel my throat starting to close up. "You're going to make me cry, and I really don't want to because I'm not wearing waterproof mascara, and I look really bad when I have panda eyes."

He lifts his eyes to mine, and they're glittering with emotion and some other thing I can't quite put my finger on.

He presses one final kiss to my hand before turning the engine on and putting the car into drive.

But he doesn't let go of my hand the whole ride there.

Chapter Twenty

"I HAD A REALLY GREAT time tonight." I look across at Ares from the passenger seat of his darkened truck parked outside my apartment building, the shadows tracing his gorgeous face.

And I really did. The restaurant was perfect. The food was amazing. The company even better. We talked about nothing and everything. Then, after dinner, we went to the cinema and watched *The Big Lebowski* and laughed our asses off.

It was the perfect date.

And he was the perfect gentleman.

But, now, we're at the part of the date where I don't want him to be a gentleman anymore.

He reaches over and brushes my hair off my face, tucking it behind my ear. "I did, too. But it's not over yet . . . is it?"

"Do you want to come in for . . . coffee?" I bite down on a smile.

His brow lifts. "Do I get sugar this time?"

"Oh, most definitely."

We get out of his truck, and Ares wordlessly follows me up and into my building. His hand is on my lower back as we walk up the stairs toward my apartment. That one small place on my body where he's touching, and everything inside of me is focused directly there.

I can't concentrate on anything but the feel of his fingers gently pressing into me.

It takes all my concentration just to get my keys out of my bag and unlock my front door, letting us in.

I close the door behind us. "So, about that coffee—"

The rest of the sentence is sucked right out of my mouth when I'm picked up and pressed against the door by a hot, hard football player as he kisses the hell out of me.

And it's the wettest, dirtiest kiss I've ever had in my life.

"I've been wanting to do that all night," he rumbles against my lips.

"Feel free to keep doing it," I say breathlessly.

A deep chuckle thrums through his chest, lighting me up. "Bedroom?"

"That way." I point.

Then, we're moving, and this man mountain is carrying me to my bedroom while I cling to him like a spider monkey to a tree.

We reach my bed, and he lays me down on it. Standing there, one knee resting on the bed, he stares down at me.

"Fucking beautiful," he says.

And my insides glow like I'm filled with a million lightning bugs.

He takes my heels off, one at a time, dropping them to the floor.

I remove my jacket, tossing it aside, and take off my necklace.

He holds his hand out for it. I give it to him, and he puts it on my nightstand. Then, he takes his wallet, cell, and car keys from his pocket and sets them beside it.

"Just so we're clear, I'm spending the night."

I raise a brow. "And if I don't want you to?" I'm teasing. Of course, I want him to stay over, but I need to exert some authority here.

"Then, we don't fuck tonight."

God, I shiver every time he says that word . . . *fuck*. He makes it sound so hot and dirty, all at the same time.

He leans down over me, hands on either side of my body, mouth an inch from mine, those blues staring right into mine. "Like I told you yesterday, the first time we have sex, we're doing it right. And right isn't me picking my clothes up at the end, dressing, and going home."

My heart shimmies in my chest. "Why does it matter so much to you that we do this right?" I ask quietly.

"Because I fucked up with you once before. I won't make the same mistake again. This . . . what we're starting here, is too important. *You're* too important."

I'm important. I don't think I've ever been important to anyone before.

Tears sting the backs of my eyes, but I refuse to cry and spoil this moment.

I slide my hand around the back of his neck and whisper, "You're important to me, too." Then, I lift my mouth to his and kiss him.

He groans into my mouth, deepening the kiss, his body settling down onto mine. I part my legs, and he settles between them.

He's hard already.

I love that I can turn him on without even having to remove a scrap of clothing. It's doing awesome things for my ego.

"I can't believe I almost drove you away." He presses his forehead to mine, exhaling.

"You're lucky I'm awesome," I joke. I don't want him feeling bad right now. The only thing I want him to feel in this moment is good.

"I really am." He kisses me again, his mouth moving a path along my chin, down my neck. Pressing kisses along my collarbone, down my chest, to the valley of my breasts.

His fingers slide under the hem of my tank, the silk dragging up my skin, the rough pad of his fingers driving me to the point of madness.

He slides down my body, pushing my top over my breasts, and starts pressing hot kisses to my stomach, making me squirm with desire.

I reach down, take hold of my top, and pull it over my head, leaving me in just my bra.

Kind of like the first time I saw him—minus being wet through.

Well, I am wet. In fact, I'm soaking . . . so I guess it is like last time.

His eyes fasten onto my breasts, pupils dilating. "Nice bra."

He licks a path up to my breasts. One hand covers my right boob, gently squeezing. The other, he sucks my nipple through the fabric of my bra. My hands fly to his hair, gripping the strands, my hips jerking up, seeking him out, needing to feel the press of him against me.

His hand leaves my breast and takes hold of my thigh, bringing my leg up, opening me to him, as he moves against me, his denim-covered cock rubbing against the spot where I need him, while he continues to torment my nipple through my bra with teasing bites and sucks.

Then, finally—*finally*—he takes my bra off, and then it's mouth on skin.

My thighs tighten around him, gripping.

"You're sensitive," he murmurs as he licks my nipple, teeth gently grazing over my skin.

"You're driving me crazy," I tell him.

All the other men I've been with in my life, it's been a quick foreplay fumble and then sex.

Ares seems to be in no rush. Taking his time with me. Getting to know what I like.

I slide my hands under his shirt, desperate to feel him.

He stops what he's doing to me, kneels back, undoes a few buttons on his shirt, then reaches back, and pulls it over his head, tossing it to the floor.

Then, he's back on me, skin on skin, and it's heavenly.

My hands roam his broad chest and back while he

kisses my neck, nipping my jaw with his teeth, and then he covers my mouth with his.

His tongue slides against mine, hot and hard, fucking my mouth like I want him to fuck my body. It feels like a promise of what's to come.

And, boy, do I really want to come.

I'm starting to writhe beneath him, needing more, wanting all of him.

His hand moves between us, fingers firmly sliding over the crotch of my jeans, pressing right where I need him. The relief of the pressure has me moaning out loud.

"You want me here, Ari?" he asks in a guttural voice.

"Yes."

"Say it. Tell me exactly what you want me to do, and I'll do it."

I meet his blazing stare. "I want you to make me come."

"How?"

He's going to make me say it. I'm not shy, but I'm also not used to vocalizing what I want. I usually just direct the guys or go with the flow.

But then I was drunk every time I ever had sex. Even when I lost my virginity, I was drunk.

This is the first time I'll have sex sober. The enormity of it hits me like a freight train.

"It's my first time," I blurt out.

His hand stops moving, his face slackening with shock. "You're a—"

"No! God, no! I mean . . ." God, this is mortifying. I cover my face with my hands. "This is the first time

I'm having sex sober. All the other times, I was . . ." I trail off, not saying the words because he'll know exactly what I mean.

"Ari."

"Mmhmm?" I reply, not moving my hands from my face.

They're moved for me and pinned to the bed on either side of my head. "Look at me."

I open one eye, peering up at him. His expression is hot and fierce.

"Both eyes."

I sigh and open the other.

"We don't have to do this yet, if you're not ready. We can wait."

"I don't want to wait. I'm ready." *So ready.* "But I just realized that I hadn't ever . . . and what if I'm not very good at it . . . sober?"

"I don't think that's even remotely possible."

"It's possible to be bad at sex."

"Not with me, it's not."

"Cocky bastard," I utter.

He grins. "Babe, when two people want each other as much as we do, there's no way the sex can be bad. It's going to be hot." A kiss. "And explosive." A second kiss. "And feel so very fucking good."

The third time he kisses me, I keep him there, kissing him back hard, sucking on his tongue.

My hands are still pinned to the bed. He starts to thrust against me. That big, hard cock pressing against my clit through his jeans and mine, driving me wild.

"I want you," I whisper to him.

"And I want you, babe. Now, tell me how you want me to make you come."

"Your mouth. I want your mouth on me."

He grins wickedly, the promise of something amazing glittering in his eyes.

He releases my hands. His go to the button on my jeans. He drags down the zipper. The sound is loud in the quiet of my room, like a needle scratching a record.

He starts to pull my jeans down. I lift my butt, giving him easier access.

My jeans are off.

And I'm in just my panties. He leans down and presses a hot, wet kiss against my clit through the fabric of my panties, making me moan.

"You're soaked," he groans, his finger drawing a line from my pussy to my clit.

His fingers hook into the elastic of my panties, and he pulls them down my legs. Then, I'm completely naked for the first time in front of him.

He's kneeling at the bottom of the bed, eyes on me. His cock straining against the restraint of his jeans. He grabs his dick with his hand and squeezes. My mouth waters.

I'm not self-conscious about my body. Yoga keeps me fit. But, even if I were . . . the way he's looking at me right now would take any doubts away.

He's watching me like he's starving, and I'm his next meal.

"So fucking beautiful." He shakes his head, like he can't believe what he's seeing.

The praise in his words and his eyes light me up inside.

He climbs back up the bed, hands pushing my thighs apart. He leans down, face close to where I want him most, and he gently blows air onto my pussy. The sensation of the cold against my hot, aching clit is thrilling.

I want him so badly.

His eyes lift to mine. "I'm gonna make you come so hard," he growls. Then, he covers my pussy with his mouth and pushes a finger inside me.

I nearly come up off the bed, but he holds me down with his other hand.

He licks and sucks and fucks me with his finger, driving me wild.

"Play with your tits."

His hoarse order has me obeying immediately. I roll my nipples between my fingers, moaning when he slides another finger inside me, two now, and sucks hard on my clit.

I'm not going to last much longer. It's been too long.

I want to move my hips, but his grip won't permit it.

He's in control here, and he's making sure I know it.

I feel the rise of my orgasm climbing. My toes curl into the bed. One hand leaves my breast, going to his head between my legs, fingers tangling in the dark strands. "Yes," I chant. "Yes . . . right there, Ares. Don't stop—fuck!" My eyes roll back into my head as the most intense orgasm of my life hits and keeps going . . . and going.

Ares doesn't stop until I'm lax in my bed, and even then, his fingers stay inside me, slowly working me.

"Jesus," I breathe, opening my eyes, looking at him. "Sweet fucking Jesus."

He laughs deeply, although there's no humor in his eyes. Only desire. Raw fucking passion.

"I want to taste you," I tell him.

And he growls. "I want that, too, but I'm big, baby. This isn't me being cocky—it's a fact—and you're small and tight. I need you to be ready to take me, and right now, you're ready." He pushes to his knees, sitting between my legs, still working his fingers in and out of me.

"I don't care."

"I do. I don't want to hurt you."

"You won't." And I'm sure of that. I know he won't ever hurt me again.

I push up to sit. His fingers stay inside of me. Meeting his mouth, I kiss him. I can taste myself on him, and usually, that doesn't do anything for me, but with him, it does. It turns me on even more.

I grab his dick through his jeans and give it a squeeze.

He moans a tortured sound. "You're killing me babe."

"Can't have you dying on me."

I undo his jeans, dragging the buttons open, and I work his jeans down his legs. His fingers slip out of me, and he pulls his jeans off the rest of the way. Then, his boxers follow.

And, sweet Lord, he's naked in front of me. Big cock jutting up, straining toward his rock-hard stomach.

His body is insane.

I've seen men's bodies like this in magazines and in movies but never in real life. He has muscles in places I didn't even know you could have them.

All that football and working out have clearly paid off.

And I'm currently getting to reap the rewards.

I have never wanted a man more or been as desperate to touch as I am with him right now.

"You're beautiful," I tell him, my eyes lifting to meet his.

Unnamed emotion flickers across his face.

I move up onto my knees to him. My hand on his chest, I run my fingers across the ridges of his body, like I'm tracing a map down to the promised land.

He cups my chin in his hand and kisses me deeply.

I wrap my small hand around his huge dick. He's hot and hard, like nothing I've ever felt before. I give a firm squeeze. He groans that tortured sound again, into my mouth.

I break away from his kiss.

The way he's looking at me . . . it's intense. Hungry.

No one has ever looked at me this way before.

Like they see only me.

I lower my head and take his dick in my mouth, sucking the tip.

A hot breath shudders out of him. "Jesus, Ari."

I wrap my hand around the base of his cock, moving it up and down, as I take more of him in my mouth and start to work him over. Licking and sucking. I taste his salty pre-cum on my tongue, and it spurs me on further.

I want to make him feel as good as he just made me feel.

His fingers tangle in my hair. The other hand teases my nipple, rolling and pinching.

I moan around his dick, and his hips jerk forward a little, giving me more of him.

"Fuck, Ari . . . that feels so fucking good."

I take my hand off his dick and place both hands on his hips. I stop moving, his cock still in my mouth, and I stare up at him, telling him with my eyes to fuck my mouth.

His gaze is pinned on me. He gathers my hair back from my face, holding it with his hand, and then he starts to move his hips back and forth, fucking my mouth.

"Shit . . . this feels so good . . . too good." He's still pumping his cock in and out. "I need to stop." He pulls out of my mouth. "Get on your fucking hands and knees—now, Ari."

Holy shit. Bossy Ares is here, and I like him a lot.

I scramble onto my hands and knees.

He grabs his wallet from my nightstand and gets out a condom.

I hear the rip of foil. Then, he's behind me.

The next thing I expect to feel is his cock. So, color me surprised when I feel the hot breath of his mouth on my pussy. From behind me, his tongue pushes inside me, his thick finger pressing down on my clit.

"You'll come for me again." It's not a request, but I'm more than happy to fulfill it.

My limbs are like jelly. I'm barely able to stay upright as he fucks me with his tongue. A blunt, rough finger teases my clit.

I'm coming apart in no time. Shuddering around his mouth. This orgasm just as explosive as the first.

When I can manage, I lift my head, staring back at him.

He's kneeling behind me. Cock in hand. "Are you ready for me?"

"Yes."

He smooths a hand over my ass as he positions his cock at my entrance.

I feel the first push as the head of his cock enters me, spreading me.

"You okay?" he checks, his voice sounding strained.

"Keep going," I rasp out.

And he does. Pushing each thick inch inside me until I'm full of him.

He's everywhere. In me, on me. And it's everything I could ever want.

Big hands grip my hips as he pulls back out and slowly thrusts back in.

"Harder," I tell him.

"I don't wanna hurt you."

"You won't. I need you. Please."

His resolve must snap because he pulls out and slams back in. The feel of his cock and the delicious sound and feel of his skin slapping mine have me crying out in ecstasy.

"More," I beg.

And he gives me what I want. He fucks me hard, and it's primal. The sound of his raw, guttural grunts behind me drive me on.

"So fucking sexy," he rasps. "I could fuck you all night."

"Yes. Don't stop."

My arms give out on me, my chest lowering to the bed. Ares pushes my ass down, so I'm lying flat on the bed, and he starts to pump in and out of me from behind. The angle is delicious, hitting me right where I need him to.

Although he doesn't stay there for long. He pulls out of me, and I'm being turned over and lifted. Up into his kneeling lap.

"Ride me," he orders.

I lower myself down onto his cock. The position putting us face-to-face.

God, he's so beautiful.

I wrap my arms around his neck. His come around my body, grabbing my ass, as I start to ride him.

His eyes are so intense on mine; it's hard to look at him, the emotions I'm feeling for this man swirling inside me like a building tornado.

Needing to break the connection, I close my eyes and kiss him, riding him hard and fast in short, shallow movements. The edge of his dick dragging across my clit.

"That's it, baby. Ride me hard." His hand slaps my ass cheek.

Fuck, that's hot.

Wanting him to do it again, I ride him harder and faster.

"You like my hands on your ass?" he growls.

"Yes," I breathe.

He slaps the other cheek, making me moan.

"My dirty girl." He bites my lower lip, sinking his teeth into it before licking away the sting.

I move, wrapping my legs around his back, and he takes over, grabbing my ass, lifting me on and off his cock, fucking himself with me.

"Rub your clit," he tells me. "I want to see you touching yourself."

I lower my hand between us and run my fingers over my swollen clit.

"Fuck yeah, baby, that's it," he rumbles. "Get yourself off." He lowers his head, taking my nipple in his mouth, sucking.

I'm overwhelmed with sensation. Full of him. With him. Wanting more. Having enough. My mind is a jumble of feelings and emotions.

"Are you close?" he asks. "I won't come without you."

"Yes," I pant. "I'm nearly there."

I rub myself harder as he continues to fuck me.

The orgasm hits me just as hard as the other two, making me scream his name.

Then, I'm moving onto my back, and he's fucking me hard with his cock and tongue. Owning me. Telling me that I'm his.

"Ari," he groans against my mouth. "I'm coming, baby." His body tenses as the first wave hits him. Hips jerking against mine as he rides his orgasm out inside me.

We're both panting, trying to catch our breaths as we come down from the most intense sexual experience I have ever had.

His lips find mine, softly kissing me. "You okay?"

"Is that a trick question?" I reply, and he chuckles. "It was . . . wow, Ares . . . just . . . wow. Three orgasms. I didn't even know that was possible. Seems sober sex is the best sex. Or maybe it's just sex with you."

He brushes my hair back from my face, staring into my eyes. "I'd say both. I'm pretty fucking awesome in the sack."

I can't even argue with him on that. So, I just pinch his ass instead, making him chuckle.

"But, seriously," he adds, "I'm really fucking glad that it was me you chose to be with the first time . . . since getting sober."

I lift my head and press my mouth to his. "Me, too."

Chapter Twenty-One

W E'RE LYING IN BED after getting cleaned up. Both naked, wrapped up together. How the hell I'm ever going to sleep with him next to me, I'll never know.

"I'm glad you're here." I press a kiss to his chest.

"I'm glad I'm here, too. And, just to warn you, it's highly likely that I'll wake up during the night, horny, and want to bang you again."

"Who needs sleep?" I shrug, and he laughs, giving my ass a squeeze.

I lay my head on his chest, listening to the gentle thrum of his heart, running my fingers through the hairs on his chest.

I can't believe I'm here . . . that we're here.

Especially after the way we started. Hate at first sight—on his part anyway.

"Can I ask you something?" I lift my head and rest my chin on my hand.

"You can ask me anything."

"When did you . . . change your mind about me?

I mean, when did you start to see me in a different light?"

"You mean, when did I realize that I was into you?"

"Yeah."

"In a way, I always knew. The first time I saw you, I swear, I thought I'd won the fucking lottery. Here was this half-naked chick, soaking wet and bent over, in the locker room—total fantasy moment right there, babe—and then you turned around and knocked me on my ass. You were so the opposite of what I usually went for, but I thought you were the hottest chick I'd ever seen."

"Sure you did." I roll my eyes.

He grasps my chin in his hand. "Believe it." Then, he firmly kisses me before letting me go. "You're hot, Ari. Even when I was being an asshole, I always thought that. I can't tell you how many times I jerked off in the shower over you."

"I can't believe you just said that." I laugh. Although the thought of him getting off to me in the shower is totally hot.

"It's true. Even when I was telling myself I hated you, I was still tugging one out over you. There were all kinds of hate-sex scenarios going on up here." He taps a finger to his head.

"We should totally try them out."

"Role-play hate sex? I'm down for that." He grins.

"So, when did things change for you? You're feelings . . . about me. I know how you feel about alcoholics . . . and I'm still one. I guess I just can't figure out what changed."

His expression turns serious. "It was never about

you. I was projecting my shit onto you. I hate that I did that." He runs a hand over his face. "Full disclosure?"

"Always."

"My dad's an alcoholic. Currently sober. It's the longest he's lasted. But, after multiple rehab attempts, I'm not holding my breath."

"I figured that you'd been around a drinker. I'm sorry that it's your dad. That's . . . gotta be hard."

"Yeah." He sighs. "He wasn't always a drinker. Once upon a time, he was a decent dad. Yeah, he liked a drink, like the next person. Then, my mom got cancer. After she died, his drinking intensified. He just gave up. So, it was down to Zeus and me to keep things together. Zeus boxed and worked a factory job to earn money. I took care of Lo and Missy. And cleaned up after my dad. It was Zeus who put me through college."

"God, I'm so sorry, Ares."

I press my hand to his cheek. He takes hold of it and turns his face into my palm, pressing a kiss there.

But he doesn't let go of my hand; he holds it in his, resting it on his chest.

"I hated him for a long time. I guess, in a way, part of me still does. I resent him. My relationship with him is . . . difficult. I don't trust him. And I don't forgive him for letting us down when we needed him most."

"Which is why you don't trust drunks."

His eyes come to mine. "I trust you."

My heart swells to the size of Texas.

"You told me the truth when it mattered, Ari. I know how hard that was for you to come to me and tell me that you'd gone to that bar. My dad . . . he never would have done that. It was lie after lie with him. That's why it's so important to me that you're always truthful with me."

"Even if it's something you won't want to hear, I'll always tell you the truth." I press a kiss to his knuckles.

"But, yeah, so because of my shit with my dad . . . I took offense with you."

"I understand that."

"But that doesn't make it right. I projected my bull-shit with him onto you. It was wrong of me. And I guess . . . because I wanted you so badly, but I couldn't have you . . . it made me angrier."

Knowing that he wanted me for all that time, it's crazy.

"Then, after the shit with your dipshit ex, I felt . . . protective over you. And the more time we spent together, the harder it was to lie to myself. And then, when I saw Luke here . . . and I thought maybe . . ." He shakes his head. "I've never felt any-thing like it, Ari. Jealousy, rage. And I don't get jealous. I'm not that guy. Well, I didn't think I was . . . until then. And that's when I had to stop lying to myself and admit the truth. I was fucking gone for you."

My heart skips some seriously happy beats. "If I hadn't come to see you yesterday, what do you think would've happened?"

"Honestly? I don't know. I'm a stubborn bastard. I would have brooded for days about it. Probably been an asshole to everyone. Missy would've given me shit about being an ass and called Zeus, and he would've come and gotten the truth out of me and talked sense into me. Then, I'd have come crawling to your door."

I chuckle. "Zeus sounds like a smart guy."

"I wouldn't go that far." He laughs. "But he's a great fucking brother."

"You're lucky to have them, as they are you. I always wanted siblings, but . . ." I trail off.

He moves down the bed, rolling onto his side, putting us face-to-face. "Tell me to mind my own business . . . but where's your mom? Coach keeps his personal life pretty private. I honestly didn't know he had a daughter until the crash happened."

I laugh, and it's not humorous. "I'm not surprised. My dad's not one to talk about his family. Or, well . . . me." I rub a hand over my face. "Full disclosure?"

"Of course."

"My mom is dead. She, um . . . took her own life. I found her."

"Jesus, Ari." He presses his hand to my cheek, thumb brushing along my cheekbone. "I'm sorry that happened . . . to you."

"She was sick for as long as I could remember . . . bipolar disorder. My dad couldn't handle it, so he wasn't around much. So, it was mostly me and her. When she was up, it was great. But, when she was down . . . it was hard. I'd been studying for a test at a friend's the night I found her. Dad was away at a game. She was hanging in their closet."

He sucks in a breath, and I close my eyes, hating that I can still see the image of her there.

"That's when you started drinking."

Nodding, I swallow. "I had my first drink before her funeral. It made things easier, you know." I blink open my eyes, and the look in his nearly slays me. *He cares about me. Really cares.* "And, after she was gone, Dad was still never home, and I was alone . . . and sad . . . and alcohol helped. I didn't realize that I actually had a problem until the accident. So, yeah . . ."

I don't realize I'm crying until I feel him brush a tear away with his thumb.

"He let you down," he says with understanding.

I guess both our dads let us down, just went about it in different ways.

I nod and bite my lip.

"Your fight with your dad yesterday . . ."

"Was about you. He . . . doesn't like me riding into work with you."

"Well, he's definitely not going to like this then."

He raises a brow, and I manage a laugh.

"Gotta say I'm a bit offended though. I get you're his daughter, and no man wants to know their little girl is doing the deed with a guy. But I've always had a great relationship with your dad."

"It's not me he's worried about."

Ares's brows pull together with confusion.

I sigh. "He's worried that *I'll* tarnish *your* reputation."

His frown deepens. "He said that?"

"Kind of."

"That's bullshit."

"No, really . . . even though I hate it, he actually has a point. My reputation is in the toilet. Yours is . . . you're a great guy, Ares. And you're in the public eye. Being with someone like me will hurt that."

"You're wrong."

"I'm right, and you know it. If I were a random

person, the news of what I had done probably would never come to light. But I'm your coach's daughter, who was charged with a DUI and spent time in rehab. The press will go after us. It'll hurt you."

"I don't care."

"You should. It's your career. I just think . . . it's best if we keep this between us for now."

"No."

"Ares . . ."

"I don't like lying, and I don't fucking like secrets."

"I know." I take his face in my hands. "But it needs to be that way—for now."

"I'll talk to your dad. PR can handle it. They're great at swinging things to fit public image."

"My dad doesn't want me riding in your truck, Ares. Trust me; he will not want this. And I want us to have a chance. Get to know each other properly before other people . . . start interfering in our relationship."

"I don't like this, Ari."

He looks away from me. So, I climb onto him, straddling his body.

"I don't either. But I just think it's the best for now."

He stares up at me. "I won't lie. If someone asks if we're together, I will tell them yes. And I sure as fuck will be telling my family that you're mine."

"Okay," I say, agreeing.

"And, in a few weeks, Ari, we're telling your dad."

"A few weeks," I agree even though I don't think it's nearly enough time for me to figure out how to handle my dad. I haven't even spoken to him since our fight, except for that text.

Ignore and pretend shit isn't happening—that's how me and my dad coexist.

"I just don't want anyone to come between us," I say quietly.

He sits up, putting us chest-to-chest, one hand curling around the nape of my neck, holding me. "No one—and I mean, no fucking one, not even your dad—will come between us. I'm crazy about you, babe. That ain't gonna change."

"I'm crazy about you, too," I whisper.

"Glad to hear it." He kisses me deep and hard, his hand fisting into my hair.

I feel his erection press into my belly.

"Round two already?" I raise a brow.

"Definitely . . ." A kiss. "Ari?"

"Mmhmm."

"You know that yoga you do?"

"Yep."

"That means you're pretty flexible, right?"

"Uh-huh. Why?"

A grin spreads across his gorgeous face. "Because we're about to get adventurous as fuck. Hold on tight, babe."

Chapter Twenty-Two

I AWAKE WITH ARES'S WARM, hard body wrapped around mine, making me smile.

My body is deliciously sore in the way it only can be from sex.

Especially amazing sex. Some of the things Ares did to me last night . . . the positions . . . my cheeks blush at the memories.

Ares really knows what he's doing in bed. I maxed out at five orgasms by the time he was done with me.

Five!

I hadn't even known that was possible.

Apparently, with him, it is.

It's still dark out, so I check the time on my cell. Four sixteen.

I carefully disentangle myself from Ares, making sure not to wake him. I grab a nightshirt from my drawer, pull it on, and then make a quick trip to the bathroom. Then, I go into the kitchen and get myself a glass of water, leaning my hip against the counter while I take a sip.

I have this permanent smile on my face and a warm glow in my chest, and it's all because of that man sleeping in my bed.

I wander through my living room and over to the window, looking outside. The street is quiet. Not a soul around.

Then, I do something that I haven't done for a while.

I take a seat on the stool in front of my easel. I put my glass of water down on the table, and I pick up a brush.

Clean and unused.

I brush it over the blank canvas, tracing invisible lines, thinking about Ares.

Him and me together.

Without conscious thought, I reach for my black oil paint. I squeeze some out onto my palette and sweep my brush through it.

And then I start painting.

The room is bright with the morning sun. I can hear the birds outside. The rumble of cars traveling down the street. And I'm still painting.

I've been at it for hours, and it's starting to take shape already. It's something new for me. It's a still, but instead of a solitary person, it's two people. It's Ares and me, entwined, making love.

I've never done anything like this before, but I don't want to stop, for fear that I'll never start again.

I'm painting for the first time in seven months, and it feels good.

I hear movement behind me, and I stop and turn.

Ares is standing in the doorway, shoulder leaning against the frame, dressed in his boxers, hair ruffled.

He looks gorgeous.

"Morning." I bite down on a smile.

"You're painting."

"I am."

He walks the distance between us, leans down, and presses a sweet kiss to my lips.

"Apparently, having sex with you was what I needed to get started again."

He grins. "My cock is pretty inspirational."

I glance down at the bulge in his boxers. "Can't disagree with that."

I shrug, and he chuckles. Then, he kneels behind me, wrapping his arms around my waist, resting his chin on my shoulder.

I stare back at my work in progress.

I'm painting again, and I have the most beautiful man in the world wrapped around me.

Life is pretty freaking great at the moment.

"I'm happy for you, babe." He presses a kiss to my neck. "And not to sound arrogant . . . but is that me you're painting?"

"It's us . . . having sex." Biting my lip, I turn my eyes to his. "I guess I was inspired by last night."

His smile is wide. "Can I have it when it's finished?"

"The painting?"

He nods.

"Well, um . . . sure, if you really want it. But it might look like crap when it's done. It's been so long since I painted."

He gives me a look. "Babe, we both know it won't be crap. And, of course, I want it. It's us. It represents our first time together. I want that fucker hanging in my bedroom."

"Then, it's yours." I press a kiss to his nose. "When it's finished, of course."

"How long will it take you to finish it?"

I shrug. "Depends. Actually . . . what time is it?" I glance around, looking for a clock.

"Seven thirty," he tells me.

"I need to get ready for work."

"How about you don't go in today?"

His hand slides lower to cup my pussy, and he groans. I'm not wearing any panties. Teeth sink into my neck.

"I have to go in." I'm not giving my dad the satisfaction of me not showing up, especially after our fight. "And you have training."

He slips a finger inside me, and I moan.

"I'll skip it."

He starts planting kisses up my neck. I tilt my head to give him better access.

"Your first game is in a week."

"I'm in the best shape of my life."

"If we both don't go in, it'll be obvious to my dad."

He sighs, defeated.

I turn my face to his and softly kiss his lips. "Quickie?" I whisper against his mouth, and he grins.

Then, I'm spun around to face him. He whips off my nightshirt. A second later, his mouth is on mine, hot and hard. I meet his kiss with the same ferocity. We're going at each other like we haven't had sex in weeks, not hours.

I've never been as desperate for a man as I am with

him. More so now that I'm fully aware of what he's capable of in bed . . .

Five orgasms.

I'm never going to get over that.

I push my hands into the elastic of his boxers and shove them down his hips. His cock juts out to meet me. I wrap my hand around it, and he groans, sinking his teeth into my bottom lip.

I wrap my legs around his waist. Then, I drag the head of his cock up and down my center.

"You ready for me, baby?"

"Always." My legs wrap around his waist.

Then, he sinks inside me.

We both moan with pleasure.

We're joined as much as two people can be. Our mouth still fused together. His hips flush with mine, cock buried deep inside me. Our chests pressed together.

I blink open my eyes, and his are already on mine.

"I'll get a condom in a second," he says. "I just want to feel you."

I run my hand around the nape of his neck, curling my fingers into the hair there. "It's okay. I'm on the pill . . . and I'm clean."

"I'm clean, too."

My lips quirk into a smile. "So then, fuck me, quarterback."

And he does.

He takes me right there, fucking me hard and fast on my painting stool, in front of the Ares and Ari work in progress.

Chapter Twenty-Three

IT'S THE SECOND GAME of the season, and I'm here, supporting my man.

I didn't go to the first game, as they were away at Dallas, playing the Cowboys. They lost that game. And I missed him when he was away. It was the first night we'd spent apart since getting together. We either spend the night at my place or his. Mostly mine, as Missy is still home. But she goes back to Dartmouth in a few days. I'm going to miss her. We've become really good friends. But Ares told me that she comes home often, so it'll be like she's never left.

We're all going out for dinner tomorrow night. I'm finally going to meet Zeus, Cam, and Lo. He's heading back to Penn State in a few days, too.

I'm kind of nervous about meeting them.

But, tonight, there are no nerves because the Giants are playing the Detroit Lions at home, and they're kicking ass, thanks to Ares throwing some great passes.

Missy and I are sitting in great seats. Ares gets two

tickets to every home game. Usually, Zeus uses them to watch him play, as he lives over in Port Washington, which is only an hour's drive away. Lo and Missy use them when they're home.

But, tonight, it's me and Missy here, supporting him.

I could have gone in the box with the wives. Not because of the fact that Ares and I are together; that's still a secret, and that's because I haven't found the courage to tell my dad despite the pressure from Ares to tell him.

But my dad is the coach, and I work for the team, so I have access anywhere. But I didn't want to sit up there. I wanted to be out here, among the action, close to Ares.

"He's been playing great tonight," Missy says to me.

"Yeah, he has." I nod.

"It's because he's happy. Have I told you how glad I am that you and my brother are together?"

"Only about twenty times." I chuckle.

She grins. "Well, it's true. I've never seen him this happy before, and that makes me happy. And, also, it makes me love you even more than I already do."

She loves me. That lights me up like the sky on the Fourth of July.

"Thanks, Missy. It means a lot. And you know that I . . . you know . . . too." Expressing emotion isn't one of my strengths.

She softly smiles at me. "I know." She threads her arm through mine and gives me a squeeze. "You mean a lot to Ares. And me. You might be a Petrelli, but you're a Kincaid now, too."

I swallow down the golf ball in my throat and blink away the tears threatening my eyes.

"The game's nearly over," Missy says. "There's only a minute left on the clock. Do you want to head down?"

"Sure." I smile at her.

We leave our seats and walk down the steps, heading toward the belly of the stadium where the locker rooms are.

We pass security with a wave of my ID badge and walk toward the locker room to wait outside where we agreed to meet Ares.

He'll probably have to do press, so he won't be out right away, but I'm happy to hang around and wait with Missy.

There's press milling around the hall, waiting to interview the players. My dad will be in the locker room. But he generally doesn't come out to talk to the press, so he won't see me leaving with Ares, which is a good thing.

But the press will see.

Yeah, but I'm with his sister, so they won't think much of it.

I've just parked my ass against the wall when Missy says, "I'm just gonna go to the restroom. Back in a few. Okay?"

"Sure." I pull my phone out of my pocket and start scrolling through Twitter, reading tweets about the game.

"You're Arianna Petrelli, right?"

I lift my eyes from my phone to see a good-looking guy—mid-twenties, messy blond hair, a tattoo sleeve on one arm. The whole bad-boy vibe going on.

Would have totally been my type prior to Ares.

"Depends on who's asking."

"I'm Leo Parsons. I'm a writer for *Athletic and Sports News*."

A journalist. Of course.

"Not to be rude ... but how do you know who I am?"

He's a sports journalist; of course he knows who you are.

"I recognized you from your photo ... in the news ... after your crash."

I tense instantly.

"I just wanted to say, it was shitty, the way some of the press went after you. You probably didn't see it, but I wrote a piece—not about you per se, but your case in point and about alcohol addiction and how society views us." He puts his hand in his pocket and pulls out a bronze chip. "Eighteen months sober," he tells me.

I relax a little, knowing this guy is part of the same club as me.

"That's amazing," I tell him.

"Still fighting every day, but you know that, right?"

I nod.

"Anyway, I just wanted to come over and say hi, and if you get a chance to read my article ...."

"Of course," I say, smiling. "I'll totally check it out."

"Great." He smiles and then leans in a little closer, lowering his voice a touch. "And I was wondering if ... maybe one night you might want to grab a bite to eat."

"Oh!" *Shit.* "I, um . . . I'm not dating right now. Still trying to get my life together, you know."

"Right. Yeah, of course." He straightens up and steps back. "Well, we could go out, just as friends."

"Um . . ." I scratch my cheek. "Okay, yeah, sure."

"Great." He smiles. He reaches into his pocket and pulls out a business card. "Here's my card with my number and email." He holds it out, so I take it from him. "So, yeah . . . hit me up, and we can go out for a burger or something."

"Yeah, that's not gonna happen."

My neck nearly snaps—it turns that quick—and I see Ares glowering down at Leo.

His eyes come to mine, and they are nearly black. He plucks the card from my hand and crushes it in his palm.

Shit. He's mad.

"Kincaid." Leo nods, clearly aware of who he is— which, of course, he would be because it's his job to know. His eyes go between us, working quickly. "I didn't mean to tread on anyone's toes. I didn't realize you two were an item."

"What? No! We're not an item! That's just . . . crazy! We're friends. Good friends. He's just being overprotective." Then, I punch Ares in the arm, like we're best buddies, not lovers. *Yep, I really did that. God, I'm a total dick.* But I can't seem to stop. "I'm actually really good friends with his sister, Missy, and here she is now. Missy!" I grab her arm and yank her toward me.

Missy is now looking at me, confused.

Leo is running a journalistic eye over me.

And Ares . . . I daren't look at him. But I can feel his

anger pulsating next to me, like it's a living, breathing entity.

What the hell is wrong with me?

I don't want to lie—I really don't—but this guy is a journalist, and I can't have him printing things about me and Ares. At least not until I've talked to my dad.

And I'm not ready yet. I just need time.

Because I know what my dad will say when he finds out Ares and I are together. I saw how he reacted to me taking a ride with him, for God's sake.

I know where my dad's priority lies, and it isn't with me.

He will do what's best for the team, and Ares not being with me is that.

I know exactly what he'll say to Ares.

And I'm scared that Ares will listen . . . and finally see sense and realize that my dad is right.

That I'm not the person he should be with.

And then he'll leave me.

Chapter Twenty-Four

T HE TENSION IN ARES'S truck is killing me.
It's so thick, you could cut the air with a knife
and take a slice away with you.

Missy is quietly sitting in the back, tapping away on
her phone. And Missy is never quiet.

Ares is a huge, raging hot flame next to me.

And me . . . I'm burning under the heat.

He's angry. No, he's furious.

Not that he's said a word to confirm this. He hasn't
said a thing to me since we left the stadium, apart
from to bark at me that we were leaving, but honestly,
that could have been directed at Missy.

And I'm going to take a not-so-wild shot in the
dark here and say he's pissed because of what I said
to Leo.

And I get it. Of course I wasn't going to tell Leo
that Ares and I were together. But I didn't have to
act like a complete dick about it. I made it sound
ludicrous—the notion of us being together. In a way,

it is because what is a great guy like him doing with a loser like me?

But, from the angry fumes billowing from Ares, he's taken it the totally wrong way, and I'm in for it.

I handled it badly, and I will apologize but not in front of Missy. Because it's not fair on her to make her feel uncomfortable while Ares and I hash our shit out, not that I can guess she's feeling at all comfortable now.

I notice that, instead of going into his building's parking garage, he pulls up outside.

My confused eyes swing to him, but his eyes are fixed ahead. Jaw working angrily.

"I'll be home later," he grinds out to Missy.

She takes that as her cue and practically jumps out of the car. I actually envy her. I wish I could leave, too.

"See you tomorrow," she says to me, giving me a look of sympathy.

"Bye." I give her a small smile.

Then, she's gone, jogging inside his building, and Ares is pulling the truck away from the curb.

"Where are we going?" I tentatively ask him.

I get no response, except for his hands tightening around the steering wheel, his jaw like steel.

"Ares . . ." I push.

"I can't fucking talk to you right now," he snaps.

Jesus.

He's so mad. I've never seen him this angry before. I've seen him frustrated and pissed off but not top-level anger.

I honestly don't know what to do or say.

So, like the little chicken I am, I say nothing and stay quiet, feeling like a convict heading toward her execution.

He turns down the street to my apartment, and that answers my question as to where he is taking me.

I half-expect him to pull over and tell me to get out before he drives off. But he doesn't. He parks his truck up outside my building, turns off the engine, and climbs out without a word. So, I follow.

We walk to my apartment in complete silence.

I unlock my door, letting us both in.

Ares follows me into my living room.

I sit down on the arm of my sofa. He stays standing. Arms folded across his chest.

"I'm sorry I acted like a dick before. That guy, Leo . . . he's press, and I didn't—"

"Want anyone to find out. Namely, your dad. Yeah, I got that."

Well, if he gets that, then why is he so mad?

"I shouldn't have said the things I said—"

"No, you shouldn't have."

"I don't know why I said them. I was rambling. But I am sorry."

"Yeah, you said."

He's still staring at me with unblinking burning blue eyes, frying me on the spot. Arms still folded across his chest. Jaw set.

"You're still mad . . ." I edge out.

"No shit I'm mad. Actually, I'm fucking furious. I am sick of this, Ari."

Panic lances across my chest. "Sick of what?"

"The secrets. The lying. You know how I feel about

it, but I've been doing it for you. Now, I'm done. I said two weeks. It's two weeks today. Time's up. I'm not hiding us anymore."

Shit, has it really been two weeks already?

"You said a few. Not two," I counter.

"Are you fucking kidding me right now?" he yells, startling me. He drops his arms from his chest and drags a hand through his hair. "I just don't fucking get it. What the hell are you so afraid of? What do you think your dad is going to do? You think he'll, what? Come between us? That's bullshit, and you know it. I went with it to make you happy, but this? This isn't making me happy."

"I'm not making you happy?"

He laughs hollowly. "Have you been listening to a fucking word I've said? I said, *this* isn't making me happy—what happened at the arena. Talking to your dad every damn day and pretending like I'm not dating his daughter, that I'm crazy about her! Watching every damn thing I say in front of him in case I slip up. I'm not that fucking guy, Ari. I told you, I don't like liars, and I refuse to be one for you anymore."

"I just need more time . . ." I push to stand, my legs feeling wobbly.

"Time for what?" he yells, frustrated.

With you. I need more time with you . . . before you realize the mistake you've made by being with me and leave. And then I'll be alone again.

I stare down at my hands, swallowing down those words, afraid to say them out loud.

"I just don't fucking get it. I don't get you! You

know what? Why don't you just fucking call me when you've figured your shit out? Because I'm done."

Done.

My eyes flash up, my chest clenching in panic, just in time to see him walking out the door, slamming it behind him.

Chapter Twenty-Five

I'M EXHAUSTED. I HAVEN'T slept all night.

I picked up the phone a dozen times to call Ares and chickened out. I don't know how to explain to him what's going on in my head. I don't want to tell him because I don't want to alert him to the one thing I'm afraid he'll do—leave.

Which is stupid because he's done that exact thing.

I didn't want to tell my dad, for fear that Ares would leave me. And he's left me anyway because I won't tell my dad about us.

Confused? Me, too.

Some great frigging logic I have there.

But then I never claimed to be smart.

"I'm done."

I don't even know if we're still together right now. I'm trying not to panic.

He never said, *We're over.* He said, "I'm done."

But then, isn't that basically the same thing?

Jesus. What a mess.

I can't believe how badly I've screwed things up.

I thought getting clean meant I'd make smart decisions. Apparently, that's not the case. I'm stupid whether I'm drunk or sober.

I had this great guy, who I didn't want to lose, and I've lost him anyway.

Now, there's only one thing that's going to fix this—I hope . . . and that's telling my dad about me and Ares.

And pray to God that I'm not too late to fix things with Ares.

I guess, if I am, then I don't have to worry about my dad getting into Ares's head and him dumping me.

That would be funny if it wasn't so damn sad.

I walk up the stairs, heading to my dad's office. Ares isn't here today. None of the players are. After a game, they don't come in to train for a few days.

So, at least it's giving me a chance to talk to my dad before I see Ares.

I knock on my dad's door and push it open, popping my head around. He's at his desk, eyes on his computer screen.

"Hey, you got a minute?" I ask him.

His eyes come to me. "Of course."

I walk in, letting the door close behind me, and take the seat across from him.

"What's up?" he asks, pushing his keyboard aside and folding his hands on his desk.

"I'm seeing Ares. I like him. We're dating," I ineloquently blurt out.

Aside from a twitch in the corner of his eye, my dad doesn't react. There's nothing—no annoyance or anger. Just an eye twitch.

"I didn't lie," I continue in the silence. "When you asked me a few weeks ago if I was seeing him . . . well, I did lie. I said Ares and I weren't friends, and we were, so yeah, I lied about that, but you didn't like me riding with him, so I didn't want to tell you that he was my friend because . . . well, yeah. Anyway, now, he's more. I like him. A lot. He's good to me." *Not that I deserve it.* "He wanted to tell you straightaway, about him and me, but I wouldn't let him because I was worried about how you'd react, that you'd be pissed and maybe . . . talk him out of being with me."

I see the first sign of reaction on his face since I started talking. His brows pull together in what looks like consternation.

"That's what you thought? That I'd talk him out of being with you?"

I swallow down my dry throat. "Yes."

"Jesus . . ." He scrubs his hands over his face. "Ari, I know it probably doesn't seem like it . . . I know my past actions have given you reason not to believe this, but nothing or no one is more important than you. You're my daughter. You have and always will come first.

"And my concerns about you and Ares came solely out of my concern for you, not that you might tarnish his reputation. My worry was that you weren't in the right place to be starting a relationship with anyone. You're just getting your life back together, and Ares, he's in the public eye, which means you'll be in the public eye if you're together, especially with you being my daughter. It's newsworthy, and I didn't want you to have to deal with the added pressure."

"Oh." I bite the corner of my lip, chewing on it, feeling a bit stupid.

Okay, stupider than I already am.

"I'm . . . sorry, Ari."

"What?" I nearly fall off my chair in shock.

My dad does not apologize. Ever.

He sighs out a breath. "I'm sorry that I made you feel that way, that you couldn't talk to me, and that you thought that Ares's reputation was more important to me than you."

I fasten my hands together in my lap in front of me, staring down at them. "Well . . . it's not like you've ever given me any reason to think different," I say quietly.

"I know."

That brings my head up. Have I slipped into an alternate world? One where my dad apologizes and talks to me?

"I'm just . . . I'm not good at this." He moves a finger between us. "Give me eleven, two-hundred-pound-plus players on a football field, and I can handle them with my eyes closed. But my daughter . . . I don't know where to start. How to talk to you. And I just . . . I want you to know that I am sorry."

Two apologies. Definitely twilight zone business here.

And it's not an apology for everything he's done wrong. But it's a start.

I nod, acknowledging his remorse, my own words stuck in my throat, which is clogged with emotion.

"Okay . . ." He exhales, sitting back in his chair. "Even though I do have my concerns for you with the press, out of all my players, Ares is the one guy I would trust with you. He's a good kid. So . . . I'll notify the

PR team and have them ready to handle it when the press gets wind of your relationship."

If I have a relationship left.

"I appreciate that. But can you, uh, wait until I speak to Ares? He's . . . not very happy with me at the moment." I fidget in my chair, putting my hands under my thighs and sitting on them.

My dad frowns. "What do you mean, he's not happy with you?"

"Well, we, uh . . . kind of got in a fight about it last night"—*a big fight*—"about keeping our relationship a secret. He wanted to tell you. I asked for more time. He got mad and walked out."

"And that's why you told me today."

I bite my lip and nod.

"I'm glad you did tell me. Where is Ares today?"

I shrug. "Home, I'm guessing."

"Okay then, I'm giving you the rest of the day off to go and see him."

"You are?" I say, surprised.

"Well, it's the least I can do. This is partly my fault."

"Uh . . . thanks."

"Do you need a ride into the city?"

"I can get the bus."

He shakes his head. "I'll drive you."

"I appreciate that, Dad. But . . . I don't think it's a good idea for us both to go see him."

My dad laughs low. "Ari, I wasn't planning on coming to have a heart-to-heart with you and Ares. I was just going to drop you off at his place and then come back here."

"Oh. Right. Well then, it's a yes to the lift." I smile.

Chapter Twenty-Six

"Thanks for the ride, Dad." I reach for the handle to open the car door. "I guess . . . I'll see you tomorrow at work."

"Ari?"

I stop and look at him.

"Could we have dinner tomorrow night? Ares is welcome, too."

"Okay." I nod slowly. "I'd like that. And I'll let you know about Ares. I guess it depends on if he accepts my apology or not."

He smiles, his eyes softening. "He'll accept it."

"I hope you're right." Then, I do something I never do. I lean over and press a kiss to my dad's cheek. "I'll see you tomorrow, Dad." Then, I climb out of his car, closing the door behind me.

I walk into Ares's building. I give the security guard a smile and a wave, and I head into the elevator and hit the button for the eighth floor.

I wrap my arms around myself, trying to contain my nerves.

Feeling like this . . . really makes me want to have a drink. Something to calm my nerves.

But I don't have that option, so I just breathe through it. In and out. I don't have time to adopt the lotus position and focus. So, good old-fashioned deep breaths it is.

The elevator pings, and the door slides open.

I'm reminded of the time when I first came here to apologize to Ares for lying about canceling on him and to tell him that Luke was my sponsor. That's the first time he kissed me.

And here I am again, walking to his door to apologize. Only he isn't waiting in the doorway for me this time.

Lifting my hand, I knock on his door and then wait.

The door swings open, but it isn't Ares who answers; it's Missy.

"Hey." She smiles widely, like she's genuinely happy to see me here. "How are you doing?"

"I'm . . . okay, I guess," I say with a shrug and a small smile. "Is, um . . . Ares around?"

"He's upstairs on the twelfth floor. He went for a swim." My confused look has her saying, "There's a gym and pool up there for residents to use."

"Oh, okay. Well, I suppose I'll go up there and see him. Wish me luck."

"Luck? But you won't need it." She smiles and winks.

I'm taking that as a good sign, as she knows her brother better than anyone, and if he was through with me, I figured she'd know, right?

"Catch you later," I tell her. Then, I turn to walk back to the elevator.

"You're still coming to dinner tonight, right?" she asks, half-stepping out into the hallway.

I turn back to her, slowly walking backward. "I guess that depends on your brother."

"Ari, you're my friend. You'd be coming even if he didn't want you there, which he totally does because the stubborn ass is crazy about you."

Another shot of hope.

"Then, I'll see you tonight," I tell her on a smile.

I turn forward and walk over to the elevator. It opens as soon as I press the button. Guess it never went back down. I get in and press the button for the twelfth floor.

I exit the elevator and see the signs on the wall outside. Apparently, the gym and steam room are to the left. Pool to the right.

I follow the sign, coming to a door, and I push it open. It leads me straight into the pool area. There's an Olympic-sized swimming pool in here. Glass windows are on either side, giving a beautiful view of the city.

And Ares is the only one in here, currently swimming a length away from me.

I kick off my heels and walk over to the pool where I wait for him to finish.

He hits the other end of the pool and stops, hand on the ledge, clearly taking a break.

I stand here, waiting for him to see me.

His head turns as he moves to return to his swim, and he finally sees me.

We hold eyes for a long beat.

I wonder if he's going to swim over to me, but he doesn't. He just stays there, the stubborn bastard. So, I swallow my pride and walk around the length of the pool to where he is.

I stop before him and stare down. Water droplets are clinging to his lashes and running down his face. His dark hair is slicked back with water.

God, he's beautiful.

"Hi," I say softly.

Hands holding the ledge, he looks up at me. "What are you doing here? Shouldn't you be at work?"

Nice to see you, too.

"My dad gave me the rest of the day off." I crouch down before him, putting us at eye-level. "And I'm here because you told me to call you when I'd sorted my shit out. Well, I've sorted my shit out. But I thought I'd come see you in person rather than call."

"Mmhmm. Right." He nods. "And just exactly how have you sorted your shit out?"

"I told my dad about us."

I don't miss the surprise that quickly flickers through his eyes. He doubted I would. But then I can't blame him. I didn't exactly give him a reason to have confidence in me.

There's a long pause before he says anything. And, when he does, it's, "Okay."

"Okay?" I frown.

"That's what I said."

"And what does okay mean?"

"I'm pretty sure it has a few definitions in the dictionary—"

"You're hilarious."

"I do try."

"God, you're an ass."

"Well, what exactly do you want me to say?"

"Oh, I don't know!" I throw a hand in the air. "Maybe, *That's great, Ari! I know how hard that must have been for you!*"

"I'm more interested in knowing why you didn't want to tell him in the first place—and don't give me the bullshit about him coming between us because, if you had any faith in me . . . in us, then you would never have thought that in the first place."

He's right. But it's not that I don't have faith in him. I don't have faith in myself.

"I . . ." I blow out a breath. "After the first conversation with my dad, about me getting a lift to work with you and he wasn't happy at the thought of you and me . . . and I interpreted it to be because of you—that I would bring negative press your way—I was afraid . . ."

I feel tears stinging my eyes, and I bite the inside of my cheek to stop them from coming.

But it doesn't work, and they spill anyway.

A shaky breath escapes me. "But that was my own negative thoughts about myself coming through. It wasn't actually my dad saying it. It was me drawing the worst conclusion because that's what I already think about myself. That I'm not good enough for you. That I'm a mess. That you'd remember all of this and all the reasons you didn't want to be with me in the first place, and you'd . . . leave me." I press my palms to my cheeks, wiping away the tears.

"You're not a mess, Ari."

I finally lift my eyes to him. He's staring at me with an unnamed emotion.

"I kind of am at the moment."

"That's true." He purses his lips and bobs his head in agreement.

"Ass." I chuckle tearfully.

"Also true." He reaches out and takes my hand. His skin is wet and cool on mine. "What did your dad say when you told him?"

"He was pretty good about it. He told me that his concern was for me. With you being high-profile and me being his daughter, the press will be interested, especially because of what happened earlier this year. And he was worried about how the press getting into my personal life again might affect me."

"That makes sense." He nods. "But there are ways to protect you from that."

"He's going to speak to PR."

"Good." He runs his thumb over my wrist.

"I missed you," I tell him softly.

"I missed you, too." He slides his hand up my arm. "I hate sleeping without you."

"I didn't sleep," I confess.

"Me either." He chuckles quietly.

"So . . . what now?"

"You could kiss me," he says, a smile lifting the corner of his lip.

"That I can do." I rest on my knees, not caring about the water getting on my legs or the hem of my skirt, and I lean down and kiss him.

He takes my face in his hands, his tongue sliding

into my mouth, sending a shiver running through my body.

"So, we're okay then?" I murmur against his lips.

"We're more than okay."

The next thing I know, his arms are hooking underneath my arms, and I'm being pulled forward.

Into the pool.

Fully clothed.

"Ah!" I scream as my body collides with his when I hit the water. "What the hell?" I yell at him.

He's grinning at me—the ass.

"I wanted you close."

"And you couldn't have gotten out of the pool?"

"This seemed like more fun."

"Yeah, for you." I slap a hand to his chest, but I'm smiling.

"It'll be fun for you, too."

Then, he takes my mouth in a deep kiss and pushes his body forward, thrusting me backward until my back hits the pool wall.

"Hold on." He lifts my hands up and puts them on the pool edge.

Then, he's gone under the water, and I'm wondering what the hell he's doing. I quickly realize when he yanks the zip on my skirt down and starts to pull it down my legs.

I wriggle, trying to stop him because, you know, we're kind of in a public place. There might not be anyone here aside from us at the moment, but that doesn't mean someone couldn't walk in at any moment.

He gives my ass a hard squeeze, stopping me from

moving, and he takes the advantage and pulls my skirt off.

"What the hell are you doing?" I hiss when he breaks the surface.

He cleans his face of water with one hand and then throws my skirt on the poolside with the other. "I thought that was obvious."

He moves in close to me, grabbing my hips with his hands and yanking me close. My hands go to his chest.

"Anyone could come in."

"So?"

"So!" My eyes nearly bug out of my head. "I don't want a stranger seeing me naked."

"You're not naked. Yet."

"Have you lost your mind?"

"Over you? Seems so. And relax, babe." He presses a kiss to my neck. "No one comes in here during the day. The pool hardly gets used during the week, except by me." His hands come around to my ass, hitching me up higher, just where he wants me. "I want to make up with you."

He pushes his hips into me, his hard cock pressing right against that sweet spot, and I have to bite back a moan.

"I thought we'd already made up." Despite my vocal reservations, I still wrap my arms around his neck and my legs around his waist.

"I want to make up properly," he says and then kisses me.

A deep, hot, sexy kiss has me moaning into his mouth.

"Fuck, I missed you," he groans.

It was only one night, but I missed him, too. It scares me just how much.

His hand moves down my ass, cupping me from behind. He shoves my panties aside and pushes a finger inside me.

I sigh in pleasure, my head falling back against the edge of the pool.

He hoists me higher, so my chest is out of the water. Then, he pushes my top up, yanking down the cup of my bra, and wraps his lips around my nipple, sucking hard.

A bolt of lust shoots through me. I grind my clit against his stomach, needing him.

He sucks the water off my breast, finger-fucking me.

"I want you," I pant, not caring where we are now.

We could have an audience, and I wouldn't stop.

I push his swim shorts down his hips, using my feet to lever them down, freeing his cock.

He kisses back up to my mouth, lowering me down to his cock. He shoves my panties aside and then thrusts up until he's sheathed to the hilt.

My screams echo around the room.

He's deep. So very deep inside me.

"Hush," he admonishes throatily, teeth biting down on my bottom lip. "You will bring people in, making noise like that. Don't make me gag you." Mischievous eyes lift to mine, sparkling with heat and lust.

I wind my fingers into the hair at the nape of his neck and give it a tug. "Fuck you," I say.

He chuckles. "There's my dirty girl." He pulls his

cock out, and in one swift move, he slams it all the way back in.

I bite my lip to stop from screaming again.

"That's it," he croons, teeth biting along my jaw and up to mouth. He takes it in a deep kiss. "Take what I have to give you, baby."

One hand tangled in my hair, the other holding my ass, he fucks me hard and desperately, like it's been a month, not a little over a day since he was last inside me.

"No more fighting," he groans.

"Not unless we get to make up like this."

He chuckles low and deep, the sound rippling through me, like the water surrounding me.

I can feel the muscles in my stomach beginning to tighten. My orgasm not far away.

"I'm close," I tell him. "Just keep doing that . . . right there."

His hand squeezes my ass, slightly tilting it, causing his cock to drag along my clit, and I go off like a rocket.

"Fuck," he grunts, eyes closed, his forehead pressed to mine. "You're making me come, babe . . ."

His cock jerks inside me as he starts coming.

We're both panting, our breaths mingling. My body humming from the orgasm.

"So, that was a first," he murmurs.

"What?"

"Sex in a pool."

"You've never done it in a pool before?"

He pulls back, and narrowed eyes stare into mine. His jaw tight. "No. Have you?"

"No. But you should see the look on your face right now."

"That was mean." He pokes me in my side, making me squirm and laugh.

"We should probably get out of here," I say.

"Yeah," he agrees. "Don't want to push our luck any more than we already have."

I pause, my brow rising. "I thought you said no one used the pool during the day."

A slow grin slides across his face.

"You asshole!" I shove at his chest. "Someone could have caught us!"

"But they didn't. And, even if they had, it would've been worth it."

"Yeah," I sigh, agreeing with him. Because pool sex with him is hot as hell.

He kisses me one last time and then pulls out of me. "Although I should probably let building maintenance know that the pool needs cleaning," he says as he hoists himself out of the pool, sitting on the side.

It takes me a second to realize what he means, and then I stare down, realizing that his cum will be leaking out of my body and into the water.

"Shit," I groan. "Just don't tell them why it needs cleaning."

"Wasn't gonna." He gets to his feet. "I was just going to tell them that my girlfriend had an accident in the pool." He grins and then saunters over to grab his towel.

I can't even bring myself to yell at him because he just called me his girlfriend.

His girlfriend.

That's the first time since we started dating that he's ever referred to me as that.

And I now have the biggest, goofiest grin on my face ever.

I hoist myself out of the pool. My top is dripping wet, so I pull it off over my head and squeeze the excess water out of it. I retrieve my wet skirt and shoes from the floor.

Ares walks over with a towel and wraps it around my body, securing it with a tuck at my bust. Then, he leans down and presses a soft kiss to my lips. "Ready?" he asks.

"Yep." I take my boyfriend's offered hand and let him lead me out of there, toward the elevator, and down to his apartment.

Chapter Twenty-Seven

"STOP FIDGETING," ARES SAYS kindly.

We're standing outside the restaurant on Park Avenue where the taxi just dropped us off, where we're having dinner with Ares's family before Missy and Lo go back to their respective colleges. I'm wearing a capped-sleeve lemon dress that's fitted at the waist and bust and flares out on the skirt, and I have white strappy sandals on that have skyscraper heels. I need to wear them if I'm having dinner with his bunch of supersize humans.

Missy told me that Cam is tall, too. Five-nine and a former ballet dancer.

I swear, I'm going to look like a Chihuahua among a bunch of Great Danes.

"I can't help it. I'm nervous." I shift on my feet. "What if Zeus, Cam, and Lo don't like me?"

"Why wouldn't they?"

"Um, a million reasons. I have a criminal record. I'm a drunk." I tick off the reasons on my fingers.

"You're not a drunk. You had a substance abuse issue, and now, you're sober."

"Semantics. They're going to think I'm not good enough for you."

"Babe, stop. I assure you, they're going to be wondering what the hell a stunner like you is doing with me. Trust me. And I'm fully expecting for Lo to actually ask that question."

"You're funny."

He takes my chin in his hand, tilting my head back, bringing my eyes up to his. "I'm serious. You're amazing, babe. They're going to love you."

Do you?

I know it's only been a short time that we've been together, but I'm pretty sure that I'm in love with this guy.

Okay, I'm not pretty sure. I am sure.

I'm totally gone for him.

But I have no clue if he feels the same.

And no way in hell am I telling him first. I'm just going to wait until he says it . . . if he ever does.

God, I hope he does.

"Where have you gone?" he asks, carefully eyeing me.

"Nowhere." I force a smile.

"Babe . . . I know we already talked about this . . . that they serve alcohol here. But, if at any point it's too much for you, let me know, and we can leave."

"I'll be okay."

"I don't doubt that. But, in the small instance it isn't—"

"You'll be the first I tell."

He presses a soft kiss to my lips. "Let's go inside."

He takes my hand and leads me inside the restaurant.

"Do you have a reservation?" the host asks when we approach.

"Yes. Under Kincaid," Ares tells him.

"The rest of your party is already here." He smiles. "Follow me."

The host leads us to our table, and my stomach is swimming with nerves.

I see them all seated around the table. Missy is already here, looking gorgeous, as always, in a powder-blue dress. On one side of her is a younger-looking Ares, which has to be Lo—seriously good-looking—and on her other side is a stunning brunette, whom I'm guessing is Cam. Next to her is a slighter bigger version of Ares, which can only be Zeus—sweet Lord, he's handsome but not as handsome as Ares, of course—and next to him is a huge blond guy, who has to be Kaden Scott. Also really good-looking.

Kaden isn't family, but he's as good as to Zeus and Cam, and I know Missy is close to him, too.

Kaden used to be a boxer until, believe it or not, a boxing match with Zeus Kincaid left Kaden unconscious and in a coma.

Ares told me how messed up Zeus had been after it happened and how he stepped up and paid for Kaden's medical bills and rehabilitation.

They've been close ever since.

"Finally! We've been dying of starvation here, waiting for you to show up," Zeus says to Ares, a lightheartedness to his tone.

"We're not even late, dipshit."

Zeus chuckles out a deep, rumbling laugh.

Ares puts his arm around my shoulders, giving me

a gentle squeeze. "Ari, this is my older brother, Zeus, and his better half, Cam. That is Kaden Scott, and you know Missy, so I'll skip her. And the idiot sitting next to her is my younger brother, Lo."

"Thanks, man," Lo says, giving Ares the middle finger.

"Hi, everyone." I smile. "It's great to meet you all."

Cam gets to her feet and comes around the table to us. "It's so good to finally meet you, Ari. We've heard so much about you." Then, she hugs me, kissing my cheek. "You were right, Ares; she's gorgeous," she says to him, leaning over to press a kiss to his cheek.

We all take our seats, Ares holding mine out for me, like the gentleman he is.

The waiter appears. "Can I get you a drink?"

A glance at the table tells me everyone has already ordered. I notice there's no alcohol on the table at all.

Did they not order any for my sake?

I know Ares doesn't drink, which is because of his dad, who isn't here tonight. He avoids all places where they serve alcohol, which I can totally understand.

I know Missy and Lo had coffee with him earlier, as they were both coming from there to here.

If they aren't drinking for my sake, then I feel really touched that they would do that for me. But really embarrassed, too.

I wish I were a different person for him. A better person. One who could come to a restaurant and order alcohol and not end up in rehab straight afterward.

"A sparkling water for me," I say quietly, feeling awkward.

"And for you, sir?" the waiter asks Ares.

"Diet Pepsi."

Ares takes my hand and squeezes it, as though he can sense my inner turmoil.

I look at him and offer a smile. It's forced, but I don't want him to worry, and I definitely don't want to spoil his evening.

"So, I have a question for Ari," Lo says, pulling my attention from Ares to him. "What exactly are you doing with my thick head of a brother? You do realize, you could do a million times better than him, right? Yeah, yeah, he might be a famous football player, but he's batting way, way above his average with you. You're like prime rib steak, and he's burger—and not even a good burger. He's like one of those shitty, skinny ones that are made mostly out of water."

Lo grins, and a small laugh escapes me.

I glance at Ares, who raises a brow at me, as though to say, *What did I tell you?*

Ares stares across the table at Lo, brow still raised. "And, just out of interest, baby brother, just exactly who fits the prime rib steak category that would be good enough for my girl?" Ares's arm comes around the back of my chair.

Lo leans back in his seat and puffs out his chest. "Well, me, of course."

He shrugs, and everyone at the table bursts out laughing.

Me included.

And, just like that, my somber thoughts are gone, replaced with happiness.

Chapter Twenty-Eight

"I HAD SUCH A GOOD time tonight," I tell Ares as he unlocks his apartment door, letting us in. "Your family is amazing."

"Yeah, they're pretty great," he says, locking up behind us.

Missy and Lo are both staying at Zeus and Cam's tonight, so they can spend some time with the kids before they go back to college.

"Although I think I'm going to have to watch my little brother around you," Ares says, coming over as I take my shoes off.

My feet press on the cool floor, and I almost moan with relief. High heels are a killer. "Don't be silly," I tell him. "Lo was just winding you up."

"Yeah, well, it worked." He wraps his arms around me and presses a kiss to my forehead. "You're mine."

"And you're mine," I say on a yawn.

"Am I boring you?" He chuckles.

"Never. Just too much food."

I stuffed myself. The food was amazing. Almost as good as the company.

I swear, I'm in love with his family. They are awesome. Watching them interact, it was how I imagined it would've been for me if I'd had a brother or sister.

"Bed?" he asks.

I nod on another yawn.

He toes his shoes off and then leads me through his apartment, turning off lights as he goes, heading to his bedroom.

I brought an overnight bag here with me earlier, as we decided we'd stay at his place tonight. So, I grab my wash bag and toothbrush.

We brush our teeth, side by side. Then, Ares disappears into the bedroom while I remove my makeup.

When I'm finished, I flick off the bathroom light, and on tired feet, I pad into his bedroom. Ares is already in bed, sitting up, chest bare, and I know he'll be naked beneath the covers, as he doesn't wear a stitch in bed. He's reading something on his phone; knowing him, it's probably the latest sports news. The lamp next to his bed is illuminating the room for me.

I remove my dress, laying it on the chair, and then take off my bra, leaving me in my panties. I can feel his eyes on me as I walk over to his dresser, grab one of his football jerseys, and put it on.

I could wear my own pajamas. But I like to wear his shirts.

And I know he likes to see me in them.

I climb into bed next to him, snuggling close, feeling drowsy already.

He puts his phone down and turns off the light. He

scoots down, putting his arm around me, holding me close. Soft lips meet mine. "Night, babe."

"Night," I murmur.

Then, it's lights out.

I wake slowly, rousing, to the feel of velvet lips pressing kisses to my inner thigh.

A hot tongue runs up my center, making me gasp. My hands reach down, running through Ares's silky hair. He moves up my body, pressing kisses as he goes, his hand pushing his jersey up my body. I lift my arms, and he pulls it off over my head.

"I like you in my jersey," he says, voice low in the dark.

I smile. "I know."

"But I like you better out of it."

"I know that, too."

His lips meet mine in a gentle kiss. I can feel his erection, hot against my thigh.

His hand comes up, covering my breast, thumb brushing over my nipple, making my hips jerk up.

"I want you," I whisper.

His hips circle, cockhead rubbing over me. Then, he slowly pushes inside me.

I'll never get used to the feeling. The euphoric sensation of him filling me so completely.

When he's seated to the hilt, he stays there, unmoving, eyes staring down at me in the dark.

I can feel the fast beat of his heart thrumming through his chest into mine.

"Ari . . ." My name is like a whispered plea on his lips. "I . . ." A kiss. "I'm . . . crazy about you."

"Back at ya, babe," I tell him, sifting my fingers through his hair.

"And I ..." A deep breath. "I think you should leave some things here, like a toothbrush."

Huh?

Another kiss.

"A toothbrush?" I murmur.

"For when you stay over. And I'll leave one at yours."

"Okay ... but are we actually talking about tooth-brushes while your dick is inside me?"

He chuckles. "Sorry."

He shifts his hips, withdrawing to the tip, and then pushes back inside, hitting me right in that sweet spot.

My legs come up around his hips, my eyes closing, while I revel in the feel of him inside me.

"Maybe a drawer, too," he says.

I pop an eye open. "A drawer?"

"For your stuff, to keep it in," he explains.

"Okay."

"And I'll have one at yours."

"Okay ..." I repeat, dragging out the word. Then, I squeeze his ass with my feet to urge him to start moving.

"Maybe a key, too. For here. And I can have one to your place. Or is that too soon?"

"It's fine." I push up onto my elbows, bringing my face close to his. "What's going on?"

"What do you mean?"

"I mean ... you're not usually this much of a con-versationalist in bed, except for the odd command, like, 'Suck it harder,' or heated praise of, 'Fuck that's good, babe.'"

I laugh, but he doesn't.

And that worries me. "Ares . . . is everything okay? Me and you are . . ."

"Fine. Better than fine. I just realized something, is all."

"What?"

"I love you. I'm in love with you. You were lying there, sleeping, and I was watching you—in a non-creepy way. And it just hit me. That I fucking love you."

My heart has stilled in my chest.

He loves me.

"You love me?"

"Apparently so."

Then, I smile big. "It's a good thing that I love you, too, then, or this would be awkward as hell."

"You love me?"

I press a kiss to his lips. "Yeah, I do. Madly, deeply, head over heels in love with you."

His hand goes to the back of my head, fingers threading into the strands of my hair. "Say it again."

"I love you."

"Fuck, that's hot. You're making me harder, babe."

"So, fuck me then, and finish what you started."

"Finish?" He chuckles a low, dark, sexy sound. "Babe, that word isn't even in my vocab when it comes to you." Then, he kisses me hard with his mouth and makes love to me with his cock for the rest of the night.

Chapter Twenty-Nine

I'T'S AMAZING HOW LIFE can change in the blink of an eye. One blink, and my hedonistic lifestyle—the one I was so sure that I loved—came crashing down around me, bringing me to a new reality. A clean, sober reality. But also a lonely, empty reality. Then, one person came along and changed everything so very completely again.

One kiss changed everything.

Now, my life is full and happy because of Ares.

Nights that I used to spend with Netflix, feeling lonely, are now spent with him. Sometimes, Netflix joins us. Sometimes, we just chill.

I've never been this happy. Ever.

I adore him. Love him . . .

And, best of all, he loves me.

Baggage and all.

Life with Ares is amazing. I'm loving every second of it.

My relationship with my dad is also better than it

was. I'm not going to say it's fixed because it's not. But it's better.

I'm still going to AA regularly. I still see Luke.

But I haven't had to call him since that one episode in the bar.

The urge to drink will always be there.

But, now, I have more in my life to lose, and it makes me work harder to never drink again.

That is why I feel confident, going alone to this silent charity auction, which my dad asked me to attend on his behalf because the team is at an away game—meaning Ares is away. If I wasn't here, I'd only be sitting at home, missing him. At least this keeps me busy and kills the hours until he's home tomorrow.

The auction is to help raise money for a children's cancer charity. The team has donated a bunch of signed memorabilia, and my dad has also asked me to make a purchase on his behalf. Mary usually comes to these things for my dad, but she couldn't make it tonight, so he asked me, and it felt good that he believed I could come here alone, where alcohol would be served.

It's a good test for me, too.

Only thing is, I haven't managed to make it to the bar yet.

It's not that I think I'm going to go over there and buy all the alcohol.

But it's just been so long since I walked up to a bar, and it just feels weird.

"Hey, Arianna."

I turn and see Leo Parsons, the sports journalist.

"Hi . . . Leo," I say, surprised to see him.

The last time I saw him was, well, a tad awkward and also the night when Ares and I had that huge fight, which resulted in him walking out on me.

Not that it was any of Leo's fault, of course. I just feel a bit weird because I told Leo that Ares and I weren't together. And, now, everyone knows Ares and I are dating. There've been the news stories about Ares dating me, the coach's bad-girl daughter. How my dad has a big problem with us dating, which he doesn't. All the speculating that the media likes to do. But, overall, it's not been too awful. And, after the initial interest in mine and Ares's private life, it has died down.

Leaving Ares and me to get on with our relationship, which couldn't be better.

"How are you?" I ask.

"Good. You here representing?" he asks.

"Yeah, my dad asked me to come on his behalf. What about you?"

"It's filled to the rafters with sports personalities. *ASN* wanted me to come cover it—see who bids on what and how much."

"Sounds . . . newsworthy."

He shrugs. "It's the kind of shit people want to know. How much a celebrity is willing to bid for charity. Gossip sells. Even in sports."

"True." I sigh.

"I saw the stories about you and Kincaid . . ."

"Yeah . . . I'm sorry I wasn't honest that night. It was just . . . my dad didn't know, and—"

"You don't have to explain it to me." He kindly waves me off.

I smile. A beat of silence passes between us.

"Do you want a drink?" He nods at my empty hands. "I was just on my way to the bar."

"Um . . ."

"Nonalcoholic. I'm the same as you, remember?"

"Yeah, of course," I say, a little embarrassed. "That'd be great. Actually, you know what? I'll come with you," I add, feeling a little braver, going with someone.

"I'm taking it, you haven't been near the bar since you got here?" he says.

I shake my head, biting my lip.

"Don't put yourself through it then. I'm used to it. But it takes time. I'll go."

"Thank you. That's really kind of you."

He shrugs. "So, what nonalcoholic beverage can I get you?" he says with flourish.

I laugh. "Sparkling water's fine."

He pulls a comedic face. "No way! Why don't you go wild and join me for a Coke? Diet, of course."

I laugh again. "Okay. A Diet Coke would be great. Thanks."

I watch him walk away in the direction of the bar, and then I turn back to the room.

I get my cell from my purse and check it. There's a text from Ares. He must have just sent it before they went on the field.

I'm so proud of you, going there alone tonight, babe. You're amazing. Love you. See you tomorrow. xx

Smiling, I tap back a reply.

I'm proud of me, too. Have a great game. Love you, too. Can't wait to see you! xx

I open the NFL app on my phone to check the score. Giants are winning.

"You look happy." Leo appears beside me.

He holds out my Diet Coke, and I take it from him.

"Thanks. Giants are winning," I tell him, and he smiles.

I close down the app and put my cell away. I have a drink of my Coke.

I wince. It tastes a bit bitter.

"Everything okay?" Leo asks.

"Yeah, my Coke just tastes a bit . . . iffy."

He frowns and then takes a sip of his own Coke. He pulls a face. "Yeah, it's not great. Must be cheap Coke instead of the real stuff. You want me to get you a different drink?" He holds his hand out for my glass.

"No, it's fine." I smile, waving him off. I feel bad that he went to get me a drink, and I'm complaining about it. I take another sip. It's actually not too bad the second time, so it must've been me. "It's actually not too bad," I tell him, "once you get used to it."

He sips his own drink, trying it again. "Yeah"—he smiles at me over the rim of his glass—"I think you're right."

I take another sip and hold the glass to my chest. "So, I know you're working, but are you going to bid on anything?"

He shakes his head, an uncomfortable smile on his face. "No . . . I think the items are going to be a bit out of my price range."

"Mine, too," I tell him, and his smile relaxes. "But my dad asked me to put a bid in for him. My choice."

"Spending the 'rent's money. Always a bonus." He chuckles.

I laugh, too, but I don't actually agree with the statement. I hate spending my dad's money. I hate that I still owe him so much money. I'm only comfortable doing this because I'm buying this for him. I wouldn't be comfortable with taking his money and buying something for myself.

"Have you had a look at the auction items yet?"

I shake my head, having another sip of my drink.

"You want to look around with me?" he asks. "I can check out the bid lists while you browse the items."

"Okay." I smile. "But you have to promise one thing."

He gives me a speculative look. "What's that?"

"Keep my bid out of your story."

He gives me a mock-affronted look, pressing his hand to his chest. "As if I'd put you in my story. We're friends . . . right?"

"Right." I smile at him before having another sip of my drink.

Chapter Thirty

LEO HAS JUST WANDERED off to go chat with a friend he just spotted. I've put a bid in for my dad on the Yankees shirt signed by the whole team. My dad might be football for life, but he's also a Yankees fan.

I'm leaning against the wall, people-watching, holding my half-drunk, now-warm glass of Coke.

I get my cell from my purse to check the scores again. It's thirty-eight to seven. Only ten minutes left . . . meaning another victory.

Go, baby!

I slip my cell back in my purse, knowing how happy Ares is going to be with this win.

Then, I feel myself sway.

I press a hand to the wall, steadying myself. I lift my eyes out to the room, and my vision goes hazy.

I don't feel right.

I hope I'm not coming down with something.

I move away from the wall and wobble unsteadily, making my way to the restroom.

The stalls are empty. I put my purse and glass down on the counter by the sink and feel my body sway again, my head feeling light. I grip the edge.

Something's not right.

I stare down at my glass of Coke.

It doesn't have alcohol in it . . . does it? Surely not.

Leo knows I can't drink.

I pick the glass up with one hand, holding steady on the counter with the other. I hold the glass to my nose, sniffing the Coke.

No, definitely no alcohol in there. I'd know.

I put the glass down with a harsh clang, like I don't have proper control over my hand. I stare at my hand, and there's a tremor to it. I look up at myself in the mirror. My eyes are hazy, and my pupils are dilated, like I'm drunk.

God, no.

I turn on the faucet. Cupping my hands under the water, I lean forward to splash water on my face, but I stumble and bang my elbow on the sink.

"Fuck . . ." My word comes out slurred.

I sound drunk.

What is happening to me right now?

I grab my purse and stumble out of the restroom. I hold the wall as I walk for support, getting looks from people passing me on the way to the restroom.

I'm starting to panic.

I don't know what's happening.

Should I look for Leo? He might be able to help me.

I stumble back into the room, looking for him, but my eyes can't focus properly.

Shit.

I'm scared. I don't know what's happening to me.

Ares. I want Ares.

What am I going to do?

Home. I need to go home.

I turn too fast and stumble into someone.

The guy catches me by the waist, steadying me. "Whoa there." He chuckles. "Hey, you okay?"

"Yeah. Sorry," I mumble out, my words slurring.

I stagger past him, needing to get out of here. I somehow make my way through the event room and out into the lobby of the hotel.

I trip my way through the lobby. I can feel eyes on me.

Fuck.

Tears sting my eyes.

I make it out of the hotel, the doorman holding the door for me.

"Night, ma'am," he says but stops with a look of concern on his face. "Are you okay?"

"Need a taxi," I manage to get out, my voice all over the place.

"Ah, little too much to drink." He chuckles good-naturedly. "I'll flag you a cab now."

I want to scream that I haven't had anything to drink. That I don't know what's happening to me, but I can't seem to form the words.

The next thing I know, I'm in a taxi. I manage to give my address to the cabbie.

He turns and looks at me. "You're not gonna puke, are you, love?"

I shake my head and immediately regret it.

Closing my eyes, I lay my head back on the seat as the car pulls away.

"That'll be fifteen fifty." The sound of a male voice jolts me awake.

Where am I?

Cab.

I look out the window.

I'm outside my building.

I rifle in my purse, pull out a twenty, and hand it to him. I don't wait for the change. Then, I fumble with the door, pull the handle, and manage to get it open.

I literally fall out of the cab. Bringing myself upright, I hold on to the car door. I get it closed and turn to my building.

The stairs look like a mountain.

I'm so tired.

I just need to get in my apartment, and I'll be fine.

I stagger up the steps of my building, gripping the railing for support.

Somehow, I make it inside and I lean against the wall, closing my eyes. I feel myself start to slide down the wall. Somehow, I stop myself. I push away from the wall and move over to my door. I dig for my keys and drop my cell on the floor.

"Shit," I mumble. I don't even have the energy to pick it up.

With a lot of difficulty, I get my key in my door. I turn the lock and open it. I fall through, losing my balance, and I hit the floor of my living room with a thud.

"Shit." I moan in pain.

I can't get up. I'm too spent.

What's wrong with me?

I manage to shut the door with my foot and just lie there, unable to move.

My head is swimming. I can barely lift it off the floor. I try, and my stomach revolts.

I'm going to be sick.

I throw up all over the floor, right where I am.

"No," I groan, wiping my mouth with the back of my hand.

What's wrong with me?

I just need to sleep, and then I'll be okay.

I hear my cell start to ring from somewhere.

I'll get it later. Too tired.

I'm vaguely aware that I need to clean my mess up, but I have no energy, so I leave it.

I slowly drag myself across the floor, crawling toward the sofa. A wave of nausea hits me again. So, I stop moving and just lie down on the floor.

I'll just stay here a while.

And then I'll be fine.

I hear my cell start to ring again in the far-off distance.

Later. I'll get it later. Rest now.

I close my eyes.

And everything goes black.

Chapter Thirty-One

HAMMERING. SOUNDS LIKE HAMMERING.
I blink my heavy eyes open.

Where am I?

I see my coffee table above my head, realizing I'm on the floor.

What am I doing down here?

Bang! Bang!

"Arianna, open the fucking door!"

Ares?

I push myself up onto my hands and knees and sit up. My head spins.

"Shit." I wince, putting my hand to my head.

What happened?

Oh God. I didn't drink . . . did I?

I flash through hazy memories. Leo . . . Diet Coke . . . feeling ill . . . getting home . . . being sick.

I turn my head and see the puke on the floor.

Shit.

More pounding.

"Arianna! I know you're in there! Open the fucking door!"

He's angry.

Why?

"Coming," I call, my voice raspy. I get to my feet with the help of the sofa. I've still got my shoes on and last night's clothes.

This feels so very reminiscent of the last eight years of my life.

But I didn't drink anything.

I pull my shoes off as I pad over to the door and open it.

The look on his face.

Disgust. Distaste. Anger. Betrayal.

He's holding something out to me. I look down at his hand, confused.

He's holding my cell.

Why does he have my cell?

"I was trying to call you all night." His voice is cold and hard.

"Why do you have my cell?"

"I found it out here in the hall. Clearly, you were that fucking wasted that you didn't even know you'd lost it."

"I—"

He cuts me off with a slash of his hand. "I don't want to fucking hear it, Ari." He storms past me into my apartment.

I close the door and turn to face him, leaning on the door for support, feeling like crap. "I don't understand. Why are you so angry?" I ask softly, my head pounding.

He lets out a bitter laugh. "Have you seen the state

of yourself?" His eyes go down to the floor, and he spots the vomit there. Another acidic laugh. "Jesus Christ." He shakes his head, like he's seen this scene a million times before.

He has.

"I was sick last night," I quietly tell him.

"Is that what the kids are calling it nowadays?"

"What?" I say, confused.

"You were wasted, Ari."

"No." I shake my head. "I swear, I didn't drink. I had a Coke. That was it."

"Don't fucking lie to me!" he roars, making me jump. "You can't fucking deny this, Ari! It's all over the internet! Jesus!"

"What? I don't understand."

My cell still in his hand, he taps the screen. A moment later, he hands it to me. It's a gossip news website; a video is on the screen, ready to watch.

"Press play." His voice is arctic.

I press play, and the video comes to life. It's dark and grainy. Like it was captured on a cell phone. But it's me, stumbling down a hall and into the party. Bumping into some guy and almost falling over. Then, it cuts to a cab, me falling out of it. Staggering up the steps into my building, and then, it ends.

I swipe the screen down to read the headline.

BAD GIRL GONE BADDER!

Looks like Arianna Petrelli—daughter of Giants coach, Eddie Petrelli, and current girlfriend of Giants quarterback, Ares Kincaid—has gone back to her partying ways. She was seen drunk and stumbling around a charity event she was attending on behalf of the team.

One partygoer said, "She's been drinking all night. Making a real show of herself. Flirting up a storm with some guy who definitely wasn't Ares Kincaid."

A staff member who was working the bar and served Petrelli numerous times confirmed this, saying she ordered "at least five vodka and Cokes."

A source from the Giants tells us that Kincaid will be furious with this news.

Let's hope Petrelli can get herself back to rehab and finally leave her partying days behind her.

Check out the video below for actual footage.

"I . . ." I stare up at Ares. "I don't understand."

"I do. It's pretty fucking clear, isn't it?"

"No . . . not to me, it's not. I don't know what happened."

He lets out a humorless laugh. "You don't know what happened? Right . . ." he says disbelievingly.

"I'm telling you that I don't know."

"So, the vodka just jumped up and leaped down your throat."

"I didn't drink vodka."

"Don't fucking lie!" he yells again.

"I'm not lying!" I yell back, not even caring that it's making my head thump and my throat sorer. "I didn't drink anything but Coke last night. One Diet Coke."

"Who was the guy?"

"What guy?"

His eyes are dark, impenetrable with anger. "The guy you were *flirting up a storm with*."

"Leo." I move away from the door, toward him, my expression pleading with him to believe me. "But I wasn't flirting with him. He got me a Coke, and we chatted for a bit. Ask him if you don't believe me."

"Leo, the journalist guy?"

"Yes."

He laughs, and I frown.

"What's so funny?"

"Nothing." He stares at me. "Not one fucking thing is funny about this."

"I didn't drink . . . I swear to you."

His jaw tightens, eyes flaring.

"I just had a Coke. Nothing else. Then, I started to feel weird, so I went to the restroom, and I-I just felt . . . off. I checked my drink to make sure there was no booze in it, but I couldn't smell anything. But I was woozy. I couldn't walk. I don't know what happened. Someone must've spiked my drink." I suddenly realize.

Ares takes a step closer to me. "You know . . . if you'd told me that you relapsed, I would've understood. Helped you. But . . . no . . . you just can't admit it, can you?" He drops his arms by his sides. "I thought you were different than my dad." He shakes his head. "But you're just the same."

"No!" There's consternation in my voice. "I'm telling you the truth."

"I don't believe you!" he roars.

Those four words are like a punch to the chest.

And they hurt like hell.

The ensuing silence in the room is deafening.

My throat is thick with tears.

"I'm going to ask you one last time. I'm giving you this opportunity to tell me the truth. Did you get drunk last night?"

I swallow back the tears and wrap my arms around myself. "No," I say quietly, shaking my head. Because I won't lie. I promised him the truth always, and that's what I'm giving him.

He exhales a harsh breath, shoving his hand through his hair. Then, he starts across the room, walking past me.

"Where are you going?" I can't hide the fear in my voice, and I don't want to.

"I'm just . . . done."

"Done?" My heart leaps in panic. "Ares . . . please."

"No, Ari. There's no coming back from this. I refuse to be with you and have you lying to my face."

"I'm not lying!" Tears spill down my cheeks.

"Stop!" he bellows, silencing me. "We're done. Don't call me. Don't come to see me. In fact . . . just forget I ever existed because that's what I intend to do with you."

Then, he's gone.

And I'm standing here, in shock, my phone still in my hand.

Confusion, hurt, and pain spill through me.

I stare down at the video.

I didn't drink.

Someone had to have given me something . . .

Put something in my drink.

Like what?

Date rape drug.

No . . .

RUSH   237

But there's no other explanation.
But who would do that?
Leo.
No. Why would he?
It's not like he tried anything. He wasn't even with me when the drug took effect . . .
Oh God. No.

I check the story, scrolling to find the writer or contributor, but there's nothing. There isn't always on these types of gossip sites.

But I intend to find out.

And I have a pretty good feeling I know exactly who it'll be.

Chapter Thirty-Two

I'M SITTING ON A chair in an examination room at a private hospital, seeing Luke's doctor, Dr. Pritchard.

Luke is here with me; he's sitting outside in the hall.

I called him after Ares walked out of my apartment, and he came straight over.

I'm here, having my blood tested for drugs. The so-called date rape drug. Because I'd already peed before I left the house, they couldn't use my urine to test, as I'd have probably passed the drug, so they had to take blood. The doctor left the room to go have it tested.

Luke had insisted I come here after I told him what happened.

He believed me. No questions asked.

Unlike the guy who's supposed to love me.

But I can't think about Ares right now because, if I do, I'll start crying. And I don't want to cry.

How he looked at me . . . like he hated me. What he said just before he left . . .

"Just forget I ever existed because that's what I intend to do with you."

Tears sting my eyes.

Shit. Don't cry.

Deep breaths. I'm okay.

I need to focus on my anger. That I was drugged, possibly by someone who was pretending to be my friend. Someone who just wanted a story and fast money and would go to the lengths of drugging me, making it look like I was drunk.

I know what a story like that would sell for.

Well, I hope he enjoys the money.

The doctor walks back in the room and takes his seat at his desk.

He turns to face me and exhales, and I just know what he's going to say.

"Okay. So, you tested positive for flunitrazepam. The showing was low, but it was there."

"What is that?" I ask through my paper-dry mouth.

"It's more commonly known as Rohypnol."

Jesus Christ.

Even though I knew this was highly likely, and I'm relieved that I'm not losing my goddamn mind and drinking without even being aware, I'm still shocked, angry, and hurt that someone would do that to me.

"As you're probably aware, it's a drug that is quite often used to facilitate sexual assault. It makes the person who has been given it look like they're drunk. They'll have trouble standing. Slurred speech. Loss of muscle control. Nausea."

"I had all of those."

"And you say all you drank was Diet Coke?"

"Yes."

"Arianna ... I know this isn't a question you'll want to hear, but I have to ask ... is there any possibility that you think you could have been sexually assaulted?"

I clasp my hands in my lap and shake my head. "I don't think so. I recall leaving the auction and going into my apartment alone. And I don't feel ... like ... you know." I nod south.

"Okay." He nods his head. "Well, either way, we can do a rape test kit if you want one done to be sure."

I shake my head again. "No. I'm sure I would know ... but thank you."

"Okay. Well, what I do suggest is that you file a report with the police. You were drugged against your will, and that is a crime. And people don't use this drug without intent. It was lucky that you managed to get out of there and get home before something more serious happened."

I know I'm lucky. But I don't feel it.

And, honestly, I don't think that was ever Leo's intent. He wanted me to appear drunk, so he could sell a story.

I knew journalists could be devious. I just didn't realize how low they could go.

"Thank you, Dr. Pritchard. I appreciate you seeing me on short notice."

"No problem at all."

"Could I ask a favor?"

"Sure."

"Would you be able to give me a copy of the test results for me to show to the police?"

"Of course."

I wait while he prints it out for me. Then, I put the test results in my bag, thank Dr. Pritchard again, and leave his office.

Luke is still out there, waiting for me.

"Okay?" he asks, getting to his feet.

"Yes . . . no." I shake my head, fingers curling into the sleeves of my sweatshirt.

I feel like I've been violated.

Like something has been taken from me.

I was lucky to not have been sexually assaulted. Leo might not have done it, but someone else could've taken advantage of me in my vulnerable state.

And I know it wasn't alcohol in my system . . . but I still had the same effects as if I were drunk. The hazy feelings, emotional and physical numbness, the vomiting. All the same results, just without the booze.

"You were drugged?"

I nod, and Luke's face tightens with anger. He walks over to me and wraps his arms around me, hugging me, and the gesture is so sincere and kind that I start crying.

"I'm so sorry." I sniffle, moving back, embarrassed at my public meltdown. "I'm getting your shirt wet."

"Don't be sorry. You've every right to be upset. I'm fucking furious, and it didn't even happen to me."

I'm so lucky to have him as a friend.

"Thank you, Luke, for everything . . . bringing me here, being there when I need you." I dry my tear-stained face with my hands.

"Ari, this is what sponsors are for . . . what friends are for. And we're friends. And trust me when I say that I've had worse things on my shirt than tears."

"Puke?" I say.

He nods, and I laugh through my tears.

"Thank you," I say again, and this time I'm thanking him for the laugh just right when I needed it.

"Come on," he says, putting his arm around my shoulders in a friendly gesture. "Let's get you home, and then we're going to figure out what we're going to do about this."

"Okay," I say, and we start walking down the hall.

"But there's one thing you can trust me on. The bastard who did this to you won't be getting away with it; that's for sure."

Chapter Thirty-Three

I SEE THE HULKING FIGURE of my dad waiting at the foot of my building steps as Luke pulls the car up.

"My dad," I say to him.

"Ah."

"I've been ignoring his calls all day. I know you wanted to talk about our plan of action, but I should talk to him."

"You should. And, Ari, *really* talk to him this time."

I glance over at him, knowing what he's saying. "I will. And thanks again. I'll call you later."

I climb out of his car and walk over to my dad.

My dad's eyes go to Luke's car that's pulling away and then to me. "Who was that?" he asks, suspicion lining his voice.

I sigh. "Luke. My sponsor."

"Nice car," he comments.

"Yeah, well, addiction doesn't discriminate. You wanna come inside?"

I walk past him, and he follows me up to my apartment in silence.

"You want something to drink?" I ask him as he takes a seat on my sofa.

"Coffee."

I go into my little kitchen and make coffee for us both. Then, I carry them through to the living room.

"Thanks," he says when I hand him his coffee.

I sit down on the chair, curling my feet under me, and hold my cup in my hands.

"So . . ." he starts.

"Can I just say something first before you start?"

"Of course."

"I know you're pissed and that you probably want to yell at me right now, but can we not?"

His brows draw together. "I'm not going to yell, Ari. I didn't come here to fight. I just came to check that you're okay. And to find out what happened."

"You saw the video."

"I did."

"Okay. So, before I talk, I'm asking, do you want the actual truth or the truth that you've already decided in your head?" *A la Ares style.*

"The actual truth."

"Okay," I repeat. I blow on the hot liquid and take a sip before speaking again. "So, here it is . . . I was drugged."

His face goes ashen, but I don't stop talking.

"I think I was drugged by a guy called Leo Parsons; he's a journalist with *ASN*. We'd met before, and I bumped into him at the auction. We were chatting. He offered to get me a Diet Coke from the bar. Aside from whoever poured my drink, he was the only one with access to it.

"A short while after drinking half of it, I started to feel weird, light-headed, and dizzy. Then, I was struggling to walk, and my speech was slurred. I knew I hadn't had alcohol, but I didn't know what was happening to me. I managed to get home in a cab and passed out, not before throwing up all over my floor." I point to the damp patch on my carpet from where I scrubbed it clean earlier. "I hadn't had a drop of alcohol." I stare into my dad's face, wanting him more than anyone to believe me.

"I've just gotten back from the hospital. Luke kindly took me to see his doctor. He tested my blood, and I showed positive for a low level of Rohypnol—the date rape drug."

His face goes from gray to white. "Were you . . ."

"No," I'm quick to reassure him.

He sits forward, putting his coffee on the table. "Are you sure?" His words are careful. "Because I've heard stories about that drug, how people are unconscious and don't know what's happening to them."

"Dad . . ." I put my drink down and move to sit next to him on the sofa. I place my hand on his arm and stare into his face. I'm surprised to see the fear in his eyes. I know he loves me. I'm his kid. He has to. But, until this moment, I didn't realize how much. "I'm sure. I left the auction as soon as I knew something was wrong. I was mostly aware by the time I made it back to my apartment. I didn't black out until I got home."

"Jesus Christ." He sits forward, putting his head in his hands. "This is my fault. I asked you to go to that auction."

"It's not your fault."

He looks at me. "You wouldn't have been there for this to happen if I hadn't been away."

"You had a game."

"I always have a game."

"Dad . . ." My mouth goes dry.

"I know I failed you. Time and time again. I know it was wrong, but I couldn't cope with your mom at the time . . . how she was . . . so I avoided being at home. I didn't think about how that affected you. I was selfish. And when she died . . . I should've been there. The guilt was eating me up so bad; I couldn't look at you without feeling shame."

"I always thought it was because I reminded you of her."

"No. Christ, no." He puts his hand on mine, gripping it. "You do look like her. You're beautiful, just like your mom. But it was my own shame . . . I failed you, Ari. And, now, I've failed you again."

"You haven't failed me." I squeeze his hand. "Truth: yes, you failed me back then, when I needed you, and I spent a lot of years being mad at you."

"Is that the reason you drank? Because of your mom?"

Tears squeeze at my eyes. "Partly . . ."

He closes his eyes and heaves out a breath. "I'm going to sort this out for you." He opens his eyes and brushes a fallen tear from my cheek. "I'm going to kill the son of a bitch who did this to you."

"No." I shake my head. "I'm going to do this the right way. I'm going to report it to the police."

"Can I . . . go to the station with you?" he asks tentatively.

I give him a sad smile. "I'd really like that."

"And Ares . . . have you spoken to him yet? He left the hotel without letting anyone know he was leaving. I was guessing he'd seen the video."

"He, um . . ." I look away from my dad, picking my coffee up and taking a sip. "He came here first thing this morning, before I went to the hospital. He'd seen the video. I tried to tell him that I hadn't drunk any liquor, but . . . he wouldn't believe me."

"Have you told him about the drug test?"

I shake my head and lower my cup to the table.

"You need to tell him."

My eyes flash to my dad's. "I don't have to tell him a thing. He's supposed to believe me. Not a drug test. He doesn't trust me, and I've never given him a reason not to. And, without trust, we have nothing."

My feelings toward Ares, the way he reacted, are turning to anger and bitterness, and I'm clinging to them because it's all that will get me through this . . . through losing him.

"He deserves to know the truth," my dad counters.

"I gave him the truth, and it wasn't good enough, coming from me."

"I know. But you have to see it from his point."

"I get that." I dig my hand into my hair, frustrated. "But he didn't even give me a chance. He came here, guns blazing. He'd already made his mind up about what happened, so it didn't matter what I said. He was never going to believe me."

"I know, Ari, but his background, with his dad . . . he has a hard time trusting people."

"Especially drunks. Yeah, I get that. But I'm not his

dad. He can't hold me up against his dad every time something goes wrong. Either he trusts me or he doesn't. And it's clear that he doesn't."

My dad drags a hand down his face. "Okay." He exhales. "I get what you're saying. I don't agree with you not telling him. But I get it."

"And don't you tell him either."

"Ari—"

"I'm serious."

"Okay," he concedes. "I won't say anything to Ares. But we should go to the police station now and report this. The sooner they talk to that little shit, the better."

We leave my apartment, and my dad drives me to the police station where I make a statement to a police-woman with a kind face. I give her the copy of the test results that Dr. Pritchard gave me. The officer, whose name is Knight, tells me that she'll talk to Leo and get his version of events and that she'll be in touch.

And that's it.

I'm frustrated at the lack of action, I guess, and so is my dad. But there's nothing else we can do.

Dad drives me home, and we pick up pizza on the way.

We sit together, watching an old *Friends* rerun— "The One With Russ." Both of us laugh through the episode, and honestly, I need the laugh after everything that's happened to me since last night.

I guess the fact that I can still laugh tells me something.

I might have been drugged, and currently, my name might be getting dragged through the mud. And I might have lost Ares, the guy I love.

But I'll survive.

I've survived worse.

When we've finished eating and another *Friends* episode starts, exhaustion washes over me. I lean my head back on the sofa and close my eyes.

"You should sleep," my dad says from beside me.

"Yeah . . ." I agree. "But . . . will you stay with me for a while?"

I open my eyes and glance over at him. His stare meets mine, eyes softening on me.

"Of course I will. I'll stay as long as you want."

Chapter Thirty-Four

I'M IN THE BATHROOM, brushing my teeth, when I hear a knock on the front door.

I spit out into the sink and call, "Dad, can you get that?"

"Yep," is his response from the kitchen where he's making us breakfast.

Dad stayed last night. He slept on the sofa. He knew I didn't want to be alone and insisted on staying, which I really appreciated.

I managed to get a bit of sleep. In between thoughts of Ares, our fight, and the tears I shed silently into my pillow, I had a few restless hours.

I rinse off my toothbrush and step out of the bathroom, heading for the living room.

I come to a stop when I see Ares standing there with my dad. The breath rushes from my body. I wasn't expecting to see him.

I look awful. I'm wearing sweats, and I haven't brushed my hair yet.

Not that he's faring much better. He looks awful.

Like he's not slept at all. Unshaven with dark rings under his eyes.

"Hi," he says low, his voice gravelly.

My skin breaks out in goose bumps.

I wrap my arms over myself as our eyes connect. Ares's eyes are somber and soulful, piercing deep into my already fragile emotions.

"I was just about to head out," my dad says, getting his jacket and keys. He walks over to me and kisses me on the forehead. "I'll call you later."

He gives Ares a sturdy pat on the shoulder as he passes. Then, he's gone, and I'm alone with Ares.

"What are you doing here?" I ask. My voice sounds as rough as his.

"Ari, I . . ." He drives a hand through his disheveled hair. Gripping the strands, he shakes his head and exhales a soft, painful-sounding breath. "I'm sorry, babe. So very fucking sorry."

He knows the truth. Someone told him.

A flash of anger runs through me. My eyes go to the door and then back to him.

"Did . . . my dad tell you?" The words are like rocks in my mouth.

He shakes his head. "No. I saw . . . Luke."

"Luke?"

"He came to my place late last night."

"How . . . did he know where you lived?"

"Money can buy you a lot of things in this city. And, apparently, my address is one of them."

"Oh."

"He came to give me a piece of his mind. And I'm glad he did. Because everything he said was right. It should've been me with you yesterday at the hospital. It should've been me listening to you when you were telling me the truth ... believing you because you'd never given me a reason not to trust you. But because I'm so used to distrusting people, I ..." He breaks off and blows out another breath. "I let down the one person I shouldn't have."

I wrap my arms tighter around myself. "I don't know what to say," I whisper softly.

"Tell me you'll forgive me."

I stare into his eyes, his endless eyes that desperately search mine.

And I shake my head. "I'm sorry, Ares. But I can't be with someone who doesn't trust me."

"I do trust you."

He steps up to me, hands curling around my upper arms. The feel of his hands on me ... it's like he's burning me.

"I just let my own bullshit cloud my judgment. I made a mistake, and I'm so fucking sorry."

"I was drugged. Do you get that? I was drugged. I was pleading with you to believe me, and you wouldn't listen! You dismissed me. Yelled at me. You didn't listen to a word I'd said to you. You once asked me for the truth, full disclosure, and I promised you that ... and I have never broken that promise."

"Neither have I."

"No. But you've let me down. The only reason you're here right now is because Luke told you the truth!" I stab a finger at the ground. "Not because you suddenly realized I was telling the truth. Not because you got over your initial anger and saw that I would never lie to you. No, you're here because Luke told you what had happened. And I have no doubt in my mind that you wouldn't be standing here right now if he hadn't." Tears are running down my cheeks now, showing my pain and frustration.

The guilt that sweeps through his eyes tells me everything I need to know. That I'm right. That he wouldn't have come. That he would never have believed what I had told him.

"You need to leave."

Panic flashes through his eyes. "Ari, please. I've fucked up, and I'm so sorry, babe. I hate that you're crying because of me." He lifts a hand to my face and cups my cheek, brushing away my tears with his thumb. His eyes plead with mine. "Please, Ari. Just give me a chance to make this right."

I look away from him. "I . . . can't."

"But . . ." I can hear him searching for words, and what comes out of his mouth next is entirely the wrong thing. "You screwed up before, and I forgave you."

"Are you fucking kidding me?" I yell. I push his hand off me. "I can't believe you! You're comparing a white lie when I canceled on you because I was too ashamed to tell you that I'd been to a bar *before* we were even dating to this!" The words roar out of my mouth.

Surprise flickers through his eyes. He's never seen me angry. I've never seen me this angry. I'm so mad that I'm vibrating with it.

"You need to leave," I tell him again, low.

"Jesus, Ari . . . please. I'm just saying all the wrong things here. I'm messing everything up."

He comes back to me and takes my face in his hands. I look away from him, hating how much I want the feel of his hands on me.

"Ari, I love you. I love you so fucking much." His voice breaks, and something cracks inside me. "I've screwed up so badly. And you'll never know how sorry I am for that. And I will spend the rest of my life making it up to you, if you'll let me."

My heart is aching and screaming and begging for me to say yes. It would be so easy to forgive him and take him back. But . . . what if he does it to me again? What if something happens again, and he doesn't believe me? And he won't because he doesn't trust me. He hurt me once, and he has the capacity to do it again. And I can't go through this again. Not with him. Because it will be even harder later down the line.

If I love him this much now, in such a short space of time, imagine how I'll feel about him in a year . . . in two years.

It would break me.

And I can't risk that. Because I can't turn back into the girl I used to be. I'm barely hanging on now. It's taking everything in me not to turn to alcohol to numb this pain.

And staying sober has to be the most important thing. If I'm to have a future, it has to be the only thing.

"I'm sorry," I say quietly, my eyes refilling with tears, blurring my vision. "I have to think of myself right now . . . my sobriety. And I . . . I can't be with someone who doesn't trust me. Someone who's just waiting and watching . . . expecting me to fall."

I blink, sending fresh tears down my cheeks, and

then I bring my eyes to his . . . and wish I hadn't. The raw emotion shimmering in his gaze almost breaks me. But I hold strong because I have to. It's the right thing to do. The only thing I can do.

So, I draw up all the strength left inside of me and say softly, "You were right yesterday . . . when you said we were done . . . because I don't trust you with my heart anymore. The one time I really needed you, Ares . . . needed you to believe me, and you let me down."

His hands slowly draw away from my face.

He swallows roughly and closes his eyes, a shaky breath escaping him.

Then, he turns and walks for the door.

I can't watch him leave. So, I close my eyes.

"Ari . . ."

I force myself to look at him. And it shatters my heart. The anguish on his face.

"I screwed up. But I never stopped loving you. And I never will." He opens the door and steps through, and then he's gone.

Out of my life. For good this time.

Chapter Thirty-Five

IN THE DAYS THAT pass, I can feel that sense of loss, like I felt after my mom died. It's a different sense of loss but no less difficult.

I guess, in some ways, it's hard, knowing Ares is out there, living his life without me.

I haven't been into work since Ares and I broke up.

My dad told me to take the next few weeks off work, and I didn't argue the point.

The last thing I need is to bump into Ares.

I honestly don't know how I'm going to handle it when I do go back. But, for now, I'm not thinking about that.

And that is one of the problems about not having to go to work; I've got time on my hands, and all I do is think.

Mainly about Ares.

I haven't seen him since the morning I told him to leave my apartment. He hasn't called or texted. Not that I expected him to.

And it's hard. His disappearance from my life. I got so used to being with him. Spending time with him.

He was my best friend. I loved him. I still love him. I'm just wondering when I'm going to stop feeling this way. Because being without him is like I'm slowly dying inside.

I've been trying to keep busy. So, I have thrown myself back into my painting.

I finally managed to finish the painting of me and Ares. I cried the whole time.

But it was cathartic, you know?

The final brushstroke was like the closing of that chapter in my life.

I have considered sending the painting to him, as I promised him that he could have it when it was finished. But that was when we were still together, and now, we're not. I don't know if he'll still want it.

So, for now, I'm hanging on to it.

Although it's in my hallway closet because looking at it makes me want to cry.

On the subject of things that make me want to cry, but more with anger . . . I received a call from Officer Knight, who had taken my statement about my complaint against Leo. She said that they had spoken with him, and he, of course, denied any wrongdoing. And they couldn't check the CCTV footage from that night, as there wasn't a working camera on the bar. So, it basically came down to my word against his. She apologized that there was nothing more she could do. I felt angry, but it's not her fault. She's just doing her job. So, I thanked her for trying for me and hung up.

My dad was not happy when I told him. His exact words were, "That's fucking bullshit."

Then, he ranted a little, and I let him. Honestly, it's

nice to see him showing me that he cares about me even if it did take such a shitty thing to happen for him to start doing so.

Do I want to drink?

More than anything.

I've had bad days, but I've handled them.

As well as painting, I've gotten back into my yoga. I let it slide a little when Ares and I started dating.

Now that I'm single . . . I'm reverting to life pre-Ares, just not as desperately pathetic.

Okay, it's a little pathetic. I've gotten reacquainted with my good buddy Netflix.

I've still got *Dexter* on there, waiting for me to watch the next episode . . . but it wouldn't feel right, watching it without Ares sitting here beside me. So, I removed it from my list.

Maybe, one day, I'll be able to watch it alone.

But that day isn't today—or anytime soon.

But I'm not being a total loser all the time. I've been spending a lot of time with my dad. Okay, that is sad. But I think he's trying to make things up to me, all his past failings, and I'm more than happy to let him.

He's the only family I've got left.

I also spoke to Luke. He called and apologized for telling Ares what had really happened to me that night.

But I understood. He cares about me as a friend, and honestly, when you don't have that many people who care about you, you hold on to the ones you do have.

Ares cares about you, that annoying voice in my head whispers.

Yeah, well, if he did really care, then he would've believed me when I told him the truth.

And, now, I'm arguing with myself.

Great.

I push open the door to the art store. I've run out of a few oil colors and need to stock up.

I walk inside, smiling at the girl behind the counter. Her hair is long and dyed different colors, like unicorn hair.

It's cool.

Not that I'd ever have the balls to dye my hair like that.

I've just walked down the aisles where the oil paints I use are when I hear my name being called.

"Arianna Petrelli?"

I turn at the voice, and a smile breaks out on my face. "Declan Wiseman."

Dec and I used to go to art college together.

"How the hell are you doing?" he asks as he comes over to give me a hug.

"I'm good." I smile at him as I pull away.

"It's been how long since we last saw each other?"

The sad thing is, I can't actually remember the last time I saw him. Because most of those years and the subsequent ones blend together.

"Too long," I say instead.

"Hey, you fancy having a coffee? There's a coffee shop a few doors down."

"I'd love that." I smile again. "Just let me grab these paints, and then I'm good."

I get what I need, and we head to the counter together. Dec pays for his charcoals. He does charcoal drawings, and from my memory, they are amazing.

I pay for my paints, and then we head out of the

store together and take the short walk to the coffee shop.

We order coffees, and Dec insists on paying for mine. Then, we take a seat by the window.

"So, what are you up to nowadays?" Dec asks me. No hint that he's seen the news stories about me recently or earlier this year.

"I was working for a gallery there for a few years, but I, um . . . lost my job . . . and . . ." I pick my coffee cup up, sipping it, delaying my words. *Be truthful, Ari. Stop hiding who you are.* I put my cup down and look up at him. "The truth is, I had a drinking problem, and I got in some trouble earlier this year, as I had an accident while drunk driving, so I had to go into rehab, and I lost my job at the gallery."

Surprisingly, his expression doesn't change. "Shit," he says. "But you're doing okay now?"

"Yeah." I smile. It's a little forced because the reality is, I'm not doing great. I have this huge hole in my chest where Ares used to be. "I'm eight months sober."

"That's great," he says, smiling. "My older brother has been to rehab a few times. Opiate addiction," he explains.

"Is he okay now?" I ask sympathetically because I know it's hard for those who deal with the addiction, but it's equally as hard for those people's loved ones who have to watch them destroy themselves.

"He's four months clean at the moment. But my mom and I have been down this road with him before. So, we're just hoping it sticks this time."

I nod, understanding.

"So, what are you doing for work at the moment?" he asks, sipping his coffee.

"I'm working for my dad."

"He coaches the Giants, right?"

"Yeah. I'm currently an assistant to the team."

"Sounds good."

"Not really." I shake my head. *The guy I love is the quarterback, and we're no longer together because he doesn't trust me.* "I mean, it's a job. But it's not what I want to do with my life."

"You want to paint?"

"Yeah . . . I mean, even just working back in a gallery would be amazing, but after the DUI, I can't get anyone to hire me."

"My mom has a gallery, you know."

"Wow. Really?"

"Yeah. It's fairly new. She opened it eighteen months ago, but it's doing well, and she is always keen to showcase new talent. And she doesn't discriminate against people with former addictions." He grins, and I smile. "I can set you up with a meeting with her, show her your portfolio, if you'd be interested?"

"Interested? Are you nuts?" I laugh. "It's taking everything to keep me in my seat right now and not grab you and hug the hell out of you."

He laughs. "So, should I take that as a yes?"

I nod manically. "You can take that as a massively huge yes."

Chapter Thirty-Six

IT'S A BRIGHT, SUNNY afternoon as I walk along the sidewalk, heading for Nuu Fine Art, my heavy portfolio bag carrying the two paintings I've brought with me to show Dec's mom, Moira Wiseman.

After coffee with Dec yesterday, we exchanged numbers and went our separate ways. I didn't expect to hear from him right away, but he texted me later that day and said his mom would see me today.

Cue my freak out.

I'm dressed in a black shirtdress that sits just above my knees and has a cute bow that ties at the neck. I've got cute beige-colored high-heeled sandals on my feet. Makeup is natural, hair down and wavy.

I want to make a good impression.

I reach the building and stop outside to stare up at it.

It's a metal-and-glass-front building. Light and airy. Some of the works are visible from the window. Paintings and sculptures.

Taking a deep breath, I push the door open and

walk inside. Soft music is playing in the background. I walk up to the reception desk.

A pretty girl around my age with poker-straight, shoulder-length blonde hair and striking blue eyes—which, for a moment, remind me of Ares—smiles at me. "Hi, can I help you?" she asks.

"Yes. Hi. I'm here to see Moira Wiseman. My name is Arianna Petrelli. I have an appointment."

"Of course." She gives me a friendly smile. "Moira's expecting you. Follow me."

She comes out from around the reception desk and leads me through the gallery, which is a hell of a lot bigger than I was expecting. She opens a door, taking me into the back area, which has countless paintings stacked up—some wrapped, some not. And maybe twenty varying sculptures are all lined up, either waiting for delivery to a customer or ready to go out for display, I'm guessing.

She reaches a door, knocks once, and opens it. "Moira, Arianna Petrelli is here to see you."

Moira Wiseman looks to be in her early fifties. She has short black hair and a strikingly attractive face.

She stands from her chair and comes around the desk, holding her hand out to shake mine. "Arianna, it's so good to meet you. Declan has told me all about you."

I don't worry or panic about what she knows about me because her older son has his struggles, too, and Dec told me that she doesn't judge a person. Only their work.

I slip my hand into hers and give it a firm but friendly shake, clutching my portfolio bag containing some of my paintings.

"It's good to meet you, too," I tell her.

"Would you like something to drink?" she asks me. "Coffee?"

"Coffee's great," I tell her.

"Ebony, could you bring us some coffee, please?" Moira addresses the girl from reception.

"Of course."

She closes the door, and Moira tells me to take a seat.

I lower my bag to the floor, leaning it against the chair beside me.

God, I'm so nervous that my insides are shaking, but I'm trying to exude calmness on the outside. I'm not sure if I'm pulling it off though.

"Thank you for seeing me," I tell her.

"Oh, no problem at all." She waves me off. "Declan was raving about your paintings, and he had me keen to see them. Only, I said to him, 'If this girl is so good, then why the hell didn't you tell me about her before?' " She laughs, and I do, too. "Men, eh?" she adds, and I agree.

"Well, I'm just glad I bumped into him," I tell Moira.

She smiles and nods. "Come on then, let's not waste any more time; show me these paintings of yours."

I swallow hard as I reach for my bag. I move it in front of me, leaning it against her desk, and open the zipper on the bag.

Moira comes from behind the desk to stand next to me.

"I only brought two paintings with me," I tell her. "I don't have a car at the moment, and they're pretty heavy to carry."

I lift the first painting from the bag, and I hear her take in a sharp breath.

Shit. She hates it.

It's the one of Ares and me.

I glance up at her and start to tell her that the other painting is much different than this, if this one isn't to her taste, but the look on her face tells me that she doesn't actually hate it.

"Can I?" She reaches for the painting.

"Of course." I hand it to her.

She moves across the room with it, sitting it on an empty easel, and then stands back, looking at it.

I move to stand beside her.

"Jesus, Ari . . . this is good. Really good." She glances at me. "I thought Declan was exaggerating about your talent, but . . ." She reaches out a hand, a finger tracing the painting without touching. "The lines here, the detail . . . I can feel the absolute passion in this picture."

I feel a lump rise in my throat. "Thank you," I tell her.

"I'm guessing this is from memory and not a still life?" She looks at me again, a grin in her eyes.

"It's from memory."

"It's personal to you though, yes?"

"Yes," I exhale.

"And how would you feel, showing this? I know all art is personal, but this one runs deep; I can tell," she says, finger moving over the painting again.

"I . . . it . . . well, I would show it, but . . . it belongs to someone else," I hear myself saying. *Like my heart.*

I didn't realize it until this moment. I'd thought I could part with this painting. But I can't. Not to her. It belongs to Ares.

Whether he still wants it or not, it's his to do with as he wants.

Because he gave this back to me. It was him who gave me back the ability to paint. The inspiration I needed. And I owe him for that.

Jesus, I miss him.

I feel my throat thicken with tears. *Christ, not here. Pull it together, Ari.*

Moira turns to face me and stares at me. "If I told you that I wanted this painting in my gallery, what would you say?"

I swallow past the thickness. "I'd say that I would want to have my paintings in your gallery more than anything. But I can't give you this painting."

"Why did you bring it today then?"

"Because . . . I thought I could."

She's thoughtfully staring at me. "You love the man in this painting?"

It's not a question. But, still, I answer. "Yes."

"I loved a man once, too. Total asshole. I hope your man isn't an asshole."

Laughter slips past my lips. "He can be." *Not that he's mine anymore.*

She laughs, too. "Aren't they all at times? But it's whether they recognize they've been an ass and stop being one or don't care and carry on regardless. Mine was the latter."

Mine is the former.

She smiles brightly at me. "Okay then. Show me this other painting you've brought with you, and let's see if it's equally as good as this one."

Chapter Thirty-Seven

MOIRA LOVED THE OTHER painting I'd brought to show her. It was a slightly abstract portrait of a beautiful woman. Totally different than the painting of Ares and me.

The woman in the picture wasn't inspired from anyone I'd seen. It was just straight from the heart. A recent painting from only days ago.

The woman is alive with color, but her eyes are closed. The expression on her face is wistful, achingly sad, and the abstract portrays her feeling of utter loneliness.

Yes, I'm fully aware of the fact that the woman in the painting represents my feelings right now.

But that's art. It's a reflection of our innermost desires, wants, needs, and feelings. It's emotional and messy. Just like life.

And Moira loved it.

She said she loved the contrast in my ability to paint, and she offered me a showing on the spot. And get this: she has an opening for someone to work sales on the gallery floor, and she asked if I would be interested in the job.

I was like, "Hell yes!"

When I walked out of the gallery, the first person I wanted to tell was Ares.

Then, I remembered.

I stood there for a moment, unsure of what to do.

But I wanted to tell someone, so I called my dad and told him the good news.

He was really happy for me. He asked me if I wanted to come home to celebrate, and I accepted.

It's not like I have anyone else to celebrate with.

So, I'm in a cab on my way to my dad's.

But, first, I've got a stop to make.

There's something I need to do.

I get out of the cab outside of The New York Giants headquarters and training facility after paying the driver the fare. I decide not to ask him to wait while I go inside, instead deciding I'll call for another cab to take me to my dad's.

I hold the painting under my arm. It's wrapped in bubble wrap to protect it and covered in brown paper. I went home first, after leaving the gallery, before heading here, so I could wrap it. I didn't want it on display for everyone to see.

It's late in the day but still light out. I wave at Josh, the night guard, and make my way inside. Because it's after hours, the main door is locked, so I have to input the key code to get in.

The building is eerily silent, as it usually is at this time of night. I'd be surprised if anyone was actually here. Thank God all the lights are still on; otherwise, I'd turn around and walk straight back out.

I'm not exactly brave.

Case in point: the fact that I'm here to leave the painting in the locker room for Ares and not take it to his apartment.

I walk to the locker room, my heels echoing loudly against the floor. When I reach the locker room, I push through the door. The light is still on in here, too. I step inside, letting the door close behind me.

I walk over to Ares's station and stand the painting on the floor, leaning it against the bench, where his cleats sit.

I just stand here for a time, staring at his team shirts hanging there, emotion overwhelming me, remembering the exact moment I met him.

In here. Me, half-naked, soaking wet, and bent over in this very spot.

So much has changed since then.

He hated me. He loved me. He didn't trust me.

I step forward, closer to his hanging clothes, and his scent washes over me, like the breeze on a warm summer day, making me ache for him. Eliciting memories so wonderful that, in this moment, it's hard to remember why we aren't together anymore.

I hear a door bang behind me. I turn, and he's there.

Ares.

Standing in front of the door to the showers. Hair wet, beads of water running down his chest. He's still sporting stubble, which is well on its way to a beard. Eyes dark, like sleeping hasn't been easy for him. A towel tied around his waist.

He looks so beautiful that it hurts.

It's been just under a week since I last saw him, and yet, right now, it feels like it's been years.

Longing so fierce jolts through me, making me want to go to him.

But I can't.

So, I dig my toes into my shoes, staying where I am.

"Hi," he says softly, looking sad and unsure, all at the same time.

"Hi." I smile, but it feels sad on my lips. "I didn't know anyone was here," I tell him.

"I stayed to do a workout. I just finished up and had a shower. Obviously," he says with a nod down at his towel, mocking himself.

There's a beat of silence between us. Silence that once upon a time ago would never have been there.

"How . . . have you been?" he asks quietly.

"I'm . . . okay. You?"

He lifts a shoulder. "I . . ." His eyes close, and he lets out a breath, so achingly somber, it makes me want to cry. His gaze comes to mine. "Full disclosure?"

I bite my lip and nod.

"Not good. I . . . miss you."

How I don't cry in this moment, I'll never know. I wrap my arms around myself. "I'm sorry."

"Don't be. It's my fault. I'm the one who messed up and lost the best person I've ever met and the best thing that has ever happened to me."

My lips tremble, and a tear falls from the corner of my eye. I brush it away with my hand.

This is killing me. Just like I knew it would if I saw him again.

I don't want to see him in pain. I love him. I hate not being with him.

And seeing him hurting is hurting me.

But I don't know how to get past what happened. Him not trusting me.

I see his eyes go behind me.

"Is that . . ." He steps forward. "Is that for me?"

I nod, biting my lip.

He walks over, close to me, and his nearness overwhelms me. He smells like everything I've missed.

"Can I . . ." He looks at me, gesturing to the painting.

"Of course."

I watch in silence as he picks it up and carefully tears the paper from the painting. He places it on the bench next to his cleats. Then, he slides his thick finger under the tape that's holding the bubble wrap together and removes it.

He drops the bubble wrap where the disregarded paper sits. Then, he holds the painting up and stares at it.

I watch him and see his throat work on a swallow.

When he lifts his eyes to mine, the raw emotion almost brings me to my knees. Tears prick my eyes again, and I bite the inside of my cheek to stop them from falling.

"You finished it?" he says softly.

"Yes."

"It's beautiful, Ari. Really beautiful. Thank you so much for letting me have it. For bringing it here for me."

"I . . . I said that you could have it when . . . and I wasn't sure if you would still want it . . . but I promised, so . . ."

"No, I want it." He stares down at it again. "It's amazing."

"I got a job," I hear myself saying. "At a gallery. Working the floor. But she wants to showcase my work for me as well."

"Ari . . . that's amazing. I'm really happy for you." And he sounds like he genuinely is.

"It was because of this painting that I got the showcase," I tell him.

I know Moira really liked my other painting, but it was this one that really caught her eye, showing her what I'm capable of.

"I . . . I started painting again because of you. And I wanted to thank you for that."

He swallows roughly. "You don't have to thank me. It was always inside of you, Ari. I . . . being with me just gave you the push to do it."

"You inspired me."

"You inspire me every single fucking day."

He puts the painting down, propping it against the bench, and walks close to me, making me tremble. He cups his hands around my face, tilting it back, so I'm looking up at him.

The feel of his hands on my skin is like fire . . . like the fire blazing in his eyes.

"I'm sorry I let you down. I'm sorry I let my past shit blind me. I was just so . . . scared you'd hurt me . . . like he used to, that I ignored everything I already knew about you and jumped to the worst conclusion. I hate myself for what happened to you. I hate that I wasn't there to protect you from that motherfucker. But I never, not once, in all that time, *didn't* trust you. I let my old habits of expecting the worst and seeing the video confirm my worst fears. And I was wrong. So fucking wrong, and I will be forever sorry.

"But I'm human, Ari. I made a mistake. A colossal mistake. But it wasn't because I didn't love you. It's because I love you so fucking much. I can't breathe without you. I always knew what it was like to be needed by my kid brother and sister, even my fucking dad, but I didn't know what it was like to need someone, and I fucking need you, Ari . . . so much."

"I . . ." I don't know what to say. I know what my heart wants me to say.

I know he messed up and hurt me badly, but he knows this. He's apologized for this. He's hurting for his actions.

And I'm only hurting us both by not giving him a second chance.

Because I miss him so fucking much.

"One chance, Ares. You screw up again, and we're done—"

I don't get to finish that sentence because his mouth slams down on mine, kissing me like a man starved. And I'm equally as hungry for him.

It's been too long since he kissed me.

"I won't screw up again," he breathes against my lips. "I swear."

And I believe him.

He kisses me again. Rougher this time and with more desperation. Teeth nipping at my lips.

My hands slide into his hair, tugging him even closer, and he comes willingly.

I'm on fire. My whole body burning with need for him.

Big hands slide down my back and over my ass, gripping hold of my dress. He lifts it up.

We part, so he can pull it off over my head. Then, our lips fuse back together.

"You're so fucking beautiful," he says, a hand cupping my cheek, angling my head so that he can kiss me deeper. Tongue plunging into my mouth.

I give his towel a quick pull, and it drops to the floor.

I'm quickly divested of my bra and panties.

Then, he lifts me off the floor, my ass in his big hands, my legs around his waist, my arms looped around his shoulders. He moves us over to the wall. My back is pressed up against the cold wall, but I can barely feel it.

All I can feel is him.

Ares lines his cock up with my entrance, and slowly, he pushes inside.

When he's buried deep inside me, he softly kisses me. "I love you," he tells me.

"I love you, too," I whisper, my eyes staring into his. "But don't ever hurt me like that again."

He presses his forehead to mine, eyes staring straight into mine. "Never. The only thing I plan on doing from now on is loving you."

And he does.

He loves me against that wall in the locker room until both of us are coming fiercely.

Chapter Thirty-Eight

AFTER ARES AND I made up, he put me and his new painting in his truck and drove me to my dad's.

He came inside with me but left the painting in his truck, as we'd agreed that wasn't a painting my dad needed to see.

When my dad opened the door to us, Ares holding my hand tight, like he was afraid of losing me again, my dad didn't say anything about it. Just gave me a knowing smile that told me he had been expecting it all along.

Then, he invited us both inside.

We ordered pizza and celebrated my new job at the gallery with sparkling orange juice.

I'm off Diet Coke nowadays.

After dinner, my dad got the playing cards out. That's what we're doing now, sitting in the dining room, playing poker, and I'm kicking both their asses.

I'm with my two favorite men. I have a new job and

a gallery showing. Life couldn't be better than it is right now.

"Do either of you want some ice cream?" my dad asks, rising from his chair, after I won the last game.

"I'm down for ice cream," Ares says.

"You just ate a whole pizza," I say.

"It was a pizza and a half," he informs me with a grin. "And your point is?"

Laughing, I shake my head at him. "Pig." Then, I ask my dad, "What do you have?"

"I'm not sure. I'll go have a look," he says, going to the kitchen, and I get up to follow him.

"I'll have whatever you're having, babe," Ares tells me.

"Makes sense. Pigs will eat anything," I tease.

He grabs me around the waist, yanking me to him. "I'll eat you if you keep up with the cheek, and I highly doubt you want me going down on you on your dad's dining room table."

A shiver runs through me. I cup my hand around his chin, the stubble pricking my palm. "No. But you can do it to me on your dining table when you take me back to your place after here."

His eyes go molten. "You can bet on it."

I plant a chaste kiss on his lips and then pull away. He smacks my ass as I go.

I walk into the kitchen, and my dad is looking in the freezer, his right hand on the open door. I notice his hand is cut up on the knuckles.

"Hey, what happened here?" I say, walking over and taking hold of his hand. How did I not spot this before?

Because he was holding his cards with his left hand.
And my dad is right handed.

"Oh." He pulls his hand back, eyes moving away from me. "Nothing. Just scuffed it. Can't even remember how."

Huh?

I stare at him, wondering how the heck he forgot how he had done it. If I had grazes like that on my hand, I'd be crying over it for days. And it doesn't exactly look like an old wound.

"Did you clean it up?" I ask him, knowing what he's like.

"Of course I did."

"Good. Well . . . be careful in the future."

Taking over from my dad, I rifle through, getting to the ice cream. He has vanilla and mint chocolate chip.

"What do you fancy?" I ask him.

"Mint chocolate chip."

"Me, too." I grin at him.

I serve the ice cream into the three bowls that he's laid out for us, and we carry them through to the dining table. I've just sat down, ready to resume our card game, when my cell starts to ring on the table.

I glance down at the number, not recognizing it. I hesitate for a moment, deciding whether to answer it or not, and then pick it up, connecting the call.

"Hello?"

"Arianna."

"Yes."

"It's Officer Knight. I just wanted to call and let you know that Leo Parsons was assaulted last night."

"He was?" I say, surprised. "I'd say I'm sorry to hear that, but I'm not."

"I didn't think you would be." Her tone is so even that I can't tell where she's going with this. "A couple of guys broke his nose and a couple of his ribs. Bruised him up pretty bad," she adds. "There were no witnesses, and he couldn't identify the perpetrators."

"Okay . . . but why are you telling me this?"

"I just thought . . . all things considered, this might be something you'd want to know."

I finally hear the inflection in her voice, and I smile.

"Well, I appreciate you calling to tell me."

"No problem. I'm just sorry there wasn't anything more I could do regarding your case."

"That's okay," I tell her. "I understand."

"Well, that was all I called to say. You have a good night now."

"I will. You, too."

I hang up my cell, placing it back down on the table.

"Who was that?" Ares asks.

"The cop who dealt with my complaint. She called to tell me that Leo was assaulted last night. Broke his nose and a couple of ribs. Beat him up pretty bad."

Neither of them says a word.

And, suddenly, the silence at the table is deafening.

My eyes move from Ares to my dad and down to my dad's cut-up hand.

Then, they fly up to his eyes, and everything I need to know is written there.

A lump appears in my throat.

I don't condone violence, but . . . he did that for me. He went there and kicked the shit out of the guy who had drugged me and hurt me because . . . my dad loves me.

It might not be the ideal way to show your love to someone. But it's my dad's way.

"Dad . . . did you . . . beat up Leo Parsons?"

His eyes slide to Ares and then back to me. Then, he shrugs. "Yes. And I'd do it again in a heartbeat. After what he did to you, the little bastard is lucky that I didn't kill him. And you know what I found in his pocket? A bag of those fucking pills that he probably planned on using on someone else."

I gape at him in disbelief, emotion swimming inside me. "You could've gotten in trouble, Dad."

"He needed to be taught a lesson."

"Hang on. She said a couple of guys." My eyes swing to Ares. "Ares?"

"Arianna."

"Did you go with my dad and beat up Leo Parsons?"

He glances at my dad before looking back at me. "You want the truth?"

"Always."

"Of course I did."

"But . . . we weren't even together then."

"So?" He shrugs. "That fucker hurt you. So, I hurt him. Multiple times."

I stare at them both, filled with so much love for them that I could burst. They risked so much for me. My dad would've been fired without a doubt and quite likely prosecuted. Same for Ares. He would have probably lost his contract and been prosecuted.

My lip starts to tremble.

"I-I . . . thank you. Both. So much." I know I'm thanking them for kicking Leo's ass, but I don't know what else to say.

"Don't thank me," my dad says roughly. I can hear emotion thick in his voice. "I'm your dad. That's what dads do." He shoves his chair out. "I need to use the bathroom."

He strides out of the room, and I stare after him.

"You do know that Coach is going in there to bawl his eyes out." Ares chuckles softly.

"My dad doesn't cry."

Ares grabs me and pulls me from my chair and onto his lap, his big hand cupping the nape of my neck. "News flash: men cry, babe."

"Did you cry over me?" I ask teasingly.

"A fucking river." He stares at me, and I gulp at the seriousness in his eyes.

I look at the door my dad just went through. "Do you think I should go check on him?"

"No." He laughs. "Give him a minute. Let him keep his man card."

"Okay. I just . . . I can't believe you both did that. Kicked Leo's ass like that . . . for me."

"Full disclosure?" he says, still staring into my eyes.

"Always."

"Believe it. Because there isn't a single thing that I wouldn't do for you, Ari. I fucking love you."

I press my lips to his, kissing him. "I love you, too."

Epilogue

Today is Zeus and Cam's wedding day. We're in Port Washington to celebrate with them. The wedding is being held in the back garden of their home.

It's a small and intimate wedding, close friends and family only.

The garden is private and secluded. It's also huge with woodlands at the back. There's a tent set up over to the right, where the reception will take place. And the section where the wedding will actually take place is adorned with flowers, hanging lanterns, and fairy lights.

It all looks beautiful.

There are seats on either side of the makeshift aisle leading up to the altar where Zeus is standing in a traditional tuxedo, waiting for his bride. Ares and Lo are at his side, both in tuxes.

Ares looks incredibly handsome. I rarely see him in a suit, but when I do, it makes my hormones go all kinds of crazy.

I'm wearing an off-the-shoulder dusky-pink satin dress with an organza skirt with leaf and flower details on it, teamed with pale pink heeled sandals on my feet.

I'm seated up front on the right, going with traditional etiquette, with the groom's side being seated here. Cam's friends and family are over on the left. There aren't tons of people here. But that's how they wanted it. Only the people who matter are here, and I'm proud to be one of those people. Kaden is sitting next to me, smart and handsome in a navy-blue suit. Next to him is Ares's dad Brett. He's a big guy. I can see where they all get their size. But they don't look like him. I've seen pictures of their mom, Grace, and they all look like her. She was incredibly beautiful.

I've gotten to know Brett a little better in the time Ares and I have been together. He's a good man who made a lot of mistakes but doesn't know how to make up for them. He reminds me a lot of my dad in that respect.

And in some ways, Brett reminds me of myself, in the difficulty he has with alcohol. I understand that about him, which is something Ares never will. Only someone who has to deal with the addiction on a daily basis will understand.

I don't understand how he could've chosen alcohol over his children. I know for sure that is one thing I would never do.

Brett is still sober, and this is the longest. I think he's in it for the long haul, like me. And, even though he's sober and trying, his relationship with Ares is still difficult. But I think it always will be. Because Ares can't find it in him to forgive him for failing them when they all needed him, and I do understand that.

Although I do forgive my dad for letting me down. My relationship with him is getting stronger each day. We've talked a lot. Mostly me about how I felt about his failings when I was younger. He's listened. And he's working on making up for it. Being a better father to me. There's no magic fix, but we're a hell of a lot closer than we once were.

I guess, in a not-so-nice way, what happened with Leo was the catalyst to finally make my dad start talking to me, opening up.

Speaking of Leo, the police never did catch the people who beat his ass that night.

I heard he left New York and moved to San Francisco for a job there.

He didn't have much of a career left here. My dad froze him out of the press for the Giants, and my dad knows all of the other teams' coaches. After a few words in people's ears, Leo was blocked out of their press access, too.

I can't say I was sorry to see the lying, deceptive scumbag leave New York.

And I'm still sober, if you were wondering. I got my one-year chip a while back. I'm hoping to be a sponsor one day. Luke continues to be my sponsor, and I see him on the regular and go to weekly AA meetings. I still need Luke's support as my sponsor and friend. He and Ares get along really well, too, which is great.

I still have moments from time to time, where I think I need a drink, although not as often as they once used to be.

And Ares is there for every single one.

He's my rock. My strength.

I look at him and remember all the reasons I don't want to drink. All the reasons I need to stay sober.

I had my gallery showing, and it was a huge success. Ares insisted that we display our painting. So, I did. Of course, it wasn't for sale, as it already had an owner. But it was right to see it there among my other paintings.

Moira was thrilled to see it hanging with my other art.

Everyone came that night to support me. Ares and my dad were there along with Missy, Lo, Zeus, Cam, and Kaden. Every member of the Giants team, including players and staff. Mary, my dad's PA, came along with her husband, Ted.

Dec was there. It was because of him I had a place in the gallery. And there were all the industry insiders that Moira had invited.

I sold out of every painting that night.

Ares and I celebrated afterward in bed.

It was a really, really good night.

I've had two more gallery showings since then. Both equally as successful. I'm more and more in demand, meaning I've had to reduce my time on the shop floor at the gallery to spend more time painting.

Although I'm still painting out of my apartment. I could really do with a studio.

Music starts to play, an acoustic version of Rihanna's "Umbrella." Everyone stands and turns to watch the bride come down the aisle.

First down the aisle is Gigi; she's holding Thea's hand, who just recently started walking. They both look gorgeous. Just like their mom. They have on bridesmaid dresses in a striking shade of blue. The color reminds me of Ares's eyes. The Kincaid eyes.

Gigi and Thea both have those striking blue eyes, and then I realize that Cam must have matched the color of the dresses to their eyes.

I can understand wanting to do that. I love Ares's eyes. In a non-creepy way, of course.

Missy follows behind them, wearing the same color dress as the girls.

She catches my eye and smiles at me. She graduated from Dartmouth and is in New York permanently. It's good to have her home. We've gotten even closer over time. She's like the sister I never had and always wanted.

I hear a sharp intake of breath and glance at Kaden next to me.

He's staring at Missy. A look of unmistakable longing in his eyes.

A look I've seen on him a few times when she's around.

He thinks no one notices, but I have.

I've also noticed the looks that Missy gives to him when she thinks that no one else is watching.

I've tried to subtly ask her if she's interested in him, but she never gives anything away. She's quiet on the matter, and that is not like Missy at all.

And that tells me everything I need to know.

I just wonder, if they like each other, why the hell are they not together?

But then the same thing could have been said about Ares and me in the beginning. So, I'm no one to talk.

Then, Cam appears with her mom at her side.

Cam's mom is actually her aunt, but she raised Cam since she was a small child. I love Aunt Elle. She's a badass cop. Running a department at the station. Cool as hell. She even offered to look into the Leo thing for me, but I thanked her and told her not to worry. I was leaving it in the past where it belongs.

But, honestly, I was more concerned that what my dad and Ares had done that night could come to light.

Cam and Elle walk down the aisle. Cam's dress is stunning. Simply elegant. It's an A-line, V-neck, sleeveless ivory tulle dress sprinkled with diamantes, followed by a sweeping train. Her hair is flowing down her back, curled, strands of hair pinned up with diamante pins. She looks like a princess.

Next to her, Elle is wearing a pale gray three-piece pantsuit with a lace jacket. And the proud look on her face is everything.

I turn and look at Zeus as he watches his bride walk toward him.

I've never seen a man look more in love than he does right now.

Gigi is at his side, and Thea is in his arms.

When Cam and Elle reach him, he takes Cam's face in his hand and kisses her. Then, he leans over and kisses Elle's cheek.

Elle and Cam hug before Elle goes to take her seat.

Zeus hands Thea off to Ares, who holds her in his arms, and my ovaries do a flip-flop. They do every time I see him with those girls.

*

The ceremony went off without a hitch. It was perfect and beautiful. And I was crying by the time they were pronounced man and wife.

After that, we all walked over to the lake across from the house and released Chinese lanterns. It was so romantic.

Then, it was time for photos and onto the reception.

It's early evening now, and the speeches and toasts have been done, food has been consumed, and everyone is on the makeshift dance floor.

Me and Ares included. We're dancing with Gigi. He's carrying her, perched on his hip, one arm around my waist, and I'm holding Gigi's hand.

And my ovaries are heading into serious overdrive.

"When are you and Uncle Ares getting married, Aunt Ari?"

Gigi has recently taken to calling me Aunt Ari, which I kind of love. Okay, I love it a lot.

But her question makes me choke a bit.

Ares chuckles as I make a strangled sound in my throat.

"Um . . . uh . . . well, I'm not sure, Gigi. One day, maybe."

I see Ares's eyebrows go up, and I worry that I've said the wrong thing. It's not like we've discussed anything close to marriage before.

"Can I be a bridesmaid when you get married to Uncle Ares?"

"Uh . . . well . . ." I'm faltering. "If I get married to your uncle Ares, then you can definitely be a bridesmaid," I tell her, gently tapping her nose with my index finger.

She giggles, making me smile.

"Gigi girl"—Missy comes dancing over, taking Gigi from Ares—"time to dance with me. Thea just ditched me to go dance with your uncle Lo. I mean, really? What's that all about? And I'm left, looking like a loser out there, on my own on the dance floor."

"Nothing new there." Ares chuckles low.

Missy covertly flips him off, and he laughs again.

"Of course, I'll dance with you, Aunt Missy!"

Gigi leads Missy off into the middle of the dance floor, and they get their groove on. At the age of six, Gigi is by far a better dancer than Missy. She's definitely got her mother's talent for dancing. For Missy . . . *talent* isn't exactly the word I'd use for her form of dancing.

I laugh silently to myself.

"So . . . what exactly did you mean by, *if*?" Ares's deep voice brings my eyes back to his.

"Huh?"

He slides his arms around my waist, pulling me closer.

"You said, *if* you get married to me. I didn't realize that was up for debate."

"I didn't realize it was a forgone conclusion."

His brow rises. "Full disclosure?"

My lips curve into a smile. "Always."

"It's happening, babe. Maybe not today, tomorrow, or next week. But it will be happening. I'll be getting down on one knee and asking you to be mine forever."

My breath hitches. "I'm already yours."

"Well, call me old-fashioned, but I want it to be

official. I want my ring on your finger and my kids in your belly."

It's my turn for my brow to rise. "We're having kids?"

"At least four," he tells me.

"Four?" I almost yell, my eyes going wide. I figured, when the day came that I had kids, I'd have two. One of each.

"I said, at *least* four."

"Sweet Jesus. What are you working toward, your own football team?"

"A life, Ari. I'm working toward a life with you."

My heart swoops and dives.

"I want it all with you . . . marriage, kids, a home—the whole nine yards."

I stare up at him, smiling, running my fingers through his hair. "I want that, too. I'm not sure about the number of kids"—I grin—"but I definitely want my life to be with you."

"We'll stick a pin in the number of kids to revisit later, but we'll keep practicing making them."

"Now that, I can agree with."

I reach up onto my tiptoes and kiss him. His fingers grip the fabric of my dress at my back, his tongue slipping into my mouth.

"Move in with me," he says out of left field.

I lean back, staring into his eyes, wondering what the hell has gotten into him tonight.

"Where's my Ares, and what have you done with him?"

He chuckles low, and my stomach clenches in the most delicious way. "Just watching Zeus and Cam today . . . I've always known I love you and that I want you, but seeing them today . . . I want all of this for us, Ari."

My lips curve into the biggest smile.

"We practically live together anyway. Let's make it official. Move into my apartment. You can keep your place if that makes you feel more secure. Sublet it or whatever. It's not like you're going to need it again though because I'm not letting you go anywhere ever again. I can turn one of the spare rooms into an art studio for you instead of you working out of that small corner of your living room. What do you say?"

He's staring down at me, his eyes so open and warm, filled with love for me, and there's only one word I want to say.

"Yes."

Acknowledgments

FIRST AND FOREMOST, THE biggest thank you goes to my husband and children, who put up with my absences, without complaint, while I spend time with my imaginary characters, building these crazy, fantastic worlds that I so very luckily get to share with you all.

My editor Jovana – I have the best editor ever. You make my life a million times easier. And you put up with me dropping last minute things on you, constant delays on delivery and extended deadlines, and you never tell me off. You are a saint!

My cover designer Najla Qamber – as always, just simply wonderful! Your talent to produce exactly what I'm wanting never ceases to amaze.

My agent Lauren Abramo – you continue to bring amazing things to the table. If it wasn't for you, I wouldn't be seeing my books in store in my home country, or in other countries around the world. You helped make my dream come true, and I can never thank you enough for that.

My Wether Girls – I adore each and every single one of you. This group is my safe haven, and man candy slice of heaven!

As always thank you to each and every member of the blogging world, who work tirelessly to help promote our books, without ask or complaint. We authors couldn't do it without you.

And lastly, to you, the reader, you're the reason I get to live my dream. Thank you from the bottom of my heart.

RUIN

Zeus Kincaid, heavyweight champion of the world,
is about to face his biggest fight yet . . .

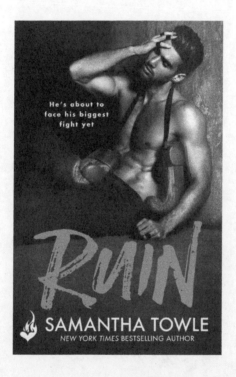

Available now from

HEADLINE
ETERNAL

BREAKING
HOLLYWOOD

Ava Simms has just hit Hollywood's resident
bad boy, Gabriel Evans, with her car. Breaking
Hollywood was never part of the plan, and neither
was falling in love with him . . .

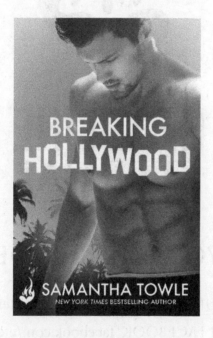

Available now from

HEADLINE
ETERNAL

HEADLINE
ETERNAL

FIND YOUR HEART'S DESIRE...

VISIT OUR WEBSITE: www.headlineeternal.com
FIND US ON FACEBOOK: facebook.com/eternalromance
CONNECT WITH US ON TWITTER: @eternal_books
FOLLOW US ON INSTAGRAM: @headlineeternal
EMAIL US: eternalromance@headline.co.uk